A SCHEME OF

SORCERY

Ennis Rook Bashe

A NineStar Press Publication

www.ninestarpress.com

A Scheme of Sorcery

Printed in the USA

ISBN:

First Edition, August, 2021

Also available in eBook, ISBN:

CONTENT WARNING:
This book contains sexually explicit content, which may only be suitable for mature readers. Depictions of

Palace squire Edwynne Dovecote has discovered her life is a lie. She wasn't born into the nobility- she's a daughter of the North, an inhospitable country where people worship a mysterious goddess. Even if it puts her at odds with her adopted family, she's determined to explore her heritage, as long as no one finds out who she truly is.

But Sariva al-Beroth, an ambitious Northern girl who's started working for the queen, is sick of rude outsiders gawking at her culture. She refuses to be in the same room as Edwynne, let alone share ancestral secrets.

Then the queen falls under a curse, and only Sariva and Edwynne can rescue her. To save their country, they'll have to survive a ruined underground castle infested with ghosts, a fascist uprising prepared to sway public opinion with mind-control magic... and each other.

For Corey Alexander, who loved hope, romance, trans representation, Judaism, everyday magic, their community, and good food.

Chapter One

Sariva couldn't finish the beaded bag before her caravan reached the castle, so she tidied away her supplies and peeked out the carriage window. "Are we—"

"Don't worry, miss, we're not going past the haunted ruins."

Strange. She'd only wanted to know when they'd arrive.

The carriage rolled over uneven streets made of pale mountain stone, passing low whitewashed houses with flat-eared cats on their doorsteps. The scent of daffodils and cyclamen filled the air as distant silver bells rang, calling people to pray to the sky. Even without the bag completed, her outfit seemed presentable. Everyone who noticed her would believe she belonged. Did she appear marriageable though? She touched the swirl of her plaits. Her rhinestone hairpins still held. Would anyone be able to tell how she'd altered her mother's old dress? Would they think of her as resourceful or unfashionable? Shining gates swiveled open, presenting a terraced courtyard, a burbling fountain, and tall palm trees in painted pots. As the carriage driver halted his bay roans, she rubbed her heirloom moon pendant for reassurance as her mother had so often done.

A slender woman with warm-olive skin hurried across the courtyard, sandals pattering on the stone. She bobbed a curtsy and shook Sariva's hand in both of hers. "So pleased to finally meet you. I've had the honor of reviewing your list of qualifications and your letters of recommendation—we've all agreed you'd be a lovely addition to the queen's service. Lady Ava of Valency, and you are Lady...Broth, is it?"

"Sorry, it's Be-roth." No one ever got her name right. "Rolled *R*, accent on the second syllable."

"Well, I'm pleased to make your acquaintance. We have a formal dinner among the court tonight—I have time to show you your quarters." They left the courtyard through an archway and turned onto a path between ornamental lemon trees.

A young woman passing by in the other direction paused with a displeased moue, raising plucked-thin eyebrows. "Oh, I wasn't aware of a foreign dignitary arriving today."

"Lisette, this is Lady Sariva Beroth. Her parents fled serving the sultan, and we're even luckier to have her at our Almesian court." Ava gestured to the woman. "Lady Sariva, may I introduce you to Lady Lisette? She is a splendid dancer."

"Bah-rroth?" Lisette's delicate features creased, perplexed with worry. "I'm so sorry, your name is just so hard to pronounce. What does it mean?"

"It means cypress," Sariva began, feeling suspicious, "but—"

Lisette beamed. "It would be so rude to get your name wrong, right? I mean, I'd absolutely hate myself for mispronouncing it. I'll just call you Lady Cypress if I have need of you, and then we can be great friends."

Did Lisette think she'd change her surname just because fools kept mangling it? Absolutely not. Sariva made herself smile. "Indeed, I do look forward to us spending time together."

"Yes, of course! Northerners are always awfully clever. If I have any figures to evaluate, I'll be certain to call on you."

She wanted to say "I'm horrid at sums" or "What next, will you accuse me of having killed infants for the Northern sultan?" Instead, she curtsied and nodded.

Even though nearly everyone who'd fled the North did so because they objected to the government or refused to serve in the military, people accused them of lying. Didn't a fortune in furs hide amongst the Northern mountains, and weren't all its inhabitants mages? Didn't most people in the North worship the Goddess of All-That-Is? How could anyone flee the North with less than a fortune in stolen gold? Once a new pupil at the village school had told all the others, "Sariva's family drinks blood. They only came south 'cause the people who didn't worship their nasty Goddess caught them. That's why her little brother is so weak because everyone else drinks his blood." Of course, a lady didn't stab classmates with pens or hit them over the head with writing tablets, more's the pity.

Magazines included subtler taunts: concern about secret mages, wealthy Northerners harming trade, assuming even refugees from the North supported the sultan's every policy. In the city, maybe people would only mangle her name, not her reputation. She remembered her mother's words: "It's much more cosmopolitan in the capitol, my dearest. Islanders, desert nomads, people of the tree faith, and of course, plenty of Northerners if you feel homesick or want others to pray with—even though many of them support the sultanate, my friends say you'll meet some lovely young radicals."

Sword crashed against sword. Voices shouted. Would she need to run for her life? "Is there some sort of trouble?" Her town's largest Northern specialty store had gone up in flames a few months ago. She'd heard about a timed fire-starting charm amongst the sacks of imported food, customers praying as they ran for their lives. Swinging her shopping sack, she'd turned the corner and stopped, mouth open. In childhood, she'd picked out ornately carved candles for the family's rituals there.

Ava gave a reassuring smile, waving off her concerns. "It's only the squires practicing. In summer they stage mock sieges in the cellars, but this time of the year, they still use the outdoor ring."

"How...nice." Her heart still pounded. Would it ever stop?

"Indeed, our knights are some of the most adept on the continent. We might go watch them if you wish."

Sariva would rather stitch a tapestry of a battle than ride off to join one, but she liked the idea of strong warriors protecting her. "Of course."

She followed Ava down the path and into a field. In a makeshift arena of packed dirt and wooden stakes, surrounded by tiers of stone benches, trainees brawled with blunt weapons.

The scrawniest one had the upper hand.

His hair shone a muddy, undistinguished color, clay and ochre; his body appeared sparse of all but knees and elbows like an over-articulated marionette. But he fought like a mosquito the bigger boys attempted to swat—dodging, weaving, shoving others in front of him as impromptu shields. One by one, the others trailed from the arena, nursing bruises and casting baleful glares.

Sariva saw the squire's face—small pointy chin, full sulky lips. "That squire, the short one...are they a girl?"

Ava smiled, evidently proud. "Edwynne's the only girl in Queensguard training. The entrance test gives an advantage to taller people, which weeds out most girls. Queen Oradel hasn't yet managed to change it."

Maybe Sariva *did* find watching combat worthwhile. She gazed unashamedly down at the girl, who flung a handful of dust at one squire's eyes, aimed a booted foot at another's ankles, and dodged away from the clumped-up melee, her sharp features tightening in concentration.

Another squire trudged out of the arena. Another limped out, swearing. Only two remained, whirlwind Edwynne and a wide young man, his bare arms lumpy with muscle.

Sariva's jaw clenched. She wanted to watch the end of the fight. She needed this squire to watch her.

Edwynne glared into the stands.

With a growl of rage, the other squire left in the arena dragged himself to his feet. He heaved his sword from the dust and stomped toward her.

Sariva's mouth felt like sand.

"Look out, dumbass!" a boy outside the arena cried. The larger squire roared, clenching his bulging muscles, and shifted to strike.

Still, Edwynne stared at her like a commander seeking out their enemy across the battlefield.

As the sword descended, Edwynne spun around. She dropped to the ground—surrender?—and rolled a perfect somersault right through his legs.

Before the larger, older squire could react, she'd kicked his knees out from under him. He sprawled in the dirt. Folding her arms, she told him, "You lost, Calder, and what's done is done."

Scowling, he got to his feet and accepted her offered hand. "Fine."

"All right, squires, get some water from the pump! I'd like to go a whole week without any students getting heatstroke," yelled a man in uniform.

The squire gulped down the cold river water and shook herself to let the droplets collect in her curls. After a quick exchange of shoves with another trainee, she threw one last handful of water on her neck and glanced toward the stands. She walked with an easy, dangerous gait...up through the arena, right toward where Sariva and Ava sat. Sariva clapped her hands to her mouth and squeaked. Goddess, she had no skill in talking to pretty girls! If only prayer could keep her from making a fool of herself. At least this problem would vanish soon since she didn't plan on marrying for love...

She glared at Ava. "Why are you bringing people to distract me? We see a great deal of each other already."

Ava sighed, her shoulders lowering though her bright expression didn't change. "Edwynne, meet Lady Sariva. She's new to the palace, and I thought perhaps you might take an interest in—"

Edwynne's eyes widened. "Does your necklace mean your family worships the Goddess? Are there any temples near here? I want to go to one."

Why would anyone want to voluntarily join an unpopular minority? Sariva raised her eyebrows, skeptical. "You're kidding."

The sunlight went out of her expression. "How come you're making me explain myself to you? I like your religion. I want to be part of it."

Sariva could handle her name being mispronounced, as usual, but this sulky, demanding girl, her stick-insect limbs and her sullen pale face, infuriated her in a whole new way. "You know what? Culture isn't a buffet. You can't grab a handful of whatever looks tasty. And if you're thinking converting will get you money or connections? Forget about it. You disgust me." She couldn't take it back—didn't want to, honestly.

Edwynne's cheeks flushed. "I wouldn't want to go to any temple that would have you as a member anyway. You're a useless, ornamental, selfish waste."

Why did she act like such a brat? "Useless? We entertain the queen, create gifts for visiting dignitaries, arrange palace festivities—"

"If you ever wish to learn something actually useful," Edwynne continued, casual, "why not join in with the pages? A girl about eight years old arrived yesterday. I think she'd have plenty to teach you."

She wouldn't let anyone treat her this way. "I believe the youngest lady-in-waiting here is around the same age. If you ever decide to trade your sword for something more practical, she'd be an excellent tutor."

"Milady, if you want my honest opinion—"

"I don't, thank you!" Her face felt hot, and not just from the sun.

"Sariva, shall we—" Ava began.

Edwynne's deep brown eyes seemed to look right through Sariva. "You'll make an advantageous marriage, stand around looking attractive, and perhaps host a few banquets. And that will be the sum total of your life's accomplishments. You think sitting around looking pretty is how you serve a deity? Well, I've saved people's lives, so there." Fuming, she swept an elaborate bow before stalking off.

Ava touched Sariva's shoulder. "Are you quite all right?"

Sariva grasped at something politely ambiguous to say. "Well, I certainly found her behavior unexpected."

"Would it help if I mentioned she's not usually like this?"

"What is she usually like?" A toad? A snowstorm? Sariva generally tried to think the best of others, but sometimes one needed the solace of spite. So much for the palace presenting an unassailable haven.

"She squires for my fiancé, and at first, I believe she quite disapproved of my presence."

Only at first?

"Still," continued Ava, "our disagreements have never gone further than uncharitable mutterings. I'm sure if you stay out of her way, she'll trouble you no further. Come, I'll show you to your quarters."

"Has she ever mentioned wanting to convert before?"

"No, I suppose she meant it as a joke."

Sariva didn't own her future. Still, she didn't submit without a fight—especially not to someone who made a joke of her faith.

A tall girl with neat hair in tiny plaits passed them, and Ava stopped her with a friendly gesture. "Mattie, darling, come meet our new friend."

The girl turned around. "Yes?"

"This is Mathilda, my sister-in-law to be. Mathilda, Sariva al-Beroth, our newest arrival. I'll let you two get acquainted."

Sariva curtsied, putting on a friendly smile. She liked the pale-green piping on the girl's simple lilac dress, and the fabric flowers woven into her three plaits made her look like a garden sprite. "Hello, Mathilda. I'm sure I'll need a lot of help remembering where everything is. You won't mind pointing things out to me, will you?"

Instead of curtsying, the girl sprinted up to her and gave a vigorous handshake. "Call me Mattie, please. My mum and da call me Mattie, and so does my brother Stellan. He's a knight in the Queensguard. You've got to be brilliant to get in the Queensguard."

"I'll make sure to remember." She searched the girl's innocent face and big shining brown eyes and revised her estimate of age downward. Twelve? Certainly not. A mature-looking nine at the most. "How old are you, Mattie?"

"Eight and a half," she mumbled, shifting from foot to foot.

Sariva sat down beside her. "That's awfully young to be sent away from home, isn't it?" The girl seemed younger than Sariva's brothers. She couldn't imagine sending either of them away to live with strangers.

Mattie nodded, fidgeting with her full skirt. "I'm a junior lady-in-waiting, more like an assistant or a page."

"You must miss your home. I know I do too even though I'm practically twice your age. My mother always tells me how much she missed her home when the prime minister forced her to flee across the mountains."

"Miles and miles! Wasn't she sad and angry? You must have been angry."

"Only at first. Then she found out there were good things about this country too."

Mattie considered this for a minute. "I suppose I like the paintings in the queen's gallery. There's one of a meadow of wildflowers, and it makes me feel peaceful."

"That sounds good. I hope I'll find things to like about the palace too," Sariva said, smiling at her.

"Did your mother ever get to go back to the North?" Melancholy tinged her young voice.

"No, the ways are dangerous. But she writes home on holidays." If letters came, they carried heavy inkblots of censorship. "I'm sure you'll get to go home eventually. In the meantime, why don't we make something for your friends to let them know you're thinking of them?" She opened her sewing satchel, showing Mattie the embroidery floss wrapped around wooden bobbins, the brand-new skeins still tied in twisted loops, and her felted needle books.

She peered into the bag and touched the different textures of fiber and fabric. "I know a few stitches. You have more colors of thread than I do though. What could we make?"

"In flower language, onion blossoms mean safety, and white hibiscus means good health. We could embroider a bouquet on a bag or a tablecloth. For now, why don't you go play?"

Mattie considered the suggestion for a moment before mumbling agreement and scampering off.

Ava took her arm. "Let's go meet the others."

She led Sariva up a swirling staircase, through a richly tapestried hallway, and into a big, sunny room with lots of places to sit and read. Ava cleared her throat, and seven women glanced up from their work. "Right, ladies. This is Sariva. She's here to help us serve the queen, and—"

A graceful crone with snowy hair who wore pants pursed her thin lips. "I didn't hear anything about a new addition."

Sariva shrugged, tried to smile. "I mean, here I am. Letter from the queen and everything."

"I mean, personally I find Northerners inefficient comrades. They're always talking about Northern issues," Lisette murmured sotto voce to a girl bent over a large book. "Solidarity much?"

The other girl nodded, wide-eyed, and fiddled with her pink-chiffon hair ribbons—purple when they caught a glint of late afternoon sunlight. Gorgeous fabric.

Another old woman, stepping forward, evaluated her. She had cerulean-dyed springy hair tucked up in a bun held by a thin metal spike. "I'm sure if Zerena is genuine, she won't mind making herself useful."

"Um, terribly sorry, but it's Sariva—" No one heard her, thankfully.

Ava had said something to the snowy-haired woman, who replied, "I can't say I've heard of the family."

Time to fling out a rapid-fire talking point. "My mother served as a former secret services operative in the sultan's government, and my father worked for the diplomatic corps—but they both left because they felt uncomfortable with the sultan's policies and felt what he asked of them wasn't morally right, and they fled to this country with practically nothing and are considered, umm, leaders in the expatriate activist community. And their opinions, I mean, the actions they've taken—it's all had a strong commitment on my impact, I mean, a strong impact on my commitment to social justice. And that's why I stand before you. Today."

She wanted to go home. Goddess, she'd rehearsed her speech. What good had it done? But the curly-haired woman, who seemed the least terrifying, softened. "Well, we're glad to have anyone who's truly committed to the work of activism, Sariva."

"Let's see. I'm Paveya, and you've met Lisette and Ava already—Fabiola is over there—"

The girl with the huge book peered up with a half smile.

"And this is Melisant. Say hello, Melisant." She elbowed the taller woman with snowy-white hair, who didn't budge.

Under Melisant's gaze, Sariva felt even smaller.

"Which policy of the queen's do you think has most impacted your village?"

A test—but one she could pass. "The additional funding for schools, even small ones like ours. We've gotten enough books for everyone and hired another teacher. My youngest brother misses a lot of school because of health issues, so having textbooks at home means he can stay caught up."

"All right. What about policies that haven't been enacted into law yet?"

Another answer she'd rehearsed.

"The Land Stewardship and Disposal of Magical Waste Act. Wizard byproducts, especially from combat spells, are hazardous. Look at what's happened to the old palace, for instance, and how many people die there yearly. It's commonsense legislation."

Please like me, Sariva prayed. *Please let me work with you. You can hate me, but let me help the cause—*

Melisant dropped a stack of papers into her arms. The weight made her stagger. "Come along then."

Sariva scurried through long, carpeted hallways behind Melisant's longer strides, heading—where? She didn't care. She'd get to stay!

★

At dinner, Sariva's legs ached, and she felt glad to sit down. She'd spent the afternoon into the evening running around the palace, carrying copies of the latest report on universal education from the printing presses, making sure all the pages were in order and tied neatly together, that all representatives from different parts of the queendom had a copy on their seat. She jotted down notes for the queen, who she'd been told was attending another meeting, as Melisant went over the queen's provided talking points, which focused on preventing misappropriation of funds on the queendom's outskirts. Later, she changed into a fancier dress for dinner, pinned the sweaty hair off her neck, and reviewed the seating chart so she could greet visiting dignitaries and thank them for their presence as they took their seats. It seemed like the ladies-in-waiting were served last.

Spoiled? Coddled? She'd show Edwynne. She'd work so hard.

Sariva kept glancing toward the wooden double doors at the main entrance to the grand dining hall. Of course, she didn't care if Edwynne and the other squires took their seats.

Edwynne swept into the room at the head of a pack of boisterous, ungainly squires laughing and shoving one another over some jest. Her curls flowed freely, and she wore a short tunic of green linen.

Sariva wished Edwynne would turn around and leave.

At least she'd gotten something she could actually eat. People tended to serve her food that she wasn't comfortable eating. She'd anticipated having to tell her dining companions, "I'm sorry, I can't eat that. No, that either. I'm guided by the laws of my people's Goddess," and then having to wait while someone improvised a meal. But before the food arrived, a chef had told her, "You're the new lady-in-waiting, correct? Don't worry, the palace hosts Northerners often. This chicken hasn't been within eyesight of dairy since it still lived." Though they gave her a different dish, her meal appeared as elaborately plated as any other. And she'd get a cake made with nut mousse instead of milk too! Her friends at home—not to mention her mother—would beg for the recipe.

The group of squires sat at the same long table as Sariva and the other ladies-in-waiting, close enough that every jest of their conversation carried. Edwynne sat down and crossed her legs, revealing sloppily tied shoelaces. Some people just didn't care enough to tie theirs up all the way.

Sariva drank from her goblet to hide the smile threatening to spread over her face. She kept eating until—"Pardon me. Dropped my spoon." With a graceful dip of her head, she slipped under the table. Slowly, she wriggled forward until she spotted a pair of sandals. She leaned forward and unknotted the hastily tied laces, then looped three together and pulled a fourth through and taut. *Good luck unpicking a complex knot with your short-bitten fingernails!* Returning to her seat, she held up the spoon. She'd slipped it into a skirt pocket. "Found it."

In the midst of a story, she snuck a glance at Edwynne. The squire laughed at a joke, unaware anything had taken place. Although Sariva ate with her typical perfect manners and decorum, anticipation secretly filled her.

A resonant voice cut into her thoughts. "Might you introduce me to your new companion?" The man who spoke seemed like he'd spent too much time indoors and overestimated his ability to grow a beard.

"Ah, yes. Delvar, this is Sariva, who recently joined us in assisting the queen. Sariva, I'd like to present to you our current court wizard, Delvar."

He had a long, pale face and a long, thin nose, and his green eyes glittered as he sketched a bow.

But the broadsheets had spoken of a witch, Izalena, at the queen's side. "It's a pleasure to make your acquaintance—only, I thought a witch named Izalena—"

Ava's face darkened like storm clouds. "Up until a week ago, yes."

"It's been an interesting new position. Lots of books, lots of room to do experiments, even if the circumstances that placed me here aren't ideal." He waved his hand. An empty chair slid over from another table. Sariva tried not to gawk as he flipped it around and straddled the back. Did residents of the capitol consider magic so unremarkable?

"So how are you adjusting to the palace? Do you like signing petitions and passing bills? Are you one of those, you know, paper pushers?" He laughed as if teasing her.

"I mean, I think the queen's done some good work."

"Sure, she's trying. We go far back—I started at the university as she approached graduation—and she used to be a lot more interesting. Now it's all who your parents are, where you come from, and how to avoid hurting people's feelings." He couldn't be too old, maybe nearing thirty, and the way he jiggled a leg, in addition to his conspiratorial smile, gave him an even more youthful air. "Did you hear what happened at the old palace?"

"I know the knights continue to cordon it off," Ava offered.

"I think it's fascinating. The magical theory of it all, how negative emotions keep them so strongly animated... Anyway, the ghosts have been quiet for a while, but they tried to eat someone alive the other day. A tourist, can you believe it?"

Ava leaned toward him, concerned. "Were you able to save them?"

He levitated a fork. It spun in lazy circles between his hands. "I mean...unfortunately, there wasn't much to save. The blood splattered everywhere, and the bite marks hit bone. The spell I used, I've been testing a new technique—"

Sariva tried to keep her face impassive, but discomfort must have showed. He caught the fork. "It's all right, not everyone has the sympathy to bother hearing the tales of an isolated scholar. I know I've got an unusual frame of reference. A different perspective on the world."

Embarrassed, she glanced at the parsley garnish on her chicken with olives. "Forgive me. I did mean to listen. It's just been a long, tiring journey. I have a lot on my mind since my family needs me to marry well."

He raised a single perfectly plucked eyebrow with impressive muscle control. "I can see you're devoted to your family. You seem like a nice, dutiful girl. I'm sure I can do something to aid you to a favorable position, and perhaps some of the nobles I know might be interested in marrying a demure good listener."

Nice? Demure? It sounded like low standards for a wife. But he seemed to mean well, and she always tried to think the best of people. "Thank you, milord."

He chuckled. "No need to be so formal! We're both here because we want to be. Where are you from?"

Sometimes people asked her "What are you?" as if playing a guessing game because she didn't look

Almesian. *Are you from the desert? Are you from the mountain provinces? No, I think that's a Northern Goddess-child nose!* Others faced worse indignities, but it still frustrated her. "My family is Northern," she replied flatly.

His austere expression softened. "Forgive me if I've hurt your feelings. Of course. Obviously, you're an Almesian citizen of the truest sort. I meant, where did you travel to the palace from? I consider myself an observant man, and I can tell you've had a long journey."

Did he look irritated? She must have imagined it. At least he didn't ask her what she thought of the sultan. "Shekhar. It's a small village near the Northern border. I'm sure you'd consider it provincial. Aside from sewing bees and the occasional traveling players, we have little in the way of entertainment. But I'm fortunate because it hosts many other immigrants from the North."

His face lit up. "You're a Northerner? Northerners are fantastic. I've always been interested in how many aspects of our own Constellation faith derive from prophets of your Goddess of All-in-All. And your country—your people have gotten so much done with surprisingly little magic. Made the wastelands into gardens."

Sariva bristled. "That's—" That's propaganda promoted by the sultan's regime and a horrific exaggeration discounting the contributions of literally everyone else who hails from the North, she wanted to say, but she forced her mouth to clamp shut.

"There's a Northern fusion restaurant in the market quarter of the city. The broadsheets describe it as quite authentic. Maybe we could share a meal sometime? I've not yet had a chance to visit the border or the North in the course of my duties, so I'd love to hear more about your family and your beautiful heritage. And I might even be able to introduce you to my Goddess-worshipping friends."

"Of course." Not wanting to get this nice stranger's hopes up, she added, "I mean, if my duties permit."

"Likewise! Anytime. It's a pleasure to see Northerners coming to court." He bowed and departed.

"So, what do you think of our court wizard? He's a genius, you know. I saw him heal a man's broken leg with a wave of his hand, even if he collapsed afterwards." Ava seemed to search her face for something.

"He seems like he'd much rather be at his books than at a court dinner."

"Yes, but you got him to talk about something besides magical theory; hence, he likes you."

He meant well. At least, he seemed to mean well. She'd rather hear "I love the Northerners" than "I hate the Northerners." Perhaps he simply didn't make a good first impression? Honestly, she had as difficult a time shutting up about embroidery as he did changing the topic away from magic. Sariva knew one could gain many advantages from befriending a well-connected wizard.

Edwynne stood, moved away from the table, tumbled, and then fell flat on her face. One of the older squires laughed so hard he choked on his food, and another boy had to thump him hard on the back. Sariva examined her bead-woven napkin ring. Quite an interesting pattern.

"What's wrong with my shoes?" Edwynne cried, expression livid as she fumbled to her feet. She clutched a chair to steady herself.

"Stars, I don't know," a skinny boy in the next seat told her, "but it looks like some sort of fancy decorative knot."

"Ugh." She kicked her shoes off and stormed away, bare feet slapping on the tiles.

"But it's not dessert yet," the boy protested.

She shrugged in a desultory fashion.

Hmm. An embroidery knot, and she'd mentioned embroidery. Would Edwynne put two and two together and suspect her? Hopefully, the squire would stay occupied with other concerns.

"I didn't see the queen at dinner," Sariva stated as they collectively returned to the ladies' sitting room.

Ava glanced toward the window. "Perhaps you'll see her later. For now, I believe we ought to let her enjoy the garden air."

"Oh, no," Paveya declared, "she's gone to bed. She's required to rise early tomorrow morning."

"What, alone?" Sariva asked, looking up at Paveya.

Paveya waved a hand, tossing her graying curls. "I accompanied her."

"Might you tell me how she is and if I could be presented to her informally? It would please me terribly to be useful." She'd journeyed here to make herself useful.

"Well, someone's behind on the news," Melisant said, turning a page in a ribbon-bound manuscript, then jotting down a note.

"Behind on what news?" Sariva felt small and stupid.

A humorless smile appeared on Melisant's bloodless features. "Haven't you heard? Court Mage Izalena cursed the queen, and Delvar banished her. Now Oradel's ill."

It explained the new court wizard. "But can I see her?"

"I'm afraid we can't have that. She needs peace and quiet," Paveya said, drawing herself up to her full height. She reached Sariva's chin, and in her flowing burgundy dress jeweled with faux garnet, she resembled an irate little geriatric pomegranate.

Sariva leaned away. "I didn't know she'd fallen ill."

Melisant didn't even blink. Like a lizard enjoying sunlight on the garden's stones. "Well, now you do."

The way Melisant and Paveya exchanged darting glances... Her parents had made eye contact with each other in such a manner over dinner, and then Sariva eavesdropped on them staying awake over pots of aromatic Northern coffee, discussing what prized family heirloom to sell next.

Even if something bad had happened with the previous court mage, why would they be keeping the queen away from everyone?

What if the queen had died?

But—no. In addition to tabulating who the people thought would rule best, the Magic Mirror of Governance announced when a ruler's soul departed. Still, what if the other ladies-in-waiting didn't have the queen's best interests at heart? She imagined writing to her family:

> *Mother, I know you intended for me to restore the family's status by marrying, but exposing an assassination plot turned out to be the "done" thing this season! Other recent trends include herbal garnishes and pastels!*

"Are we planning any sort of diversions for the queen? I mean, we have many creative minds among us— I'm sure you're already thinking of something lovely. If there's to be a masque, I could make the costumes or even read through the queendom's history to choose an appropriate scene."

Melisant shook her severe gray head. "The queen would be too busy. However, if you want some extra work, there are some tasks that would be wonderful additions to your workload."

"You'd do a great job taking care of this for us," Paveya added. "Letters to sign, dossiers on diplomats to compile, the menu and logistics for a few upcoming feasts—in addition to your work summarizing the queen's policy briefings, proofreading her speeches, and making sure sufficient rooms are free for government meetings."

Some of the other ladies-in-waiting watched their conversation.

Sariva took a deliberate breath, caught between angry and impressed.

However, turning down their offer would reflect badly on her reputation. Staying modest would make her look overly diffident, as if she performed shyness to manipulate others. People would assume she said cruel things about herself in expectation of being reassured with compliments. Turning the offer aside outright would make her seem selfish or snobby, dangerous shards of gossip. A wrong word now might ruin everything for the next Northern noble-in-exile who hoped to come to court, leading to a bad assumption such as *greedy Northerners don't pull their weight, they just want to exploit the labor of others,* et cetera.

She imagined drafting a letter home:

> *Dear Mother, I have met my match in the form of two small old women who eat poppy seed biscuits. Please send more thimbles. I suspect I will be engaged in a great deal of nervous sewing.*

If only the norms of etiquette allowed sprinting away from a stressful conversation! Curse this. Curse it all.

"I'd be happy to help."

Chapter Two

Throughout the week, one thing sustained Edwynne: She got a few hours off.

Older squires calling her a weak, whiny girl if she didn't perform a sword exercise perfectly, kicking the training-yard dust in her face? Miserable drunk tourist wandering into the haunted ruins, the smell of their puke attracting ghosts to drain their life force? An instructor cursing the trainees with a double-sided five-sheet essay on which held more importance, the Magic Mirror of Elections or the charm to remove horse shit from the city's stone streets?

Edwynne endured. (And then fantasized about satisfyingly grisly vindication, single-handedly rescuing the palace from evil when she lay in her bunk at night.)

She picked up her sword and stepped through the moves for as long as it took, hauled the tourist out across her shoulders, stayed up until dawn researching and scribbling notes. She'd get a half-day off at the end of the week. And when enough weeks had passed, she'd join the Queensguard and prove all those hulking boy-men wrong. She just had to keep her head down until the queen gave her a knighthood and a smart green uniform.

But a chunk of time off meant strolling into the city with her best friend, spending all their allowances, flirting with any pretty girl.

Climbing onto the bottom bunk next to hers, she rubbed her knuckles against her best friend's hair. "Tolliver! Wake up!"

He gave her a pale-eyed glare and yanked the thin pillow over his head. "Fuck you. It's dawn. We get to sleep until the next bell."

"It's dawn of our half-day off. I thought we were going to the market to watch street performers risk their lives for fun and eat all the delicious food we can carry and kiss kittens on their little fuzzy heads. But I can go alone if you can't be bothered."

He startled fully awake. "It's the week's end. You're right—"

"I'm always right." She cuffed him across the head. Tumbling out of bed, he aimed a kick at her shins, but she dodged and stuck her tongue out at him.

"Wait, where are my boots?"

She flung the shoes in question at his head. "Catch." He'd put them in her drawer by accident again. But at least he'd closed the drawer before falling asleep. The squires in the year above them seeing her breastbands, maybe even stealing one for a laugh? She'd sooner drown.

They both got dressed, and Tolliver headed toward the barrack door.

Edwynne stopped him. "Wait. We're allowed to wear our short swords off palace grounds now, remember?" How could he forget so casually?

"You can take yours. I don't want to risk forgetting mine if I try on clothes."

Like all squires, she had a standard-issue blade: blank metal, straight cross guard, unadorned grip. Plain, sure, but she'd earned this sword.

Winter in Almesia meant constant rain. In summer everyone slept later and stayed up later to skip the day's heat. But spring in Almesia? When you could pet new kittens and swim in the river and let the wind dry your clothes? Nothing compared.

They hurried through the blooming palace gardens, past orange trees and cacti, olive trees, and palms.

A gate guard leaning on his spear narrowed his eyebrows. "Why's a servant going out the armory entrance?"

Edwynne fumbled with the leather cord around her neck and thrust out her squire's medallion. "With all due respect, because I'm not a servant." She'd lived at the palace since childhood. If people wanted to act shocked seeing a girl squire, screw them. Almesia could have a queen—why not female warriors like amongst the Desert Peoples too?

"She has a temper," Tolliver apologized as they went through the gate.

"I do not have a temper," she snapped, fighting the urge to box his ears. Or scream. She felt like screaming often these days.

A few streets of parkland surrounded the palace, but soon, they came out of the trees. The gentle slope before them led down to gleaming buildings of creamy stone, white-painted cottages with colorful tiled roofs, terraces touching balconies touching courtyards, layers of life like giant stairs climbing up the hill. And at the end of it all, the wide, glimmering river that poets called Almesia's turquoise thread...and the blank patch of eerie, crumbling ruins.

But a half-day off meant not having to think about the ruins.

Tolliver jogged her elbow, his exotic red hair shining in the morning sun. Overhead, dawn turned the sky colors Edwynne never wore, pinks, purples, and orangey-peach. "Race you to the marketplace?"

"You're on."

They ran past streets lined with palm trees and little kitschy shops selling trinkets to travelers—"genuine war relics!" that probably weren't. Jostling each other, they shoved into a narrow side street that opened onto the big covered market.

Fish straight from the river, their stinky silver bodies displayed like treasure. Spindly shellfish trying to climb out of buckets. Turmeric and za'atar heaped up like sand.

Tolliver hurried her on. "Come on, we're not getting anything to eat here."

The air smelled much sweeter near the fruit and candy stalls. Pieces of dried kiwi dangled from booth awnings, strung jewels, stained glass. Dried apricots reminded her of a dragon's treasure. (Of course, no one wanted an actual wild dragon to land in the market.) Piles of nuts gleamed in huge wicker baskets, and a man with a big knife whacked the top off a skinned coconut and handed it to a customer.

"No river seeds? I love cracking the shells," Tolliver griped. "And they're so sweet this time of year."

"So are other fruits. Maybe the shipments from the North just haven't arrived yet." The North being at war? One more fact of life, like spring being kitten season.

A thought twinged at her like a splinter: *Did my parents sell blue river seed fruit? If I'd inherited a taste for it, how would I know?* She blurted out something unrelated, "Hey, what if I put my hand in one of those baskets of nuts? Don't they look so smooth?"

"You want to get kicked out of the market, be my guest."

They bought a pomegranate to crack open and picked out the seeds until their hands ran red and sticky with rivulets of wine-sweet juice. Edwynne liked to take out all the seeds and then crunch a big handful, while Tolliver didn't mind accidentally biting the pith. Three turnings down, the pastry seller Flavian's cat had given birth a few weeks ago. Flavian let them sit behind the counter and marvel at the tiny wriggly kitten infants and stroke the sand-colored mother's long, regal face. The kittens' pink forepaws moved rhythmically as they suckled. The cat blinked at them, disdainful, indolent: *You see what I'm forced to deal with?*

What did I look like as an infant? Does anyone remember me tiny and toothless? Fuck, why couldn't she stop thinking about it? She'd already had weeks to get used to the truth. It shouldn't bother her. She shook her head and tugged on Tolliver's tunic. "Let's go see the street performers. I bet they've started already."

"So what? We can get to the front if we want."

"Yeah, well, not everyone is as tall as you."

They rinsed the cat hair from their fingers at a public fountain before biting into pistachio-honey pastries oozing with sweetness and heading to Amaldia Square. The narrowly packed stalls and shady awnings gave way to a big, open plaza.

Tolliver, who could more easily see over the crowds, scanned the area. "I heard there's a sword swallower."

Swords didn't belong in bodies. The idea disgusted her. "I bet you want to see a sword swallower because you want someone to give you a blow job."

"You just think sword swallowers are gross."

Would this turn into a wrestling match? Good. She wanted to fight, not think. "You calling me a coward?"

He wiggled his hands in front of his face mockingly. "Long sword...scary."

They laughed and shoved each other until they bumped into a passerby, who gave them a dirty look. Eventually, they settled down to watch the acrobats.

"Okay! Before our next routine, we're going to pass the hat around! Please throw in your coins—we'll do something extra spectacular if you manage to fill it to the brim! Clap your hands!"

The hat passed the two squires and their empty pockets. Tolliver turned to her. "So how are you feeling about, umm—"

Edwynne clenched her fists. *Please don't bring up the last thing I want to hear...*

"—that thing with your birth parents being Northerners? And it's wild that you didn't even know you were adopted until the last time you visited Dovecote Manor. I mean, it must be a huge shock. If I found out something so shocking, I'd—I don't even know!"

She jerked one shoulder up in a shrug. "Does it have to be a big deal? I mean, whatever they named me, I'm still Edwynne. I'm still myself."

But everything around her had changed. Her loving family—the people who raised her—had cut her off from her heritage. The way of the Goddess didn't admit outsiders. She couldn't show up and say, "I think my parents were your sort," without proof, and she didn't even have the grave of her birth parents as evidence. They'd want her to study, convert, pour over big books with small print. Without any tangible way to prove her heritage, her own people would see her as a suspicious outsider.

"Mom and Dad didn't want your parents' religion—what people might think about them, about you—to keep you from becoming a knight," Stellan had explained earnestly. "I know you're upset, but they meant well. I mean, they raised you after your parents died in the plague instead of bringing you to an orphanage. They wanted to give you the best possible life."

Her parents had never felt like "meant well" people. They were people who did good. How could she look at them—at herself—the same way?

Tolliver nodded, his squint giving him an owlish look. "You're still the same old punk-ass bitch," he pronounced wisely.

Finally, a return to normal. "You're a punk-ass bitch," she told him, giggling, and they tried to shove their middle fingers in each other's faces. Discussions about family? About feelings? Who'd ever prefer those over play fighting and making jokes?

Most girls, in Edwynne's experience, would. Girls sat around talking about things and making handicrafts. Being friends with girls probably sucked.

The acrobats still clapped their hands and called out to the crowd, urging more generosity.

"Want to come back when they continue their routine?"

"Sure."

Pushing through the crowd, they passed a juggler in an old-fashioned jester's costume flinging cloth balls in impossible loops. A woman played sweet, sad music on a harp.

Tolliver nudged her. "Ring any bells?"

"Maybe." The music didn't sound familiar. It didn't call any lullabies her parents might have sang to mind. She wished it would awaken something in her.

Northern Goddess-kind music always had an air of melancholy, even when the lyrics went like "You are my beloved, and I will embrace you." Did the street musician strum a love song or one of mourning? Edwynne only knew Almesians couldn't even copy Northern words' sounds. The high, lilting melody still captivated her.

"Tolliver," she said, turning pleading eyes on him. Meaning *I've spent all my stipend on fruit and pastries. I have a satchel full of sweet things and no coin to spare.*

"Fine, this once."

But they lent each other money all the time and never kept track.

Edwynne elbowed her way toward the harpist. "'Scuse me, move over—thanks—hey, watch your feet!" The crowd parted, leaving her standing before the sweet-faced woman. A little sign near her read "Zulpha Behr—Northern Folk Music—street art sponsored by Queen Oradel." Palms sweaty, Edwynne crouched and laid the coin in her harp case. "*K'shava*," she said loudly, carefully: the one word of the musician's language she knew. *Thank you.*

The woman's eyes lit up. Playing with one hand so she could gesture at Edwynne, she let out a torrent of excited speech.

"I don't understand. You're mistaken," Edwynne mumbled, ducking into the crowd.

Northerners didn't believe in burning corpses, but her parents had been burned in one of the plague pits outside the city. How could she prove she'd been born to a Goddess-worshipping family?

And her family—

They'd gotten Edwynne from Elyanit because the Goddess-kind language didn't have the letter *W*. Now whenever someone said her name, the *W* sat in the middle: *You're not who you thought you were. Those who loved you first died far from home.*

Tolliver found her and put a hand on her shoulder—prelude to another play fight? Instead, he ruffled her curls, murmuring, "Hey."

She leaned against him. "Hey, yourself."

"What say we start for home? My calves are still sore from the last time we had to sprint to afternoon practice. And we can try to find the noblewoman you're hooking up with. Didn't she say the other day that men demean themselves by working out shirtless? An absolute fountain of weird opinions. She doesn't deserve you. Unless she happens to be magnificent in bed. Is she though? Why do you keep going for snobby bitches?"

Edwynne laughed as she shoulder-checked him and knocked him off balance. She broke into a jog, calling, "Shut up. You don't know what kind of women I like."

He kept pace with her. "Soft breasts, frilly dresses, talks radical politics but only if the queen's there to impress. Admit I understand you."

Leaning into the uphill slope of the road away from the market, she flipped him off as punctuation. True, she always fell for women who were feminine and emotionally unavailable. Goddesses impossible to attain. Fine ladies to admire and serve.

But fuck him for noticing the blatantly obvious.

Edwynne spotted Lisette under a peony arbor in the gardens. Her long brown hair fell in rippling waves, and her dress accented her curves, presenting an absolute vision.

"Stay here," she mouthed at Tolliver and sprinted toward the woman. What would she say? She discarded options before jumping on the obvious. "Good morning, Lisette. Are we going to kiss?"

Lisette clapped her notebook closed and pursed her lips. "Edwynne...we need to talk." Her spread-out skirts covered the bench, leaving Edwynne nowhere to sit.

"Sure." Hopefully, Lisette wanted to talk about kissing.

Lisette twirled her hair, crossed her ankles, sighed deeply, and finally declared, "The thing is, I mean... honestly, I don't feel comfortable dating someone who's more marginalized than I am. I mean, you're a foundling, your family is only minor nobility, and you only have one house? I'm just so aware of my privileges around you. I feel like that guilt is inherently harmful. I need to be working on myself and my aspirations."

Edwynne couldn't even laugh at how "aspirations" contained the word "ass." Nothing Lisette had said made any sense to her. She blurted, "Can we still make out?"

At once Lisette's deep brown eyes smoldered with anger. "And that's another thing. You're so predatory. You're like a man. Always talking about not being like other girls, and your best friends are boys. I don't feel like you stand with women politically."

She wanted to exchange a glance chock-full of words with Tolliver. Out of the corner of her eye, she saw him shake his head, like *I can't help you.*

"But I am a woman."

"You wouldn't get it. You basically have male privilege. Look, Edwynne, I'm doing this for you, okay? I feel sorry for you. You haven't had the same education as I have. You don't feel comfortable in my circles. I take you to the right sort of cocktail parties, but instead of discussing where we're going as a movement, as a society, you just want to eat the food and leave."

"It's good food," she said helplessly. Little triangles of pita and big bowls of hummus. Cherry tomatoes stuffed with bites of soft herby cheese. She knew nothing about modern art or socioeconomics or anything else they discussed, and no one expected her to do more than nod when she kept her mouth full.

"That's what I'm saying, Edwynne. You're so materialistic. I need to evolve into my best self by—"

Lisette dripped with jewelry. Fine silver lace coated her dress. Edwynne had been to her chambers and seen an entire vanity full of skincare products, delicate glass bottles lined up in the sunlight. She gave a disbelieving laugh. "I'm materialistic? Me? Go fuck yourself."

She wrinkled her perfect nose. "This is what I'm talking about. You're always so impulsive, so disrespectful. You interrupt people. You don't pay attention to my boundaries—"

"Lisette, I'm sorry, I really am—" As soon as she reached for Lisette's hand, she regretted it, guilt heavy on her shoulders.

"Do you think I still swoon for your kisses? You...you vulgar boor!" After jumping to her feet, she drew back her hand as if preparing for a slap.

Edwynne flinched.

Lisette turned on her heel and flounced away.

Today felt like too much. The truth about her birth parents, who she couldn't remember. The woman at the market who tried to speak to her in a language she knew nothing of. And then *impulsive* and *vulgar* and *disrespectful* and *basically male*—

Edwynne flopped against a decorative hedge. Her knee patches thunked down in the clover.

Tolliver's arms came around her. "Can I give you a hug?"

"Fuck you," she sniffled, hugging him. "I hate how they get tired of slumming. I hate how they pretend to care. Tolliver, I quit."

"Quit what?"

"Pretty noblewomen. I won't even flirt with them anymore."

He tensed around her, trying not to laugh, and she shoved at his sturdy chest. "I mean it. I'll ward them off as if with a spear." And she'd bitch them out first.

He scoffed under his breath, an attitude she'd accept from no one else. "Sure."

The palace bells sang out low dings. Almost practice time! They needed to hurry and grab their armor. Edwynne swiped at her face until the tears went away.

Loping alongside her, Tolliver pointed out, "You know, you could always develop better taste in women, Ed."

She snorted. "Remember yesterday's military strategy lesson? Stellan specifically said don't overestimate your forces. I know my type."

Practice fights with blunt, weighted weapons always made Edwynne feel better. She could test out new maneuvers and leave anything bothering her on the battlefield. Even when she lost, she still got her adrenaline up. So what if the instructors went harder on her than anyone else because she had a Queensguard knight for a brother? So what if the older squires laughed at her and tried to shove her into the dirt? Nothing could ruin physical training for her.

Well, almost nothing.

Because the girl Ava had brought to see the training brawl made Edwynne weak in the knees. Her olive skin had these undertones that caught the light, making her cheeks seem decorated with powdered diamonds and sapphires. (Maybe they were!) The way her high-waisted gown hugged her ample figure? Ugh. Incomparable. And the way her lips were parted ever so slightly and her midnight-dark eyes widened as she leaned forward, seeming engrossed in the fight? Only one word for it— unfair.

Why did the stars beam such misfortune down on her?

To make matters worse, Ava condescendingly went out of her way to introduce them. Typical predictable, meddling Ava, with her insincere attempts at being nice. She thought of frivolous women who turned up their noses at her for causing trouble, for being an orphan, who wanted her to devote her life to pleasing them and become one more ornament on their jeweled hands. This petite, exquisite noble, who'd gasped in disgust at Edwynne's presence, had rubbed her the wrong way. She felt like a cat whose tail had been pulled one time too many.

Did she have the right to treat a stranger so viciously? To guess what would make her most insecure and then strike without hesitation? She didn't know. Didn't care. Insulting a noblewoman— even one who could give as good as she got—hardly fell under "knightly deeds." But if cruelty could spare her from being discarded, maybe it became worthwhile.

A few days after Edwynne's humiliation, she figured out how to get back at the little snob. Midmorning, after a lunch of half-stale sesame seed pastry, hard cheese on flatbread, and pomegranate juice, she had the perfect opportunity to put her plan into action. After an excursion to the stream running through the garden, she snuck up the servant's stairs to the quarters of the queen's attendants, sticking close to the wall so the boards wouldn't creak under her sandals. She carried a drawstring bag lined with waterproof leaves. Emerging, she slid into a fine hallway. Tapestries of unrealistic nature scenes lined the walls. The Greensea without any fish boats, a desert sunset with no camels to be seen.

Fancy ladies seemed obsessed with decorating their rooms. Opening one door after another, she could tell which room belonged to the newest arrival because its walls were bare of paintings.

Her parcel wriggled. "Shhh," Edwynne whispered. She found her target: a pair of fine slippers peeked out from under the bed.

Perfect.

She didn't have land or riches. But she didn't need either to defend herself.

★

Dear Mother, Sariva wrote, *I've found court lovely. While I miss your cooking, I'm sure I won't starve! In response to the question I'm sure you'll be asking, I haven't yet seen the Magic Mirror, though of course I'd love to see such a famous artifact.*

She jammed her pen into its stand. Could she trust no one would intercept her letters? Her family, her community, would pore over each letter, waiting to hear about her duties for the queen. They'd want to know about the queen's clever remarks, her habit of helping common people with their everyday duties, and her habit of wearing fabulous jackets with trousers. Except the queen had been avoiding everyone. Sariva only saw her handwriting on notes and heard her voice drifting down the hallway.

The grounds have so many different types of plants from all over the queendom and its allied lands, and the other ladies-in-waiting have been kind to me. Sending my love and prayers! Always, Sariva.

She wanted to write, *I am in over my head. I feel like my colleagues are lying to me—like I'm being herded. This is the first time I've had a few moments to myself since coming here.* But then she'd receive a letter in reply saying, *Sweetheart, of course if you're struggling, you can come home.*

Her family needed her. She couldn't let them down. She'd do her best.

"Sariva! We're all heading down for dinner," Ava called.

Might as well. She slid her feet into her slippers.

Something small and wet pressed against the top of her foot—shifted, exploring between her toes—and sunk tiny slippery teeth into her skin.

Screaming, Sariva kicked off her slippers and gasped in horror. Frogs! Poisonous frogs?

Ava rushed in at once in a rustle of skirts and concern.

Sariva tried to form a coherent sentence but could only point repeatedly at the frogs. "Someone, look, they must have—why would anyone do this to me? And now my slippers are ruined!"

Ava shook her head, wincing. "I'll lend you a pair. Our feet are almost the same size, aren't they? Wait here." She brought shoes in a completely different shade of green.

Later, she lay awake in bed, contemplating the horrible frogs. What if Edwynne had been responsible? Maybe she suspected Sariva of tying her shoelaces together... *But why did she have to target my slippers? Doesn't she understand how important they are—how much time I spent on the elaborate embroidery? And now, it'll take days to remove the frog scum.*

A strange sound rang through the air like a finger on a wineglass or a flute carved from bone, a high tremolo, and a soft cry of pain.

Sariva knew none of the ladies-in-waiting had dragonets to shriek at night, and there were no rooms directly above hers. She peered out the door: no one in the hallway. No one below her window either.

Hadn't the old palace fallen apart like this? Magic upon magic upon magic until the illusions and ghosts started luring people in to devour.

Maybe someday this palace would be a ruin too.

She spent a few hours reading *The Battle Enchantress*, a biography of a famous mage-admiral, until the accounts of panache and wizards' duels helped her feel bold enough to sleep.

Maybe someone else had heard the possible ghost? The queen had risen early to confer with a few trusted counsellors. Still, Sariva aired her thoughts to the other ladies-in-waiting over a light breakfast in the sitting room. "I heard an odd noise last night."

Melisant glanced up from a half-written letter to a diplomat. "Servants?"

"No, or at least I don't think so. I thought someone was injured and weeping outside my window or in the corridor. But I only saw the moon."

"I didn't hear anything, and my chamber's right alongside yours. Be careful you're not drinking wine instead of grape juice or eating enchanted mushrooms," teased Ava.

Sariva, unamused, smiled anyway. "Honestly though. Did anyone hear anything, see anyone?"

"I certainly didn't. Then again, I'm a heavy sleeper." Paveya followed her sentence by yawning into her political correspondence as if to emphasize her point.

Melisant signed her letter with a flourish. "Don't doubt your sanity. You might have some dormant trace of magic, and if so, there's a perfectly reasonable explanation for everything. People worked enchantments here since before this castle even stood. All those ancient spells bouncing off one another where they weren't properly shielded... It's a wonder we're not all hearing things. People know how perilous the old palace is, but this palace holds danger too. The next time a mystical voice calls out from the twilight, I'd advise you to put a pillow over your head. Older and craftier than yours have lost their lives to the ancient secrets of this city."

"I promise," she lied.

A letter waited in her room from one of the people she'd written to before leaving home.

Sariva—

We'd be happy to have you at our Full Moon celebration. What's it like being a follower of the Goddess in such a small town, and how does your family worship the Goddess? Do you have any song-prayers you want to teach us? You're welcome to share whatever you'd like.

My house is at 2 Nuwit, right past the big tree with the birdhouses in Pomegranate Plaza—an easy walk from the palace, more or less. We'll start with some opening songs around when the local six o'clock bells fade out. If you knock and no one answers, come around to the back and tap on the kitchen window.

Remember to bring something for the table— and, if you can, a donation for one of our allied organizations because they're campaigning to elect more Desert People to city council!

See you soon,

Vered

Lots of carriages were parked outside the palace gates, waiting to take workers to their homes, diplomats to their inns. Sariva waved her arms to get the attention of a driver, who made a motion with his chin as if to say *Come on, hop up.* She got in the back of the carriage.

The driver glanced at her, graying eyebrows raised under his cap. "Where you headed?"

She double-checked the paper, though she knew the answer. "Um, 2 Nuwit?"

"East Nuwit or West Nuwit?" And, taking pity on her confusion, "Which side of the river?"

The city had parts? "It's by Pomegranate Plaza," she offered helplessly.

"Good, I can take you there. Dunno about some of my colleagues—they're younger men, haven't been around as much as I have, haven't seen as much—but I don't like crossing the river by the old palace this time of night." He turned to face the road and got the horses moving.

What did he mean? Sunset hadn't arrived yet...but she'd keep her mouth shut and tip him.

The carriage stopped at a little house made—like all others in the city—from irregular, time-worn blocks of creamy stone with a porch out front and a railing around the flat roof. Hopefully, her hosts liked flowery pink wines like the one she'd bought. Sariva passed some money up to the driver and stepped out, trying to keep a not-nervous smile on her face as she cradled the wrapped bottle like she used to carry her baby brothers.

Chapter Three

Edwynne polished her mentor's armor until she could see herself pulling faces in the gold willow emblem on his white steel breastplate.

Then Stellan strode in, all chiseled features and flowing hair. He cracked his knuckles. "Looks ready. Did you—"

What would he ask? *Did you see Mom and Dad's latest letter? Did you change your mind about apologizing?*

Edwynne cut him off. "I might not see you for weeks and weeks. Can we talk about the mission? About palace gossip—anything but that, please?" She helped him pull on the undershirt of mail, then each individual piece of plate, and tighten all the straps. He'd put on the helmet once he left the city.

"But the mission—there's not much to talk about... The queen wrote a letter. I've got to go see some wizards about a spell." A vague explanation, probably a lie.

"Sounds dangerous." The one wizard she knew acted vindictive as a wasp. Except wasps couldn't sentence you to latrine duty for swatting them.

A smile creased his face. "How long have you known me?"

"As long as I can remember. Nearly."

He tapped her nose. The bright steel, enchanted to prevent heatstroke, chilled her skin. "And have I died yet?"

"No." But didn't that apply to everyone living?

Her parents, for instance. They'd died.

"Exactly. My track record's fantastic. Come on, you can help me check over Austri." Edwynne and the strong dappled horse held each other in mutual regard. She helped Stellan saddle up and made sure Austri's saddlebags were even. Heading out of the stables, they ran into a woman and a girl.

Mattie, her beaded plaits swinging, leapt to her feet. "Stellan, are you really leaving? You said you'd take me into town this weekend, and one of the other ladies is helping me make a package for Rinan at home—"

"I shan't leave you, at least," Ava said, putting a perfumed arm around Mattie. The gesture just happened to show off her sparkling engagement bracelet. Mattie nodded forlornly and cuddled into her while Stellan's gaze softened as he beamed down at them both, and Edwynne rolled her eyes.

It ought to have been the three of them. Stellan Dovecote and sisters, mincing interloper not required.

Edwynne had been four when Stellan turned twelve. Having only known him as her foster-brother, she kicked anyone who misgendered him in the shins. He'd taught her how to fence under the willow trees in Dovecote manor, first with sticks, then blunted swords. They'd built forts among those trees, rode their ponies until sunset, and tried to catch rabbits. They evaded lessons and called the tutors names. He didn't even mind her being taller. Edwynne always tried to show Mattie similar patience.

And then Stellan had returned from a top-secret mission with this condescending stranger and her wardrobe of fine gowns. She'd called the trees at Dovecote Manor unnerving, the moss hanging down creepy, and deemed the weather too humid to watch him train. During her stay at the manor, Stellan had been too preoccupied with her to pay attention to Edwynne or the willow trees. She might as well have cut them down.

Leaning down from his horse, Stellan called Ava all sorts of absurd pet names. *My oasis, my queen, my peony, my basket of figs.* Edwynne headed for the gardens. She could tell when no one wanted her.

"Hold on, Ava. Edwynne, what's wrong? Look, I'll come home soon, don't be upset—"

"No, it's fine, you're busy," Edwynne called in her airiest voice.

Stellan's armor clanked as he dismounted. He sprinted after Edwynne and caught her before she could vanish between the trees.

"Edwynne..."

She folded her arms and glared. Three guesses and the first two don't count—he just had to tell her about poor Mother and Father and their hurt feelings.

"I know you asked me not to talk about it, but I might be away for quite some time."

"Good," she muttered, kicking the ground.

"Edwynne, can't you at least write to Mother and Father? Tell them you're doing all right and your studies are going well. Whatever you bought from the market on your last day off."

How could he say that with such a concerned, innocent look? Edwynne felt herself surging beyond spur-of-the-moment anger into a cold, deliberate cruelty as cold as the old palace's haunted cellars and forgotten stones. She kept her voice pitched low, a fierce whisper no one could overhear.

"Sure. I'll act like everything is all right. Like I'm all right with being lied to my entire life. They looked at me and told me I came from them. They didn't even try to give me back to my people."

"Edwynne—"

She wanted to stop herself. She couldn't. Stellan stood in front of her, and therefore, he'd take her fury on full blast. The words fell out of her mouth. "And I can't trust you either. Because you knew. You don't have the honor of a knight, the honor of a magpie. I bet when you and Ava have kids, you'll find some way to lie to them too."

"Edwynne, let's talk about this, please." He sounded hurt. Like she'd stabbed him. But apologizing in front of a dozen knights? Might as well keep digging her own grave. Edwynne thrust a rude gesture back at him and stomped away. She wanted to keep walking—out of the palace, out of the city, into the plains or the mountains where no one would look for her. But she couldn't bring herself to go farther than behind the stables. She curled up into a ball, glared daggers at a shard of rock in the dust, and tried to eavesdrop.

In the courtyard, Ava still spoke to Stellan. "I'm not going to pry, but...poor kid, she seems like a wreck. Are you sure you can't give it another try?"

A wreck? Admittedly. But Edwynne didn't like hearing Ava point it out.

Stellan sighed. "I can't spare the time. The curse is too dangerous. But we'll get through this. I think we just need to give her some time to calm down. After all, being sixteen is difficult."

Being sixteen wasn't difficult. Your brother ignoring you because he'd fallen in love and trying to spoon-feed you blatant lies? *That* was difficult! And what did he mean by a curse? Screw this. At least she had the evening to herself and a plan to visit friends outside the palace.

Vered—

Hey, long story short, I'm interested in learning more about Goddess worship and what it's like being from the North. Last time we spent time together (say thank you next time you drink half my juice, by the way!) you mentioned you planned to host some sort of prayer thing? A casual prayer thing?

Anyway, you can say no, but I'd like to come. If only to hum along and eat your food.

Can you ask your housemates what they think? And tell me if I need to wear anything or bring anything special.

-Ed

Hello, you!!

So, we're not doing anything serious—mainly saying the typical full-moon prayers, praying for those who're trying to bring more justice to the government, singing some songs—okay, singing a lot of songs—and everyone says you're welcome to come. We could do with another bottle of something to drink, but of course, you can't buy alcohol yet, so bring whatever you can. I'd say, "Wear a skirt or long robes," but I know you hate formal dress, so wear a head covering.

I'll lock the doors at around six when we get started. If you arrive afterwards, climb in through the window like you always do.

-V

"You look suspiciously free of dirt," said Tolliver, who'd caught her brushing her hair in a corner of the barracks as other squires headed to dinner.

"Guess so. Is my head covering centered? I'm going to a thing." The round silk cap came from an hour of rooting through the palace chapel on a hunch that a diplomatic party of Northerners might have left something behind. Pastel green. She hated pastels, but beggars couldn't choose.

"Aren't you supposed to hold the covering on with hairpins? This boy at my old tutor always lost his."

Fuck Tolliver for knowing something about Goddess worship she didn't. "Well, I don't have hairpins. Save me some dried fruit if they have any, okay? But no dried plums. Or pears. Those are nasty."

"Fine, but I get first dibs on the figs."

"Go for it."

The walk to Vered's house took her through the palace gates, down the hill separating the palace and its surrounding buildings from the city, through an intersection where some drivers argued over a crashed carriage—she vaulted the tipped vehicle like she learned in training—and down a few alleyways of closed shops. One, a pastry seller she often visited with Tolliver, had dimmed the lamps and started closing.

She ducked under the half-closed shutters to lean on the counter. "Ma'am, can I have some of yesterday's cookies? They're only a little stale, right? And it would be easier to give them to me than go all the way down to the bin on the corner to throw them out."

The proprietoress tried not to smile. "All right, since you're such a good customer. But only what you can carry."

"Thank you! My friends won't even notice they're past sell-by. I'll send them all here as soon as they get paid." Edwynne ran out with a bag of pastries tucked under each arm (pistachio cookies on the right, rosewater wafers on the left) and a ripped-off piece of braided cocoa cake in her mouth, thin layers of flavor rippling through the sweet bread.

Evening lights reflected in the streets, the stone like a cream river. Around the corner, she came to a trolley stop. This late, she'd find herself alone in most carriages, so she sprawled across the whole waiting bench. From a nearby rooftop, someone plucked out a tune on a stringed instrument, mournful notes twanging into the starlight.

"Cheers, well done," Edwynne bellowed when the music stopped, and maybe the player heard her or maybe not. Some drunk university students staggered by, singing the same song in different keys, before the public trolley came.

She showed her squires' pass and got off at Pomegranate Plaza, three blocks from Vered's. The breezy air felt perfect on her bare arms. Under the spreading tree with colorful ribbons and birdhouses dangling from its branches, people sat on rugs, drinking and chatting. Meanwhile, at the edge of the plaza, old men played board games. Edwynne touched her hair, making sure the little cap still sat in place. At least her hat knew what to do. Everyone seemed carefree, but she walked on, hoisting the two bags of sweets. Finally, she came to the little house where Vered lived with other artists and radicals. Edwynne loved when they could sit out on the porch, passing around a bottle of wine, complaining about voter registration or recounting a rally while the transient strangers sleeping in the guest hammock—some visitors from the university, others travelers passing through—always wanted to draw her or tell her fortune with carved stones.

She knocked—locked already. Of course. No matter. From the chatter, she guessed people had already sat to eat and talk before prayers. Edwynne went around the back of the tumbledown house and hoisted herself onto a rock, shoved her bags of pastries through the half-open window, and wriggled in after them. She landed near the food table, her thump on the floorboards rattling trays. Everyone else sat around a longer table with a bright-green tablecloth and mismatched dishes, Vered at the table's head, shimmery pigment on her cheeks and ribbons woven into her short hair.

Edwynne stood up. "Thank you for inviting me. I brought pastries." She locked eyes with the woman sitting right off Vered's shoulder.

The last person she wanted to see right now. Or ever.

Sariva's shocked, disgusted expression seemed to express Edwynne's thoughts: *What, it's that bitch?* A silent panic-scream welled up in her. This couldn't be happening. "What is she doing here?" she wanted to shout. Instead, she grinned at the group. "Hey, all. Did I miss any prayers?"

"We're finishing dinner, and then we'll bring out the sacred bread, the candlesticks, everything. I'll make sure you get a pamphlet with the prayers."

"Let me take these." Vered's housemate Nyssa whisked the bags from Edwynne's grasp and darted for the kitchen.

"I didn't know you knew...her," Sariva told Vered. Someone who didn't know what to look for would miss the subtle menace, but Edwynne knew her tells. She glared.

"Edwynne, why don't you go light a candle on the altar? Take a few deep breaths, clear your mind from the day." She gestured to the small table parallel to how everyone sat.

A few seated wore formal religious garments—hand-dyed shawls, the colors running into one another like water, over white robes. She touched her borrowed cap self-consciously.

"I mean, I think you have to remember your dreams in order to manifest them," said a man in a blue-green shawl.

The woman next to him, wearing a pink-and-purple shawl, shook her head. "But don't the Teachings say that sleep is one-sixtieth of death? I think even for dreams we don't remember, their energy still goes with us."

The dozen or so candles already lit brought a soft glow to the faceless stone Goddess statue, the glinting marble curves of a woman transforming into a tree. Someone had calligraphed a short prayer on a bit of scrap watercolor paper—*Wherever we go, may we share our rituals to heal the people of that land. There is magic in our collective travels.* Below that, something in Northern Edwynne couldn't read.

Edwynne didn't feel ready for "our rituals." She hardly even knew what those rituals entailed.

"Tonight, we bring divine peace into our home and our minds," Vered always prayed. But Edwynne couldn't imagine being peaceful. She tugged on her head covering, found the matches, and lit a little beeswax pillar. *Dear Goddess, please make Sariva stop annoying me. I could cope with life if only we'd never met.*

The man in blue-green pointed his fork at his companion. "Right, but you assume your dreams are enacting channels from the Divine Force."

"I mean, technically, we're not ever separate from the Divine Force of the Goddess in the first place—"

"What prayer book translation are you using, anyway?"

Edwynne bit her cheek to keep from laughing as she headed to Vered's part of the table. They sounded like wizards, prone to quibbling over footnotes...although wizards had much bigger egos.

"Edwynne's known me for years. She's a great kid—sorry, you're sixteen too, right?"

"Seventeen," Sariva replied, barely civil. She gave Edwynne a look like *Being compared to you insults me.* Edwynne returned the expression.

Vered smiled at her plate, doodling patterns in the sauce with her fork. "It's funny, I've known Edwynne for so long, part of me will always see her as the scrawny thirteen-year-old with a sword too big for her, who saved me from some sons of bitches when I was in my first year at the university. Edwynne, where do you want to sit?"

She gestured to the spot on Vered's other side. "With you, if that's okay."

"Sure, pull up a chair."

Edwynne fetched a chair from the other end of the room, then heaped food onto her plate and in her bowl (white with blue edging, Vered knew she didn't like anything fussy or girly) and sat down. She never glanced away from Sariva.

In her frilly pastel dress, she resembled a layer cake. A satisfying mental image flashed: Sariva disheveled and teary-eyed, petticoats ripped to shreds and braids unpinned.

Which. Okay. Scrap that, weirdly personal. She'd just pretend she never had that thought.

Maybe a horse could trample her.

Sariva had to listen to how Vered and Edwynne met, although she didn't seem to like the story. And why would she? It presented Edwynne as an absolute badass.

"So, on my first day old enough to actually drink—my dorm matron told me to watch my cup, but of course I thought she wanted to scare me—I left my drink on the bar while I tipped the musicians, and then I take one sip, and my head starts spinning."

Edwynne, smirking, devoted herself to the tomato stew.

"This older guy comes up to me and puts his arm around my shoulder. He's maybe thirty. He tells the bartender he's my lover and he'll help me get home. As I stagger onto the sidewalk, him practically dragging me, I see this little kid with a big sword. She's all, 'Unhand the girl or you will pay; she didn't arrive with you and she doesn't want to go with you.' I'm trying to tell this kid, 'You should go home,' but of course I can only manage random syllables. But without even drawing her sword, she beats up this man who's twice her size and then sits with me on the curb, making me drink water until I start feeling better. Of course, I had to take her to meet my roommates, if only so I knew she wasn't some kind of drugged fever dream."

Sariva nodded and sipped her tea. "One moment, I think my napkin fell under the table." She ducked beneath the tablecloth.

Fool me twice, shame on me. She wouldn't fall for the shoelace trick again. A rustling from underneath her—Edwynne swung her leg out. She got a thump of impact and a satisfying girlish shriek.

Sariva popped up, aghast. "You kicked me!"

"Sorry, I thought I had more room," she lied.

Nyssa and Corinth, another one of Vered's housemates, went around the table clearing the plates away.

Sariva fidgeted with her napkin. "Vered, can we talk in the other room—the sitting room—for a moment?"

"It'd be no trouble at all."   ◆

After they left, Edwynne counted to five. "Be right back." The bathroom filled with fake flower arrangements, which shared a wall with the sitting room, would be perfect for eavesdropping. She closed the door and moved a vase of silk lilies to press her ear to the wall.

"I just... I don't feel safe being in the same space as Edwynne, especially on a night that's supposed to be joyous and relaxing. She's tried so hard to drive me away from the palace even though I've done nothing to her." Sariva's voice.

"Can you tell me more about what happened?" Vered sounded concerned but not worried.

"She was so mean to me. She said I wasn't contributing materially to the revolution as an assistant to the queen and I was a waste of space who wouldn't accomplish anything with my life. And tonight—I literally wasn't doing anything, and she kicked me in the head. Entirely and completely unprovoked." Sariva sounded teary-eyed. Crocodile tears.

Vered would see right through this nonsense.

"Thank you for sharing your feelings with me, Sariva. I'll have a talk with her and let her know we don't condone such behavior. It's important to me that..."

Have a talk with her. Have a talk! Like a parent with a misbehaving child! She stomped to her seat.

Returning, Sariva gave Edwynne a look. The slightest smug smirk. *See?*

Edwynne's hands clenched into fists beneath the tablecloth. She wouldn't put up with this. As Vered sat, she piped up, "Hey, Vered? Got a second?"

"For you, always."

They went into the sitting room.

"I actually wanted to talk to you. Sariva—the new girl at the palace—she mentioned you hurt her feelings—" Vered started.

"Not as much as she hurt mine." Edwynne could cry on cue nowadays after learning of her birth parents' death and her adoptive parents' lies. She blinked. Tears rolled down her cheeks. *Outdo that, Lady Sariva.* Her voice shook. "You think converts are valid, right? I want to explore different religions and find one where I feel at home. You always talk about how important it is to believe in something. To find hope."

Vered held out her handkerchief. "Yes, and—"

Edwynne took it and blew her nose as loudly as possible, hoping Sariva heard. She let her voice shake as she continued. "So when Sariva came to the palace and I saw her necklace, I asked her about the Goddess, and she accused me of being dishonest and culturally appropriative and wearing her culture like a costume. I feel like I'll never be accepted anywhere. I mean, the other day at the palace, she crawled under the table and tied my shoelaces together!"

"And how do you know she did it?"

"Because it's an embroidery knot, and she does embroidery." Her argument felt less airtight out loud, Vered's contemplative expression reflecting its flaws.

"I hear you, but..."

Edwynne scowled, crossing her arms. "No, I get it. She hasn't done anything wrong here. Yet." And as a community leader, someone who got paid to organize things,

Vered had to maintain an impartial position, but she'd eventually realize the truth.

"Ed, if she bothers you, of course I'll ask her to leave."

Only a matter of time.

"Goddess," Sariva muttered with a roll of her eyes when Edwynne and Vered emerged from the sitting room. Edwynne smirked at her. *Guess who's still here!*

If Vered saw the rancor bubbling between them, she chose to ignore it. She stood, looking down the table. "Thank you for spending the moon night at my house. We're going to move on to prayers now, and we'll start with the angel song." Nyssa came from the kitchen, carrying a dish covered with a brightly colored patchwork cloth patterned with flowers and doves. Glass beads glinted on its surface. Corinth followed her, holding a peacock-colored pillar candle, its flame soft on their face.

Everyone started singing a sweeping, winding, wordless melody, sad and happy at the same time, and quiet like a secret. It reminded Edwynne a little of shanties she'd heard near the docks. Someone—the girl in the shawl or the slight youth across from her—started a high harmony, winding through and over everything. Nyssa and Corinth put the items down in front of Vered, who smiled at them.

"Sariva, as our newest guest, will you do the honor of unveiling the bread?"

"Of course," she said, rising from her chair. She pinched a corner of the brightly beaded cloth and dramatically whipped it off, then flicked it across the table.

The beading on the cloth caught Edwynne's eye. It stung, and she clapped a hand to her face, mouth dropping open. Sariva had smacked her with the bread cover!

She couldn't put up with this anymore. "You flicked me on purpose, you absolute bitch!" she cried out. Her hurt eye watered.

Sariva made a face, affronted. "You kicked me in the head on purpose. If I hit you in the eye by accident, it's only fair!"

Her air of snooty indignation? Unbelievable. "I wouldn't need to kick you if you hadn't tied my shoelaces together and made me trip," Edwynne shot back.

Sariva gasped. "What shoelaces? You should have believed me. I'm the one who didn't do anything wrong!"

"She's trying to sabotage our friendship. She wants me to be miserable!" Edwynne yelled over her.

Everyone had stopped singing by now.

"Both of you," Vered said, "sit down and be quiet." She didn't raise her voice, but she didn't need to.

They sat down, mouths closed.

"I don't know what's going on with you two. I don't know why you have so much drama. But I'm not going to let you sit at my kitchen table and try to play me against each other to prove some no-context petty point. You don't have actual accusations. You have activist jargon you're throwing at each other to try gaining my sympathy. Both of you—leave. Get rid of this chip on your shoulders. Ask for another invitation when you can actually focus on food, prayer, and song."

Edwynne couldn't believe this. "Vered, you know me! You know she should leave. She's a total bitch!" Every guest stared at her. She didn't care.

"You know, the sun's already set," said the man in the blue-green shawl with an undertone of *Let's start praying already.*

Vered pushed her bangs aside with a sigh. "As the event host, I have policies I need to follow. I'm not saying our friendship is over or that I won't give second chances. But I want both of you out of my house." And she gestured to the front door.

They glared at each other. Edwynne didn't want to admit defeat by leaving first, but Sariva wouldn't budge.

"What do you want me to do, close my eyes and count to three? This is ridiculous. You're both acting like children."

They bolted for the door at the same time, shoving each other as they went. Edwynne, with a well-placed pointy elbow, got out first.

Outside, the sun had set, the cafés were closing, and the street musicians had gone home. She sagged to the ground, a tight deflated feeling in her chest. Her first chance to connect with her heritage, and Sariva had ruined it! "I didn't get to hear the songs or the prayers. I didn't even get to eat the sacred bread," she whispered, tugging at the ground cover. How could Sariva do this to her?

Sariva scoffed. "If it's so important to you, have my stupid piece of bread. Braided yeast bread with extra egg yolks won't magically make you Northern." And she threw the bread into the dusty soil at Edwynne's feet.

Edwynne snatched the bread up and ripped a piece off with her teeth like a wild animal, glaring daggers at Sariva. Fuck her. It tasted excellent, sweet and melty with juicy golden raisins.

Did my mother make bread like this when she lived? She closed her eyes, chewing even slower. Did it taste familiar because all bread tasted a little alike, or because someone had fed little bits to her when her first teeth were growing in? But she had no way of finding out.

And when she opened her eyes, Sariva had left.

★

Sariva stood at a street corner. In the dark, it seemed identical to any other street corner. Where could she catch a carriage uphill to the palace, and why, oh, why had she stormed off without asking directions? She could either stand here, feeling like an absolute idiot, shivering in her party dress, or pick a direction at random and walk. The latter at least meant taking action. She headed toward the river, the easiest landmark to spot.

Horrible Edwynne! Sariva hadn't even done anything to her. Well, hardly anything. Now, instead of an evening's worth of valuable connections, she only had a bruised forehead. Her dignity hurt even worse. A cool breeze off the river soothed neither.

A signpost at the edge of the sidewalk only said how the old palace's visitor center could be found four blocks away.

She glanced out over the river. Lights shone on the other side, and a pale shape trembled over the water. A veil? A cloud of smoke? Shuddering, it seemed to resolve into a humanoid shape, but only its eyes appeared human—an insubstantial, melting body, a gaze filled with pain. Sariva froze. *Goddess, help me...drive away this evil presence!* Maybe whatever loomed above the depths would lose interest? Instead, it drifted closer, icy fog trailing from its clawed hands. It spewed cold air like an open door in winter, reaching out to touch her. Perhaps to rip her limb from limb.

A carriage turned the corner, wheels rumbling on the cobblestones, and rolled to a halt right by Sariva. The figure vanished, and the carriage door opened. A cultured male voice rang forth. "Sariva, is that you?"

Tension sagged from her body as she regarded Delvar. "You have no idea how happy I am to see a familiar face."

"How happy would a ride home make you then?"

"Extraordinarily." Her hands trembled with relief as she climbed into the carriage.

"Drive on," Delvar called, and the horses clip-clopped on.

Awkward silence lingered until she banished it. "What were you doing by the river this late at night?"

He smiled indulgently. "You're so cosmopolitan, I keep forgetting you're an out-of-towner anyway. The curses on the old palace have been acting up. One of my jobs is to keep unquiet spirits bound to the stones. They've been wandering from the old palace. Sometimes—at night—even blocks away."

"I did see something," she admitted, hands tangled in her lap. The strange chill still lingered.

He gasped. "Did it speak to you? Touch you? Are you hurt?"

"None of those! The specter only stared at me... It seemed terribly sad."

"Nevertheless, I'm glad I got here in time. You could've been ripped limb from limb." He retrieved a sealed jar from his robes. "Want some mulled wine? A new bar opened near my favorite magical supply shop."

"Yes, please. And I'd love to hear more about what you did tonight to bind the spirits." She welcomed a hot drink and the change of subject. Thankfully, he didn't ask her why she'd been alone on a deserted street.

Ava, on the other hand, asked. "Back early? Did you dislike the party?"

Answers jostled for priority. "Your stupid sister-in-law is ruining my life." Or "Does Edwynne make you miserable, or does she just hate me specifically?" Or "I'm going to crochet a child leash."

But she probably shouldn't bad-mouth Edwynne to her brother's fiancée. "I don't want to talk about it," Sariva replied, heading for her room. Her usual evening primping seemed exhausting. She could only muster the energy to take off her makeup and put on a nightgown, then collapse into bed without moisturizing her skin or brushing her hair.

If you ever have a problem you can't solve, Father had once told someone seeking spiritual guidance, pray to the Goddess's angels to bring answers in your dreams.

Well, Sariva possessed bushels of problems.

Several letters to prospective brides had gone unanswered. No one would introduce her to the queen. And then, on top of it all, Edwynne, everything about her a problem, from her look-at-me auburn curls to her smug freckled cheeks and sulky, sneering thin-lipped pout.

Sariva tried to empty her mind and fill it with prayer.

"Angels on the right of me, bring me wisdom. Angels on the left of me, discernment. Angels before and behind me, clarity. And below, above, and within me, the Goddess's gifts." Feeling no different, she stared at the ceiling. At least all days, even horrid ones, ended.

Sariva watched herself slip through the palace gates by moonlight, gliding down the big hill with outstretched arms, leaping from rooftop to rooftop, running on the river like a road.

A sprawling, dilapidated building lurked beside the water. The old palace. She floated under a crumbling archway, then sank through the ground, filled with an odd, detached curiosity.

The glowing eyes of a huge dragon. Cold talons piercing her. A lake like black glass.

And in the center, the queen, suspended from a cavern ceiling in iron chains, curls undone, limp as a doll. She turned to Sariva. Her lips seemed parched, her eyes glassy. "Help me. Please, you must try."

"Where are you?" Sariva didn't know this place.

"Help me," she repeated more insistently.

"Help you how? What is it that you want me to do?"

The queen pointed behind Sariva. "You must go. He's found you!"

Sariva turned and woke up in her bed.

If the bells hadn't rung yet, that gave her a bit longer to sleep.

She lay back down, but her head clunked against something hard. What lay under her pillow? Lifting it uncovered a dirty rock the size of her fist. "This reminds me of the stones from the ruins in my dreams."

She wanted to say, "another prank," but no one would go to this much trouble. Edwynne, for all her seeming omnipotence, couldn't see inside Sariva's dreams. And Delvar had bound the ruins ghosts last night. This had to be a sign from the queen, from the Goddess, perhaps even both. She needed to start with Ava and seek out the truth.

Sariva brought *A Young Lady's History of the Embroidered Arts* to the sitting room. While they examined a two-page spread, their heads side by side, she struck. "By the way, is there anything you might wish to tell me with regards to the queen?"

The smile dropped off Ava's face like fruit ices melting in sunlight.

"Please," she added, not meaning it.

Ava handed over the book and rubbed her eyes. Her face had an ashen cast under her freckles. "I assume you've heard rumors, so I might as well tell you the whole story."

Sariva sat up straighter.

"The queen is recovering from an illness. If it were known, the populace would worry, the merchant princes might make power grabs in her absence, and the provincial governors would return to old conflicts."

It made sense. "The anti-immigration faction would try to slip through some proclamations, and I bet the counsellors would start squabbling. Besides, so many people think being ill is a sign of weakness."

"Exactly."

Sariva thought about what she knew of Queen Oradel. Considering that a monarch lived her life in the public eye, in newspapers each week with commemorative crystals and transcripts of their speeches, Sariva felt she knew a decent amount. Beautiful, kind, funny, and eloquent, she could stare down wealth and power without so much as a blink. Sariva remembered things she had said: *Ignorance is only a virtue in children and courtesans, and you, sir, are neither.* Or, *If I truly am a religious extremist sent to destroy this country, I do think someone would have made me aware of it.* Or her graduation speech at a local finishing school: *You are braver than you believe yourselves to be. You are the ones who shall go forth and change our world.*

Many of Sariva's friends had sewn that phrase into their samplers.

According to the Magic Mirror, people had chosen Queen Oradel specifically to wrangle the old-money nobility and merchant princes into cooperation with the common folk. Could any ruler be as clever and as well-loved all at once? How long would it take for the various factions to provide candidates to present to the Magic Mirror? The queendom might fall into civil war.

She shouldn't push, but...

"Ava, pardon me, but I'd be honored to help you attend the queen this morning. I could just stand and watch, and that way I wouldn't make any errors you might have to take the blame for. I know I'd learn a great deal from watching you." Flattery could get one anywhere, right?

Ava bobbed an apologetic curtsy. "I wish I could offer you the opportunity, but she's been awake for hours. I'm merely bringing her a letter." She continued. Sariva bowed her head over her embroidery until she was sure of being alone. Then she drained her entire teacup in one irritated slurp.

"Might I wait on the queen at lunch?" she asked when Ava once again passed through the sitting room.

"She has a great deal of correspondence to attend to, so she'll be taking lunch in her chambers."

"Do you think you could ask the servants to send lunch up to me as well? I'm a bit dehydrated from the heat up here, and I feel a trifle unwell." She ducked away before Ava could rest a sisterly hand on her forehead, adding, "I'll be in my room if anyone wants me."

Looking over her belongings, Sariva wondered if she should disguise herself. Or would that seem more suspicious? Better not. She set her shoulders and crept toward the door—

A rap on the window. She jumped, her mind swirling with excuses before realizing only a bird nudged the glass. She kept going.

At the top of another staircase, a guard in a faded uniform leaned against the wall, picking his nails. "If you're with the diplomatic delegation, your quarters are in a different wing of the palace." He seemed polite but dismissive. All right. She could work with this. She put on a confused expression and copied her father's trace of an accent. "That's what I'm concerned about. I think there's a ruffian sneaking about in our quarters. Some jewelry has gone missing, and it seems like our furs have been rifled through. Is there some sort of form I can use to report it?"

He seemed doubtful but still nodded. "I can't go far from my post, but I'll go down the hall and get a bit of paper for you. You'll stay here, right?"

"Of course." She wouldn't. With a silent prayer of thanks, she slipped through the unlocked door he'd been guarding.

Light sparkled through glass vases, and silk thin enough to pull through a ring draped a canopy bed. Sariva's slippers sank into a brightly woven rug. A figure stirred in the bed.

One outstretched hand, brown and slender. A spill of night-dark hair. She wanted to drop to her knees in reverence or even start crying. How did people even cope with such proximity to someone who had done so much to change the world?

Melisant stepped out from behind the bed. "What do you think of these letters from the Rethan ambassador?"

Sariva ducked between the door and the wall, hardly daring to breathe.

"The what?" The voice sounded quiet, emotionless. With no identifying inflections, it could have belonged to anyone.

It belonged to a tall, beautiful woman with dark hair and skin who stared absently into a speaking crystal. Sariva recognized her from a thousand pictures—her elegant features and the waterfall of her curls.

"The ambassador to Retha. Their parliament wishes to renew the trade pact from before the wars."

"Indeed, it seems thus." A classic Plains filler phrase. "We might renew the pact under conditions such as the protection of established territories, laws to keep children out of the sweatshops..." She seemed to lose interest in the conversation, sighing midsentence.

"Are you all right, Your Majesty?"

She hugged herself and rocked. "Whether they live or die, isn't it pointless? So many things might kill a child. I suppose you might as well deal with the policy minutiae..."

What had gone wrong? Couldn't a mind-healer help? *But the queen has access to the best healers...*

At last, Melisant left. The queen, with no one to keep her awake, resumed sleep. Sariva counted to a hundred and made a run for it.

Like a deer fleeing the hunter, she sprinted through the corridors. Would she be heard? Seen?

Somewhere distant, women laughed together. Sariva tried to breathe deeply, which came out as a sob. (Queen Oradel seemed so tired and apathetic, and yet, Ava said nothing! Goddess, why had they all lied?)

Her hands shook as she hurried toward her own room. She needed to embroider something. She rifled through her workbag, spreading tangled floss over the floor. A spool bounced and rolled away. Pins she'd forgotten to stick in a pincushion jabbed into her hands. At last, she found a half-finished wall hanging of a dove, a bird the Goddess cherished. She separated the pieces of an embroidery hoop and pressed the fabric in.

The world resembled a tangled skein. The seams holding her life together frayed more every moment. This country would tear apart if something happened to the queen. No more free schools for children, no more protections for those from far away. As a Northerner, she didn't even have the most to lose. She would be able to survive. But what about other people who would face more danger?

Sariva shook her head. She could only keep working.

Curves of the bird's delicate body remained unsewn. She completed it with satin stitches, the rhythm helping slow her heart. Normally, she preferred more difficult ornamental embroidery to filler stitches, but now she clung to the pattern. Stitched feathers grew across the linen.

Why had the other ladies-in-waiting concealed so much? Would the queen die?

The Magic Mirror of Governance resonated with the queendom and its rulers. As well as tabulating whom the people wanted to rule, it could reveal when someone needed to step down.

Afternoon deepened into evening. This, at least, she could plan for, wrapping an embroidery hoop with blue ribbon and hanging it. She'd wrested some measure of control from the darkening sky.

Chapter Four

The roof of the squires' bunks on Palace Hill overlooked the glimmering river, the ruins of haunted old buildings like crumbling teeth. Edwynne liked to sit on the roof and watch the world.

Often, she, Stellan, and Tolliver, along with the knight who mentored Tolliver, visited the city. This week, Stellan had promised to take her to a dance performance: an Islander troupe whose beautifully dyed outfits boasted garlands of glimmering shells.

"Hey," Tolliver said, pulling himself up on the roof. "Hey, you. Still want to go to that performance?"

"Maybe."

"It's been cancelled. I asked around last night while I helped watch the docks. Apparently, they couldn't get permission to come into the city. They were turned away right at the gangplank. Something about their papers not being in order, and from what I've heard, that's been happening more and more often."

Despite the warm weather, Edwynne's shoulders prickled. "And they couldn't even plead their case?"

"I don't think so. There's a lot of new city guards. Haven't seen any of them wearing recording gems. Creepy, right?"

Edwynne wanted to have a glorious day to spite the bastards, to wave her joy in the face of anyone who wanted it gone. "Creepy and unfair. Let's just go to the market. Browse the stalls, eat lunch, feed the birds...and hopefully not run into any of those new guards."

Edwynne sprinted down the busy road into the city, Tolliver at her heels. She loved feeling her sandals smack against the slippery cobblestones, her muscles working to keep her from stumbling. They eventually reached the market where people stood in a long line at the entrance. Small children tugged on their tired parents, whining and crying, and merchants stooped under the weight of their goods. Some university students passed around a bottle. Cheap mead, probably.

Edwynne, scowling at the scene, ran to the front of the line. A bored guard leaned against a hastily built fence. She got his attention. "Hey. What's the problem? Did something catch on fire?" Why this strange scene?

He frowned at the squires, evidently unimpressed, and drawled, "End of the line, both of you. All people entering the market must be searched for contraband, by order of the queen."

"Bullshit!" she burst out, stamping her foot. "The queen would never order something so unfair."

"Signed and ratified proper." Looming into Edwynne's face, he brandished a scroll, embellished with the royal seal. "End of the line, brat."

She squared up, muscles tightening. "Let me see that scroll. I bet it's fake and you're only here to get money out of—"

Three more guards in clean new uniforms came out from the market. One raised an eyebrow at Edwynne. "Is there a problem, little missy?"

"Ed," Tolliver said, low with urgency. "Let's forget it. Let's go."

"Fine."

He wove back through the line, and she stomped after him until they got free of the crowd.

Tolliver sat on the curb next to a potted palm. "We ought to go somewhere else."

She wouldn't let a few suspicious jumped-up creeps ruin her day. "Yeah, like what?"

"The docks?"

"It won't be fun if all the ships are getting turned away. We'll get soggy and smell like fish. I want to go to the market." If they visited their favorite stalls, maybe listened to the street musicians and drank mint lemonade, that pinched nervous expression would leave Tolliver's face.

He rolled his eyes. "You're such a brat."

"You're such a brat," she mimicked and giggled as she pulled him to his feet and tugged him toward the line. She'd bite Sariva for saying that, but Tolliver could get away with it.

They slipped in behind a merchant, a stooped old man with long gray hair. Slowly but surely, the line moved. At last, the main guard peered into the old man's wheelbarrow full of sacks. He sniffed the contents of one sack, sifted a handful through his fingers. "This," he declared, "is contraband."

The old man quavered. "It's herbs. Culinary herbs. I've got a stall. Some of the best cooks in the city come there for—"

Another guard poked the same sack, frowning. "These could be poisonous. Or illegal spells."

"What are you—"

"We'll go through every sack until we find evidence," said a third guard. He hauled another sack out of the cart and upended it. Dried leaves fell into a dirty puddle.

People murmured in shock and dismay, and Edwynne, face hot with anger, dove forward. They could pick on a poor old man but not a squire of noble birth. "Hey! He said he's an honest merchant. I've seen him before loads of times. He's got a corner stall, and sometimes he sells dried fruit!"

The first guard leaned down, putting his face close to Edwynne's again. "Are you obstructing the activities of a government official?"

Fuck this. She headbutted him in the nose. He yanked two fistfuls of her hair, sharp pain exploding through her scalp, and shoved a boot into her ankles. Around them, people shouted, and footsteps rushed. Edwynne only cared about landing the next blow.

They tumbled to the cobblestones, trading blows. The fancy bastard punched her in the throat. She managed to get on top of him and knee-slam his crotch, but he recovered and yanked the front of her shirt.

"Ed," Tolliver said. "Ed, the other guards, they've got swords—"

Fist raised to smash the guard's nose in, she slowly turned around and shifted her weight. Two guards had hands on sword hilts. Another had forced the old man, now bleeding from a head wound, to his knees.

Her mouth said, without any input from her common sense, "And what are you going to do about it?"

They drew their swords on her. They actually drew their swords! When Stellan found out...

Tolliver stepped between her and the guards. "Please. She's simpleminded and a noble. I'm her minder. The Dovecote family pays me three gold pieces a day. She doesn't know her own strength—"

"Dovecote's an old family," one guard muttered.

"Yes, she's got the crest on the other side of her squire pendant. Show them, Ed."

She fumbled for the pendant in her tunic and held it out. The guards blanched, recoiling, and the one under her squirmed in panic. "Your ladyship—ma'am—I didn't hurt you too badly, did I?"

She relaxed her knee-hold on his rib cage and let him fumble out and scramble away. "I've had worse." Any ordinary person would have been roughed up by these thugs, maybe led at swordpoint to the dungeons. But she had the right accent, the right face, the right ostensible family, and at the sight of a noble sigil, their mean attitudes turned into "Sorry my face collided with your fist, Lady Whatsyourname!" And she hadn't earned it. She'd gotten lucky. Her skin crawled. Did the people gawping at her realize the bullshit unfairness of it all? Fuck, she hoped so. For a moment she wanted to go somewhere hidden and cry.

"Three gold pieces a day, you say?" one of the guards murmured, giving Tolliver a look. The squires got one gold piece per week.

Don't, she wanted to say, but he searched in his pockets and handed a coin over. "Yes, and here you go, for your kindness in allowing everyone to go about their business."

"All right, people," barked the guard with the shiniest shoes, who seemed to be in charge. "You two, go report this to field headquarters. All you civilians, get back in line!"

But they didn't.

People helped the herb seller to his feet, fetching his scattered bags and sachets from the square.

"Does anyone have clean cloth for bandages?" one university student called.

A woman carrying an infant unwound her shawl. "This ought to do." Slowly the crowd coalesced, passing over a hip flask to use as disinfectant, some leaves for a poultice.

A scruffy kid slipped into the market and brought vessels of tea.

A burly man unloaded a rug from his cart and draped it about the poor herb seller's shoulders like a blanket. "Seems most of your goods are still all right, Uncle." He received a tentative smile in return.

A gray-haired woman in metal-toed boots stomped over and peered down at Edwynne. "Are you all right?"

Edwynne blinked.

Tolliver poked her. "She's talking to you, dumbass."

"I've been better," she managed. The scruffy kid darted over and pressed a little cup into her hands. Jasmine tea with a swirl of raw honey. Every sip lingered in her mouth.

She glared at Tolliver's freckle-spotted face. "You know I hate being called simpleminded."

"Yeah, well, you're still here to be pissed off. I had to stall for time some way or another."

"Okay. Figure something out for next time."

He sat beside her with a deep sigh. "Please tell me there won't be a next time."

She focused on the tea. Light green. Flowery. The cup warm in her hands. The kid went around, snatching up empty cups, and Edwynne caught their eye to hand hers over.

While the remaining guards still interrogated people about what they were doing here and poked through their belongings, they no longer had the force of numbers to rough anyone up.

But in her beloved city, while she wore the palace's colors with a woman from the "low-class" Plains province on the throne, her entire brain yelled swear words of incomprehension. This sort of thing didn't—shouldn't—happen nowadays. Not here.

They got into the market. The busy plaza felt dampened, empty tables scattered between boarded-up food carts.

Tolliver went to one of the remaining carts and stomped back over, eyes narrowed. He slammed a plate of chicken kebabs onto the table. "Ed. What were you thinking?" Not a joke. Not teasing. Real anger and worry. "If they'd thought your medallion was stolen or a fake—if I hadn't been there—you could have gotten seriously hurt, you know?"

"I suppose I wasn't. Thinking, I mean." Only felt the wave of anger surging up. "I mean, I never think about things like that. You know I don't."

He sighed, mollified, and picked at his food. "Yeah, well. Maybe even people like us aren't as safe as we used to be. Things are changing, Ed."

Afterwards, they drifted over to the square to see the street musicians. Edwynne tried to find the Northern woman who'd attempted talking to her. She spotted an instrument case, still lying on the plaza, and her sign—tattered and stomped on—but not the musician herself. Maybe the new guards took her away. Edwynne broke her kebab stick into splinters. "You know what? Fuck it. Let's go home."

"Sure, as long as we don't go past the old palace. It scares my freckles off."

She rolled her eyes but followed his path. "You're probably safe with me though."

"Nah. What about the ghosts who eat energy? I like better odds than 'probably' for keeping my soul in my body and my flesh on my bones."

★

The next morning, before going to join the other ladies at their letter writing, Sariva put on her best gown. "Paveya, you're connected to the tourism committee, right? Well, my mother loves history, and I promised I would view the Magic Mirror for her."

"Occasionally, high-ranking ladies and court officials are permitted to take sightseers through. You'd have to sign up months in advance, of course, but it's something to write home about."

"Sounds lovely." And inadequate.

Asking around at the tourism office—"double-checking the schedule"—proved more productive. An Islander trade delegation had tonight's slot, and she bribed an intern for her ticket with goldwork embroidery. The place—an unused tower—and the time—sunset. She arrived in the small waiting room early. For some time, the Islanders filed in, chatting in their own melodic language. Sariva admired the jewel-toned geometric patterns of their brightly dyed clothing.

The door opened again, and Ava came in. "Right, that's everyone. Sariva, you're here too! I didn't expect to see you here."

"Oh, I wrote ahead before I came here. My mother's quite the fan of history, so I've been planning this for months. I didn't expect to see you here either."

"Well, I studied political history and government, so I fill in for tours sometimes. Part of my duties. We're ladies-of-waiting-of-all-work around here, aren't we?"

"Don't I know it." Keeping her talking seemed best.

After checking tickets, Ava produced a tiny silver key from the lining of her boot and unlocked a closet door to reveal a spiral staircase with a low ceiling. To Sariva's surprise, they emerged into a grand, sunlit room that didn't seem present from outside the tower. Large oil paintings adorned the walls.

"All right, everyone, thank you for coming on today's tour. As you can see, these works of art recount the history of the Magic Mirror."

Instead of merely buying the tragedy's sheet music, Sariva had read primary sources. She recognized each painted figure. Amaldia pouring over a map, her dark eyes burning with concentration. General Moonflower slouching thoughtfully, considering all viewpoints; Rhysling unobtrusive with paper and quill. Plains Corinne with her war hammer, and Spymaster Lockhart with his exotic straw-colored hair.

"Amaldia, who came to our shores as a Northern mercenary quartermaster, was described by her sworn companion Rhysling as a polymath strong of both feature and character." Sariva stood on her tiptoes for a better view of the portrait. She loved how Amaldia resembled no one but herself in the picture, big hawklike nose and all. Ava continued with textbook facts. "Amaldia helped Rhysling trick the invading armies..."

Evidence shows Amaldia loved and slept with women, she wanted to add. But, like Amaldia, Sariva needed to hide in the shadows for her mission to succeed.

"The mirror is practically indestructible by nonmagical means. In fact, it's the most accurate, least corruptible system of counting votes in the world and deduces when new elections need to be held."

The party of traders exclaimed in amazement.

Ava leaned forward to unlock a tiny door set into the wall. Sariva estimated they'd ascend another winding staircase to an antechamber. Instead, they poured into a grand room of pure white marble. Sunlight streamed through the stained-glass windows.

Ropes blocked off the mirror, and a filmy curtain fell over its surface. Everyone squeezed close as Ava gestured to the magical artifact.

"For years, the mirror has observed the leaders of our towns and provinces. Out of all those leaders, it helps Almesia pick one best suited to rule. Two hundred years ago, General Moonflower forged this artifact to stop a civil war, which had spilled over into the surrounding countries," Ava continued.

In the mirror, misty forms swirled. Sariva knew nothing about spying, but she understood manners. "Oh, bother," she cried as the group moved on. "Hang on, my slipper's unlaced."

"Those delicate slippers are awfully impractical," sniffed a trader in sandals. Sariva gave a nod of rueful assent and crouched down.

Under the braided ropes, she stared into the mirror. Her own reflection blinked back. She waited until the group went to the next room, then whispered, "You answer questions about leaders, don't you? Where's Queen Oradel? Is she fit to rule?"

A ripple of sound acknowledged her question, rushing water and bamboo chimes. Her own reflection winked and dimmed.

Blue lights hummed like a singing bowl as a pale-skinned spirit peered out. "She has eyes dark as lodestone. She is thinking of the way a flower breathes in the sunlight." They giggled and vanished.

"Go on," Sariva said. "Is she all right?"

With the rustle of leaves, a gold-gowned spirit perched on air. "She is thirty-seven years of age. She is contemplating the shine of semiprecious stones under dim candles." She disappeared as if windblown.

An unearthly male spirit with gorgeous dark skin and stars in his curls regarded her. "Her name is Oradel Elestren, bird charmer and world weaver, First of the Sapphire Throne. At present, her strengths are persistence and argument. But a weakness sits in her heart like a snake among reeds, forming the web she is trapped in, the bars of her cage. Her hope has been stolen."

Many voices resounded around the chamber, quietly echoing one another's words. "The queen is in the palace...the queen is in the palace..."

For years, the mirror had flawlessly described rulers. Why had its prescience suddenly stopped? She glared at her reflection and whispered, "You're no help at all!"

A touch on her shoulder. Ava smiled down at Sariva, her voice a firm whisper. "Would you please follow me once the tour is over? Melisant and I were discussing an issue relating to you, and I'd love to make sure your opinion is heard as soon as possible."

The calm expression in Ava's eyes, a certain no-nonsense tone to her voice, told Sariva she'd been caught. "I'm sure I wouldn't want to impose."

Ava grinned at her. "Oh, do please come with us. We have rainbow pastries, and I'm told that's a terrific delicacy where you come from."

Refusing a formal invitation? Almost as rude as snooping on sacred artifacts. As the traders walked back to the main palace, she offered her arm and allowed Ava to lead her. After all, she had no choice.

Ladies-in-waiting filled the sitting room. Melisant, like a war-empress, held fish spines for a ragged cat to lick. Paveya's knitting needles clicked like an executioner's footsteps. Golden bangles wound down Lisette's slender arms like snakes. Several more ladies-in-waiting ringed the room. Melisant furrowed her brow, and Sariva longed to sprint for the door. But her gaze focused on Ava. "How much have you told her?" Melisant asked, her tone harsh.

Sariva wanted to melt with relief. Perhaps she wouldn't face a reprimand.

"Only that the queen is ill," Ava stammered.

"And you?" Paveya used her needle to point at Sariva. "How much do you know?"

Sariva, fidgeting, wondered if she wanted to take a rainbow pastry. Had someone poisoned it?

Amaldia, in this situation, would already have made a witty speech. Amaldia would already have some hold over the castle staff to keep colleagues from poisoning her food. But Sariva, lacking these skills, had to improvise. "It has been brought to my attention that you may have spread dishonest statements about the nature of the queen's illness." When they failed to reply, she risked continuing. "It seems you've concealed the true nature of her illness from people and sought to conceal the queen. What the queen's become."

Paveya leaned forward. "How did you figure things out?"

"Observation when unobserved." It sounded better than "I snuck in."

Melisant stroked the cat. "Hence why we want you on our side."

She hadn't expected that. "What?"

"Anything you can find out may be of great use because we—and by 'we' I mean a significant percentage of the queen's political allies—are similarly worried."

"But she's Northern," Lisette said, crossing her arms. "No offense. How do we know where her loyalties lie? After all, the Northern sultan hates our queen…"

You can be two things at once, Sariva wanted to snap. Yet a retort wouldn't win her sympathy. She settled for turning the question around. "The queen's policies have helped many who worship the Goddess. Whatever my loyalties on a larger scale, I'd always want to help her."

"Yes, of course," Lisette murmured, fluttering her long eyelashes like *See? I'm harmless.*

"But how do I know all of you have the queen's best interests at heart? I have significant reasons to doubt all your loyalties." And she tossed her plaits for effect.

Melisant raised an eyebrow.

Sariva backtracked. "I'm sorry, it's been a long day."

"At first we all suspected our fellow ladies-in-waiting. But the queen may have done this for some reason of her own," Ava observed, her voice soft.

"She at least knew this would happen. See for yourself. She left us books of instructions with advice, such as what to say to whom and letters to be mailed in her absence." Paveya passed Sariva a few notebooks.

Paging through one revealed a table of contents in neat writing:

> *For when the Minister for Economics wants to hear monthly report.*

> *For when peace talks in the North resume.*

There were some envelopes tucked into the cloth binding of the books, and those made even less sense:

> *Open if you are reunited with the witch in the woods.*

> *Open if large-scale magic damages weather patterns.*

> *Open if anything in my chamber explodes.*

She wrinkled her nose. "Did she have someone who could foretell the future working with her?"

"We don't know—even Izalena never told anyone the extent of her powers—but we welcome your fresh perspective."

"But—" How could she possibly help with such a strange situation?

Melisant laid a hand on her shoulder. "Sariva. Rest from your duties. I have great hope for your presence here. You may notice something we have not yet seen."

The queen had put herself into some sort of fugue state for unknown reasons. The ladies-in-waiting were hiding her illness because the queen had requested they do so. And everyone wanted answers. How could a newcomer like her do anything to help?

As other ladies-in-waiting departed from the sitting room, Ava leaned in. "Sariva, would you perhaps like to sit with the queen tomorrow?"

"Yes, please." She could investigate properly instead of creeping around.

Inside the queen's ornate room, silence hung in the air like dust.

The sun shone through vases on the windowsill, which held tiny delicate blossoms, wildflowers from where the queen had grown up.

Queen Oradel stared blankly at Sariva. She reached out, but her arm fell limp as if the movement drained her energy.

"I suppose I should, umm, introduce myself?"

No reply.

"I am the Lady Sariva... I am new to court and a loyal citizen. It's an honor to be introduced to you, Your Majesty..."

The queen took a deep breath like the leaves of a dead palm tree rattling in the winds. Then she closed her eyes and sank onto the pillows.

Ava opened the door. "How are you getting on? I know it can be quite a shock."

"I'll manage... Do you think she might notice if I bring her some fresh flowers?" Having to ask such a question felt awful.

"It's the thought that counts. And don't be put off if she stares. I don't think she means to."

"How can you possibly be so calm?" She folded her hands in her lap and squeezed them together until her knuckles hurt.

Ava shook her head. "We found a note by her bedside. It stated she had subjected herself to this state to avoid a greater danger and told us to treat this with as much secrecy as possible." She perched on the edge of the bed as Sariva sat on a rocking chair by the nightstand. "Only...if the worst happens, you don't think the mirror might nominate me to be in the government, do you?" Worry creased her perfect face.

"I'm sure you'd be a splendid ruler." Her attempt at reassurance missed its mark.

Ava sighed. "I don't even want to be in parliament. Yes, I can manage people and supplies and camels, and technically, I've ridden at the head of an army. But staying cooped up in the palace would destroy me. I want to marry Stellan when he returns from his mission and start a family where my mother and grandmother grew up. Right now, I can't even meditate about my problems. Whenever the star-leader of our worship services says something about remembering a happy memory, I think about sailing down the river with Stellan. The rowboat's about to overturn, but we're laughing so hard. Being with him, feeling free in the desert...those are my glad places. I might lose both."

Sariva held Ava's hand. "I'll pray for you. My mother always says even though people may have different gods, there's only one fate."

"Thank you, Sariva. You're such a help. Let me know if anything changes, all right?"

"Of course." She bid Ava farewell.

Sariva dug around in her workbag until she retrieved her latest project, a series of small cross-stitches for brooches. She placed the fabric in a hoop, threaded her needle, and went to work. Ought she use variegated thread for these embellishments or all one color? Variegated thread would provide a more graceful effect, but how much would she need?

Something exploded.

Her chair flung her off like a wild horse, and she hit the ground hard. Ears ringing, head pounding, she blinked and tried to sit up.

The four-poster bed had collapsed, pillars toppling outward, canopy falling to shroud the queen's form. The windows had shattered, letting in wind, and the pretty vases on the windowsill lay in fragments on the floor.

I ought to go for help. The entry in the notebook... But she couldn't move.

Footsteps thumped toward her. "Sariva! Oh, stars! Are you all right?"

The room spun like a carousel. Something trickled down her forehead. She touched it and blinked at her smeared palm: blood mingled with gemlike shards of broken glass and an embroidery needle embedded through one fingertip, parallel to the nail. Her chest hurt like a burn. She glanced down to see another piece of glass jutting from above the neckline of her dress.

So much blood, all hers... It reminded her of another time and another place. Of feeling more helpless than a trapped mouse. "Her Majesty," she tried to ask Ava. But fuzzy grayness filled her vision, and her body toppled over.

Had Queen Oradel survived?

Chapter Five

Most Almesians stayed away from the old palace's ruins—except tourists who didn't believe the rumors, archaeologists who didn't mind a few flesh wounds if they got tenure, revelers too intoxicated to ignore the ghost-whispers, and the knights assigned to watch the ruins.

And Edwynne.

One knight sprinted into the training yard. "Edwynne, they need you down at the ruins! You're the smallest squire cleared for ruins work—"

"I'm on it."

In the ragged courtyard of crumbling stone, knights surrounded a plump youth clutching a notebook and a case. "Stars, I thought we'd be fine. We were just there to retrieve some scrolls. We took all the precautions," they managed, rocking.

"Have some mint lemonade. You're dehydrated," one knight offered, but they burst into tears. "My colleague loves lemonade with mint."

Catching sight of Edwynne, they seemed newly alert. "Is that her?"

Edwynne ran across the courtyard, sandals slapping stone, and crouched beside the panicked academic. "I'm the squire. What happened to your friend?"

"We're historical researchers from the university. My name is Calder. My friend Valency..." Calder started hyperventilating. Hiccups turned into sobs.

Better stick to the facts. "Where is she?"

"We were excavating on the first level down. Around—" They pointed to a spot on the map.

"Good." Farther down, people died faster.

"Valency's tiny. I couldn't fit through the route she took, so I waited as nearby as I could. But then she tripped, and I think she broke her arm. She passed out. I couldn't help her. I just ran..." Another round of sobs shook their body.

"I'll do everything I can."

The tunnel's dark entrance resembled an open mouth, and magical torches at the entrance gave the off-white stone a sickly gold glow.

Inside, water rushed through a channel between stones, foaming and churning. Someone—something?—cried out in the distance, the sound not quite words. The tunnel narrowed.

A broad-shouldered man—someone like Stellan—would have needed to sidle through. Edwynne strode on. Her torch flickered, plunging the narrow tunnel into darkness for a moment. She swallowed hard.

She came to a bend where the water-pitted stone bulged and curved. The close walls seemed to pulse like a heartbeat. If she touched the stone, would it feel soft like skin? If she scraped the lichen, would it bleed? Other knights had told her of such happenings. What if she walked into a giant mouth? *The woman needs me. She's even more scared than I am.*

Edwynne touched her short sword and continued.

"Oh, fuck, my arm... Calder, are you there? Please be Calder," came a voice from nearby.

"Where are you?" Edwynne turned around, trying to pinpoint the source of noise.

A sharp intake of breath. The voice sounded more frightened. "You're not Calder. Are you going to kill me? I feel awful."

Edwynne tried to listen to where the voice was coming from—seemingly through a solid wall. She crept nearer to that part of the chamber. "My name is Edwynne. I'm a squire from the palace. I'm here to help you get to the surface for medical treatment."

"Thank the stars you're a human." The voice came from a gap in the stones just small enough for a narrow person to slip through. Beyond, a worried face peered out. "You're just a kid though! Is it safe for you to be down here?

"I'm part of the patrol and rescue team. Grab my hand. I can't promise it won't hurt, but I'll try to free you."

Struggling through the crack, she bit back screams. At last, Edwynne managed to pull her free, damp and muddy and much the worse for wear. She cradled her injured arm and trembled with pain. "I don't know how I fell so hard. It's like something pushed me. I swear I felt cold hands moving on my back just before I tumbled against the stone."

Edwynne took hold of her unhurt side. "Stay calm, we'll be back on the surface soon. Lean against me as much as you need to."

Whenever something moved in earshot, even if Edwynne identified the sound as only water dripping or the knights above, Valency flinched and whimpered. She kept stopping to dry-heave so hard her eyes watered. Once, she even fell to her knees.

"I'm not trained to heal. If you want your injuries treated, get back up and keep moving, or you might get hurt worse."

"I'll try," Valency quavered, but Edwynne's threats had motivated her. She stumbled to her feet and limped forward once more.

On the surface, in the sunlight, the wizard Delvar yelled at the assembled knights. "I'm putting my foot down. No more research, no more tourism. Not even on levels we've agreed are safe! I want carriage drivers warned and the guard increased." Circling the group, he spotted Edwynne, and his pale eyes narrowed. "Why is a scrawny child here? This is ridiculous."

Edwynne wrinkled her nose. "I'm a squire." And he'd seen her around the palace too! He just loved condescending to anyone he outranked.

Delvar turned away, uncaring. "Take this woman to a healer. Knights, get back to the perimeter. And all of you, be careful. Remember, this place doesn't want us here." His robes whirled around him as he turned on Calder, who hovered at their mentor's side. "What are you all doing here? I just sent out a memo stating research needed my approval. You should have known better."

"But you specifically referred to nonessential expeditions," Calder spluttered. "The city charter says magical-historical research is—"

"Also nonessential from now on." He went to the archaeologist, snapped light into his fingertips, and shone the glow at her eyes. "You're unwell. Why?"

"I drank some of the water. I figured it came from the river, so I'd be all right, but I've started coughing up the most awful things," she stammered.

"You lot should put out more warning signs," he scolded the knights before passing her a luminous glass bottle from his robe. "Drink this. You'll be all right soon enough."

She gulped down the potion, and he patted her shoulder.

At least his attention had left Edwynne, but he turned on her, face stormy. "You're coming to my workshop, young lady."

He strode ahead of her. She walked backward, mimicking his haughty bearing, and mouthed "young lady!" with a face like she'd licked a lemon. One of the younger knights stifled a laugh.

If only Stellan were here! He wouldn't put up with Delvar's condescending bullshit.

Edwynne had some scrapes on her arms from the narrow passageways, nothing serious. But back in his workshop, Delvar prodded at her with stinging disinfectant, and she flinched.

"Can't you stay still for one minute?" he snapped.

"Why can't I just go?" She didn't feel too badly hurt.

"Insolent girl—you could have all manner of infections. Drink this." He shoved a flask bubbling with lumpy green liquid into her hands. She glared at him but chugged it down.

Ugh! It tasted like rotten onions, tree bark, and grass. She held the flask far from her body, grimacing. "Is this poison?"

A sniff. "Don't be ridiculous."

So, she held her nose and forced herself to chug the rest down. If only she could have a sweet to get rid of the taste! Izalena, the former court witch, always had sweets.

Plus, she used to let Edwynne rummage through the little drawers of herbs, crystals, and animal bones. (Some animals even had bones in their dicks!) She'd even let Edwynne use a mortar and pestle to help crush resin. And she never complained if the squires flinched.

"Can I have a glass of water?"

"*May* you have a glass of water? Not right now."

Stupid pretentious wizards. She tried to distract herself by examining the room. Delvar had moved into the court wizard's quarters recently. Big crates stamped with labels held his personal possessions, a beige-and-black screen-printed tapestry showed complex magical diagrams, and an antique glass-front cabinet held fancy wizard shit: carved wands, crystal orbs, glass decanters, the works. It seemed he'd unpacked in his workshop but not this visiting chamber. Did he plan on actually decorating or just throwing up some more mass-produced posters trainees kept in their university dorm rooms and calling it a day?

Halting footsteps came down the hall, accompanied by Ava's voice. "It's all right. Delvar will have something for the pain. Come on."

He hastened to the door. Edwynne jumped down and followed. What if Mattie had gotten hurt?

Ava had her arm around a shaken, bloodstained Sariva.

Delvar carefully took one of her hands in his. "Gods, Sariva, you poor dear... What happened?"

Ava glanced at Edwynne before telling Delvar, "Let's talk later *in private*."

He seemed to remember Edwynne's presence. "Right. Of course I'll have to treat Sariva's injuries first. Stay here but try to stay out of my way."

Fine! They could treat her like furniture, but she'd just saved someone's life, and they hadn't. She didn't care what they thought. She certainly didn't care if prissy nobles and the pompous new wizard excluded her.

But what topic required such serious faces? And why were they all in on it?

He led Sariva into the treatment room and helped her onto the examination table. She seemed to have fallen through a window. A closed one. Shards of glass shone in her updo and on her skin as if making fun of diamonds.

"Wait a moment, I'll mix something in my workroom to close your wounds."

She gave a shaky nod, her face ashen, as he slipped into the inner chamber, shutting the door behind him.

Within moments, Edwynne couldn't stand the silence. "What are you doing here?"

Sariva looked bitter—and too pathetic to hate. "Leave off, Edwynne. I'm not in the mood." Red-rimmed eyes, makeup smudged in tear-trails down her cheeks, even a path of dried blood from her aristocratic nose.

Who'd done this?

How had they gotten away with it?

Why?

Sariva flinched from Edwynne's gaze. "Go ahead and gloat. It's not like I can stop you."

Her posture and expression suggested defeat. But Edwynne couldn't find joy in the aftermath of someone else's victory.

How long had she been staring? "There's glass in your hair," she blurted.

Sariva tucked her knees to her chest—or tried to. The movement aggravated some open cut. She whimpered, an abandoned-kitten noise.

Edwynne hadn't expected her to sound so helpless. So young. "Stop crying," she snapped, reaching out, then rolling her eyes when Sariva flinched. "If you're going to just sit there feeling sorry for yourself, at least let me get the glass!"

Sariva just sat there as Edwynne worked the shards free of her thick, wavy hair. The stillness made her skin prickle. She wanted to grab Sariva and shake her by the shoulders: *Who are you, and why are you taking a break from trying to ruin my life?* Sariva was like a dead squirrel in the gutter, and Edwynne the street urchin poking its corpse with a stick: *Wake up, do something* or *stop being weird.*

"That's the last of it." How far could she throw these tiny pieces of glass? Only a few feet. She kicked one under the table, another beneath a cabinet. "How'd you get those cuts, anyway?"

Sariva shook herself, seeming alive again. "At no point did I request your grubby little fingers poking around in my hair, you absolute..." She trailed off, lips moving, silent and irate.

"Bitch?" Edwynne suggested helpfully. "Bastard? Daughter of a bastard? Son of a bitch?" She'd always been more attached to the concept of pissing people off than the concept of gender.

"I'm not going to sully my mouth with base language," Sariva insisted in the tone of someone who wanted to.

Edwynne leaned closer. She had nothing else to do except bother Sariva, and her scrapes—though she hated to admit it—stung like insect bites.

So Edwynne baited her. "Don't you ever just want to say fuck?"

She scowled and folded her arms. "Young ladies don't swear."

"I'm not talking about young ladies. I'm talking about you." Goading Sariva felt like climbing out of the old palace, stepping on firm, familiar ground.

"I think swear words show a paucity of vocabulary."

"Scared you'll get caught?"

"I can think of more creative insults."

"Like what?" Maybe if Sariva lost her temper, she'd let something slip.

Today her rage ran cold, her posh voice even. "You're an oversized toddler. You're a wild animal on a chain lashing out at whoever comes nearest. You deserve to muck out the entire royal stables and fall in a pile of horse droppings and suffocate and die. I hope you never even consider touching my hair again."

Not bad for a noble, but it didn't satisfy Edwynne's curiosity. "So, basically, you do want to swear, but you're just a little lady," she shot back in a singsongy voice.

Sariva leaned close enough to headbutt. "Fuck," she pronounced in her careful cut-glass accent, "you. With extreme thoroughness and to the utmost extent."

She should have let the conversation fade. Moved to her own side of the table, waited for Delvar to return with the potions, savored her victory. Instead, she leaned in further, eyes nearly crossing—Sariva's perfume even smelled expensive. Her mouth drawled, "Is that a threat?"

Sariva made a strangled squeaking noise, her eyes wide, and scuttled away, nearly falling off the table. She caught Edwynne watching her and scowled. "What?"

Edwynne drew out the word deliberately. "Nothing." But—ha!—she'd embarrassed her. "So, are you going to tell me who beat you up? Will they face justice?"

Her expression closed off again, posture deflating. Edwynne had overplayed her hand. "Leave off. We've already established I can say fuck."

She'd get no more information.

On his return, Delvar plucked one last shard from Sariva's abundant hair, teasing, "I hope the queendom's least obedient squire didn't torment you too much."

"I'm all right, thank you." She smiled at him, an expression he returned, leaning in close to dab waxy ointment on her neck. *He's just sucking up to the nobility like always.*

Edwynne's skin crawled. She turned away.

"Those should heal in a day or two. Come see me if they don't."

"Either way, I'd be happy to see you."

Ugh.

Sariva hopped down from the table and left, full skirts swishing, and Delvar's attention narrowed in on Edwynne.

"Now can you sit still for five minutes for once?"

The door swung shut. Edwynne stayed still but not silent. "Why's she such a mess? Did someone jump her?" Sariva's blood-smeared face wouldn't leave her thoughts.

"I'm not at liberty to say."

"One of the older squires? Or someone from the city?" Evidently, Sariva hadn't stood a chance.

"Why do you have such a bee up your bonnet, anyway? What is she to you? Another one of your lady-in-waiting obsessions?" He scrubbed too hard at a scab. Blood trickled down her calf. She wanted to kick him in his smug, aristocratic face. "I won't give you more ammunition to pester her."

"But we're—she's—" Edwynne's sprinting mind caught up to her mouth and stood there like an idiot. She and Sariva had nothing in common. Shared nothing. They didn't even like each other. She ought to shut up.

She settled for sitting there, expression mutinous, kicking her legs.

★

When Sariva and Ava returned to the wizard's sparsely minimalist workshop, Delvar didn't have a solution, which concerned her the most. He only possessed the same knowledge as anyone else in the queen's circle. She'd been found in a swoon one morning with Izalena gone from the castle and cryptic letters heaped upon her desk.

"I know, Sariva. This is hard for us all. At least I can make sure nothing untoward happens again with some protection spells and keep your wounds from troubling you." He'd even offered them a fruit tisane and time to rest in his workshop. But at last, they had to resume work. Today, they would proofread letters.

"Oradel used to write her own speeches. I think she wants to spare us the work of putting words in her mouth...at least on some level," Ava had explained.

Sariva held the paper up to the light and squinted at it. The queen had run out of ink but had evidently lacked motivation to get a new pen.

Ava pushed another piece of paper toward her. "I'm not sure how to complete this sentence. Any suggestions?"

The staggeringly elegant sentence trailed off into lackadaisical scribbling. Sariva made out the words *another* and *pointless*.

"Perhaps let's settle for 'to be edited later.'"

Knights galloped into the courtyard below, their armor glinting in the sunlight. "Ava, didn't you say Stellan would be returning soon?"

Ava leapt to her feet. "Let's see if he's with them!"

They collected Mattie and rushed outside. There, Sariva tried to pick out Stellan. Ava always talked about his stunning good looks, close-cropped hair, and hints of stubble on a finely chiseled face.

Ava hurried up to a rider. "Kerrich? Where is the rest of your squadron? Where's Stellan?"

Mattie peered up at him. "He has presents for me, right?"

Kerrich fiddled with the studs on his leather armor. He rummaged in his saddlebags, farm-boy face a mask of concentration, and emerged with a crisply folded letter on fine parchment. Government parchment. "My ladyship, Miss Mathilda, I'd like you to read this, please."

Mattie rocked on her toes. "When is he coming home? Did something keep him?"

"Hush, let me read," Ava told her, unfolding the letter. Nearby sparrows scattered.

Mattie tugged on her skirt, shifting from foot to foot, and whined, "What? What is it?"

Ava's face went motionless and statue smooth. She shook her head, murmuring, "Oh," refolded and unfolded the letter without looking, then read it again, wide eyes skimming the words as if willing them to change.

In that moment, Sariva knew.

"Finally!" Edwynne, laughing, darted around the group of knights and riders. "Stellan! Fight me, you asshole. Let's go spar."

Several knights shot increasingly frantic glances at one another. One stepped forward, resting an armored hand on Edwynne's shoulder. "Edwynne, I..."

She tried to lean away. "Yeah?"

"Edwynne," he began, "I'm so, so sorry."

She waited, stone faced. Sariva imagined her snapping, *Get it over with.*

"We were attacked by magical monsters. Ibex the size of full-grown dragons with armor like turtle shells and horns like swords. There must have been at least two dozen. Maybe three. The only chance was for one of us to stay behind, hold the mountain path, and give the rest time to escape."

Edwynne chuckled. Her expression didn't change. "You're kidding, right?" She glanced from one face to another, at first as if searching for a punchline, then as if searching for an escape route.

Sariva wished she'd stayed in the sitting room.

Edwynne's wild scream broke into words. "He can't be dead! You've seen him fight bandits. You've seen him fight. He's never lost!"

Another knight moved toward her, hands out in consolation, and she flung a punch at him.

He caught her fist, turning the blow aside. "Edwynne, please—"

"I hope you die in a hole. The most you could do with your life is—is if my brother stepped on your bones! You're nothing. You're nobody. You're dust and dirt, and this is all your fault." She kicked him in the shins and darted off.

Ava and Mattie held tight to each other, caught in the shared flood of their loss. Sariva rubbed the lace on her sleeves. She couldn't bring herself to approach them but took a step after Edwynne. She'd felt unmoored with terror after the explosion in the queen's rooms. Edwynne had distracted her, made the world normal again. But she ought to stop poking at Edwynne the way one of her little brothers would pick at a scab.

Especially now.

If Aziz died...she'd want to be alone too.

"I..." She looked between Ava and Mattie and the knights, who all just stood there. "I'll go fetch some tea and handkerchiefs."

Ava spent the next few days receiving one visitor at a time, giving them quiet responses of one or two words. Mattie kept telling people she wanted to go home even though flooding this time of year blocked travel.

Sariva made a lot of tea and wished she felt sad because everyone else did.

Guilt filled the void. She took over as many of Ava's responsibilities as possible—if she couldn't grieve with her, she could at least ease one burden—which meant double shifts sitting with the queen. Hopefully, Delvar's improved protection spell would work.

Queen Oradel drifted between sleep and waking, all movement seeming to exhaust her. Occasionally, prompted, she pointed to things, like motioning to a book that held the answer to a question of state or blinking at the drawer that held a lost piece of correspondence. Sometimes, she even murmured answers to questions, though only regarding matters of state. After these slight acknowledgements of reality, she slept for hours.

During her stints in the queen's sunny chambers, Sariva always talked. Sometimes about government duties, sometimes merely rambling to fill the silence. Today, rambling about embroidery. "The next stitch I learned was a raised satin stitch. I thought it was stumpwork, but it's actually a basic technique—"

Sudden movement. Not an explosion, but the queen grabbing her wrist. Upright, she seemed powerful and dignified as ever, her dark eyes intense. "I keep trying to talk. Is it working?"

Sariva nodded, heart galloping under her corset. "I'm listening, I promise."

"What you need to know is I fucked up."

Goddess, have mercy. The queen spoke? Or, more precisely, the queen swore?

Her mouth took over for her stunned mind. "Yes, Your Majesty?" Or ought she to have used Your Highness?

"I trusted the wrong mage—my soul's out of my body, wandering. Couldn't free it in time. You have to find the shards of me while they still hold. Get something to write this down. "

Sariva dove for the nightstand, moving silver keep-sakes and tiny jars of scent. At last, she grabbed the pad and fumbled up a quill. "Ready."

The queen's head lolled. For a moment, she slumped over, but she gritted her teeth, holding Sariva's wrist tight enough to hurt, holding herself in consciousness through sheer force of will. "You'll want to go to places of great power in the city. Ancient gardens and splendid ruins. I was born under a constellation of rainstorms, so follow the turquoise thread. Follow the rose, then water, then the vein of gold. Always follow water. Watch out for the serpent—watch for the wraith with a hole in her heart."

Sariva didn't know what she meant but scribbled everything down.

"Gossip about this and the last of my magic will smite you." Her dark eyes bored into Sariva, scarily intense. "Only tell one who can aid you, whose aid you need—" Then strength tumbled from her body. She flopped onto the pillows, gasping for air.

Sariva leaned over her. Oh, Goddess. Would she die? "Please say more. Please let me help you."

Breathing calmer, she blinked up at Sariva as if waiting for her to leave.

"Hello?" Sariva whispered, wondering if the queen could still hear her. "Do you also find it difficult to act like a proper lady and not say fuck?" Nothing.

She folded the paper and slipped it into her bosom below her pendant's steadying weight. What in the world?

The door creaked open—Ava, with soup. "Are you all right? I thought I heard—"

Did she trust Ava? The queen had told her to say nothing. "I'm fine, but what about you? Is there anything I can provide today? Help choosing a mourning wardrobe, or if I can take a carriage into the city and fetch anything..." The soup smelled good though. She could already taste the little translucent triangles of squash.

Ava shook her head. "At this point, being in my room alone is just making us feel worse. Mattie's at lessons; I'm trying to be useful. Thank you for taking my shifts though."

Queen Oradel had seemed so lucid. What if she could learn more about the strange goings-on in the castle?

She'd start with the first part. Perhaps investigate a fabric shop—maybe one with a rose as its sign. "I have a question about the city. Are there any fabric shops with the sign of a rose? Especially old ones."

"I visited all the best shops when I first came into town. But one with the sign of a rose? No, I'm sure there aren't any."

"Do you happen to know where I might find...an old cornerstone by a shop that sells turquoise thread?"

Ava nearly smiled.

Confusion ran through Sariva like cold water. "What's funny?"

"The river running down from the hills and through the city. In old songs and legends, it's called the turquoise thread of Almesia."

Sariva nodded. "Like how one of the largest cities in the North is called the Ruby City because so many of the roofs and doors are painted red. So, what's the oldest structure along the river?"

"Surely the old palace. It was in use for thousands of years before the ghosts began to walk the passageways."

"Doesn't seem like a popular tourist spot then." She tried to smile.

"Guards make sure people can tour around the outside safely. Of course, you don't want to go in."

Crumbling pillars, ghosts, old magic. Yes, she had her destination. Surviving inside? Hopefully, she'd be able to manage that challenge as well.

Sariva bought a cheap pamphlet on the ruins and skimmed through the pages as the horse-drawn trolley clattered down toward the river. No trolley wanted to take a passenger all the way there. She'd only gotten this far through extensive pleading and her sweetest smiles. *A few scant sections of restoration, open to sightseers. The rest...* She flipped through a long list of hazards. Carnivorous plants with hankerings for human flesh? Wild dragons? Flooded dungeons? Ghosts?

At least she could bribe her way past the guards.

Chapter Six

At her usual lookout post, Edwynne sprawled across a white stone bench. She took a few pieces of dried pineapple from her bag and crunched the sweetness. *One moment at a time. One bite at a time. If I keep going, if I work hard, maybe Stellan will come back...*

It was a quiet day in the palace of death. Sometimes whatever lurked beneath the polished stone settled a little.

A woman screamed.

Edwynne jumped to her feet, a hand on her short sword. "Hello? Where are you?"

Soft sobbing. Whatever the woman had seen had frightened her too badly to speak. Edwynne closed her eyes, trying to pinpoint the sound.

A familiarly prissy little shriek cut the air.

Ah, fuck.

She found Sariva huddled next to a wall, talking to herself. "Okay, I need to keep going. That was a chameleon, not a ghost..."

Resisting the impulse to draw her sword, Edwynne pointed. "You."

Sariva swept around, fake innocent. Just like she'd stood there so innocently when the knights claimed Stellan wouldn't come home. News Sariva had learned first. "Me?"

"Unless there was someone else with you? Someone else screaming?"

She shifted into a haughty, cleavage-out posture. "Nothing of interest to you."

"I'm the guard here. You not dying is of interest to me!" Sariva could drop dead, but not where Edwynne worked to save lives.

"On my honor as a lady, this has nothing whatsoever to do with you. I know there are ghosts here. I'm not stupid." How dare she look offended?

Edwynne scowled. Not stupid? Debatable.

"I just... I wanted to be alone."

Edwynne's bullshit detector screamed at the eyelash-batting. "So, your idea of solitude is being tormented by the cursed dead?"

"I'm not here to die! I have a duty. And an annotated map. You can even escort me out afterward."

Beautiful dreams overtook Edwynne's thoughts.

Sariva shrieking ineffectually as a dragon crunched her up. Sariva wailing as she tumbled headfirst down a pit. Choking on acid as it ate her throat lining. Running, shrieking, from a scorpion.

Except Edwynne couldn't passively watch anyone die. Knights-in-training always protected the helpless. Sariva? She didn't stand a chance. Sure, she had a large frame, but only in a "pillowy breasts, wide hips, tummy you could fall asleep on" way.

"I don't like this either, but you can't come in here and tell me to not do my job. That's bullshit," Edwynne explained.

They glared at each other.

Finally, Sariva gave in, shoulders slumping. "Fine. What's the way out of the ruins?"

"I'll show you." She grabbed Sariva and frog-marched her to the outskirts. "Go straight on this path to an archway out. A few streets down, you should be able to find someone to take you uphill to the palace. Whatever you're doing here isn't more important than your life. Go get a cup of tea, embroider a sampler, anything."

Sariva regarded her, smooth, enigmatic. "And you? What will you do?"

Edwynne ran a hand through her curls. Being a knight meant trying to extend chivalry to all, so she'd save Sariva whether the girl wanted to be saved or not. "I don't know, my actual job?"

She loved watching Sariva walk away. Not because it meant staring at her butt. Because it meant she'd leave. Time to get out her bag of delicious dried pineapple and bask in the sun. Humming, she headed for her lookout spot. She could find a whippy rapier-sized stick and charge into battle against dead trees, an important phase in the life cycle of all sticks.

A cry of pain and fear tore through the air. Not "I've seen a spider" fear. Closer to "I'm going to die." Horror fought fury as Edwynne sprinted. "Sariva?" Her voice echoed off stone walls.

"Help!"

The damn noblewoman hadn't left, just gone around and back tears, white knuckled, and didn't budge.

Edwynne had to try something else. "All right. I can't swear on my family. I'm not from some fancy dynasty like you are. But I swear on the Queensguard and the knight I serve—" I'll protect you? It's safe to let go? Would Sariva buy any of that? She settled for the truth. "I'm not a murderer."

Sariva grimaced, eyes squeezed shut, and released her grip one finger at a time.

Edwynne hauled up the larger girl. Her muscles burned in memory of every pull-up and squat she'd ever done. Slowly, carefully, she inched away from the pit's lip. At last, they both stood on solid ground.

Sariva's silence set Edwynne's teeth on edge. The frilly bitch owed her an explanation. "You're welcome," she prompted.

Sariva smoothed her skirts. "I retract my plan to dye all your garments lavender. I'll be on my way."

Edwynne shoved her against the wall. "Not until I get an explanation. You strolled in here as if you planned to have a picnic."

Sariva's gasp made her breasts heave. "This is hardly chivalrous."

"Chivalry? This isn't a ballad. People don't enter the ruins on purpose. Why are you here?"

"I'll tell you, but swear to secrecy. On your neck, on generations thereafter. In my language too." She followed the sentence with liquid sounds Edwynne couldn't understand.

Edwynne hated her clumsy mimicry of the Northern words.

"To form a proper alliance, we'd go to a priest and sign something, break bread, drink wine together, and pet each other's hunting dogs. But you need to pretend we've done all those things. For the sake of our queendom, you can't say anything."

Sariva had this facial tell when trying to prank Edwynne, a slight smirk she couldn't hold back. Now, though? She seemed completely honest.

Reluctantly, she took a step away. Then another. "Fine. I swear."

Sariva told a whole story, ending with, "To sum up the situation, the queen is under attack. Magical attack. From the exiled former court wizard."

It would explain Izalena's exile but little else. "And she told you to save her instead of the actual court wizard? Or a knight? Or anyone else?"

A helpless shrug. "He's been trying. Maybe she suspects other ladies-in-waiting of being traitors. I'm new to court...and I'm the one who was there when she got up the strength to talk."

"Then it's that bad?" *Dying* bad?

"She said I needed to go to places of power and recover bits of her soul." Not an answer.

"Sounds cryptic."

Sariva resembled an indignant marshmallow. "I know where to go. All I need is someone to watch my back. Even if you don't care about me, you care about the queen, right? I know your family. Your sister wants to be a lady-in-waiting when she grows up, and your brother was the youngest knight ever appointed to the Queensguard. Obviously, heroism isn't genetic, but you'll help Almesia. Even if you don't give a shit about me."

Nothing's genetic. I'm not related to my family. I resemble them through happenstance. They said "We didn't want you to feel like you stood out" and "We didn't want people to discriminate against you" and lied about having a baby while in quarantine. My birth family was Northern like yours. And I should know the oath you swore.

"You're right. You're a huge bitch, but I love my country."

"So that's why I'm here," Sariva finished. "Because the queen told me to come. I think I can help her."

Having directions didn't mean knowing how to follow them. "And you thought you'd, what? Wander into sinkholes and snakes until maybe you stumble across something magic?" Edwynne wondered if Sariva would make excuses: *I don't stumble* or *You're discussing this too negatively.*

Instead, Sariva raised her chin. "For the sake of my queendom? Yes. I would."

Edwynne glanced away first. "You're either brave or stupid." Her voice sounded hoarse, unfamiliar.

"Well, could you have done any better?"

"Yes. You said you were searching for a rose, right? I know where we're going. I know more routes through the ruins than anyone. I'd say if you're with me, you have a high chance of surviving."

She glanced away, eyelashes casting long shadows over her cheeks in the sunset. "My life in your hands then. And the queen's as well."

Edwynne felt unsure about leading someone unprepared into the dangerous ruins. But...rescuing the queen? She'd be granted a full knighthood for sure.

They picked their way through long-deserted corridors, all dust and bare stone.

Edwynne wanted to fill the silence. "So, you grew up speaking Northern?"

Sariva shook her head with a rueful smile. "My parents tried to speak Almesian around us so we wouldn't have an accent. Now it's my Northern where the consonants aren't quite right."

I wish I knew the language my parents had spoken. Edwynne bit her lower lip. *I wish they'd survived to speak it with me. I wish I wasn't so afraid to talk to my own people.* "You're lucky though," she murmured.

"I suppose I am. Where are we headed, noble squire?"

"Plants don't flower here. If there are roses, they'd be in the old art gallery."

They descended further into the ruins. A skinny feral cat hissed and darted out of their way. Sariva moved toward a staircase, then peered down the slope.

Edwynne stepped in front of her. "Careful. We might be attacked. I should go first."

"Yes, the art gallery at the bottom of these stairs seems so dangerous. I can see why you'd be worried, brave knight," Sariva deadpanned.

"Fuck you." But Edwynne still went first. The gallery held no giant spiders or wild dragons or pits of acid, only fading murals and tattered canvases in splintered frames.

Sariva darted about the chamber, peering at frescoes. "Rubbish. The frescoes are all of landscapes."

"Maybe the rose is a metaphor, and she's speaking in code? The hills in the south are always called the yellow-rose hills—it grows there, it's where the queen comes from. Maybe we need a picture of those."

"That one?" An eastern hillside, speckled with olive trees and gamboling goats.

Edwynne scrutinized the canvas. She wanted a sign saying, *It's Okay to be Here, Despite Murderous Ghosts!* Something unambiguous to chase her worries away.

Instead, she had Sariva.

"I hoped we'd find the queen's missing spirit here, and we could get everything fixed by suppertime." Hearing Sariva's doubts threw Edwynne off guard. Almost. "I remember something about the Moonflower General though. She had the palace built with secret passageways. So maybe..." She pressed on the frame. The large painting swung back, moving an unswept hallway's dusty smell toward them. Sariva curtsied. "After you, brave knight."

The dim corridor sloped downward. Stagnant puddles gave way to a few inches of water, and they splashed through. A ledge along the wall showed the opaque water deepening.

Sariva pointed toward a door barred with dark metal. "I think we need to get there."

Something moved in the water. Something besides the current.

Sariva's eyes widened. "What was that?"

Edwynne manhandled her to a dry patch before she swooned. "Like I said, this isn't a tourist destination."

"But the queen gave me directions. You wouldn't disobey an order from someone you trusted, would you? There must be a way we can go further along."

Edwynne squinted down the corridor. "There's a pressure mechanism, a button, to open the door. Maybe once the door is opened..."

She remembered her training—

Don't get overconfident.

Don't take unnecessary risks.

—and the wizard's threat.

If I see you back in my workshop...

But Sariva refused to abandon this dangerous quest.

"Wait here." Edwynne drew her sword and stepped onto the ledge along the wall. She sidled forward, pressed against the bricks.

"Edwynne—" Sariva quavered.

Something wet slid along the tiny gap between her trousers and her boots. Fuck! She kicked out, swiped with her sword, and stumbled hard into the knee-deep water.

Its coldness seeped in from the top of her boots, making her socks squish and cling. Something rippled. "Did you see something?" If only Sariva had actually warned her!

Sariva wrung her hands. "I don't know! A tail—maybe an eel?"

The ledge came to her waist. She tried to boost herself back up, but water made her boots too slippery. This eel swam in somehow, right? She'd disturb the water flow and make it swim out. Edwynne hurried over the uneven bricks.

Her foot connected with something thick and squishy, like a giant slug. She nearly overbalanced. Caught herself on the ledge. "You were right, for once—"

Needle teeth chomped through her boot leather, sinking into her skin. "Fuck!" She stifled an undignified shriek of pain, jabbing her sword into the water. She sliced through nothing. Nothing again. Connected with solid meat just as the maybe-an-eel swiveled in for another mouthful. It dove into a drain, a slimy dark tail flashing above the water.

Would more creatures come?

"Why didn't you just run to shallower water?"

She hadn't thought of it. "Fuck you, that's why." But she retraced her steps to where Sariva stood and clambered onto the ledge.

She dug her fingernails into tiny cracks between the stone, using every muscle to stay upright and balanced. Finally, she could punch the button. The door creaked open, and the water seeped down the passageway, its level evening out.

Edwynne jumped down. "Come on!"

Sariva ran along the ledge. They both slipped through the heavy door. Surprisingly, Sariva had planned and brought a spell-lantern. "This tunnel looks...small. And dark."

And if it flooded, they'd drown. "You have a reason for being here, right? You're welcome to leave if you don't."

Sariva lifted her head, seeming steadier, as if Edwynne's spite gave her something else to focus on. "But who in their right mind stocks a palace with underwater snakes? Or casts a...carnivorous poisonous snake spell?"

"The point is they didn't build it like this. If you use enough magic to kill people, it keeps killing." Lethal spells, mixing, mutating. Side effects of the wars they'd studied.

Sariva jumped, the water splashing around her.

"What is it?" Edwynne whispered. The tunnel felt like a throat working to swallow them whole. Already, she had to stoop so her curls wouldn't brush the moist roof.

"I think I stepped on something."

They were trapped in the darkness on the same mission as Stellan, so whatever imperiled him could endanger them as well. Edwynne grasped at a familiar argument. "Probably just a rock."

Sariva scowled, but her frantic, hunted expression ebbed. They padded forward, footsteps splashing.

No one would find their bodies if they died. No one would dare go this deep in the ruins.

They trudged through the next stretch of flooded tunnel. Edwynne liked water, but not this stagnant sludge. "So, are we almost there?"

Sariva bit her lip. "I...I'm not sure."

Turning a corner, they reached a small dry area. Murky water lapped at the edges, surrounding them in all directions. Above them, on the roof of the underground chamber, stalactites sputtered into a sickly greenish glow.

A beautiful young woman with umber-dark skin and long curly hair hovered above the water. "Help me," she whispered.

Edwynne recognized her.

Sariva peered out at the underground lake, eyes wide. "Queen Oradel—it's a piece of her soul! We have to get her. Can you swim?"

Edwynne didn't think so. "Sariva. Give me your handkerchief."

"Why?"

"We can't trust the water here."

Sariva scowled as she muttered but handed it over. "I spent ages embroidering this, you know." Edwynne wadded it up into a ball and tossed it into the water.

The handkerchief began to shrink and smoke, browning at the edges. The bloodstained part burned first. Its flame tinted the water red.

"Part of my prison," the queen whispered. "Danger for this fragment of my soul to leave, in the crystal or out of it. Danger for anyone who tries to come help."

"But there must be a way to help, right? You wouldn't have brought me here without a solution. I know you," Sariva said, fists clenched. "I know how brilliant you are."

The queen closed her eyes, shuddering. Her form wavered. "I can bring stepping-stones up...but only for a few moments."

Edwynne took off her sandals. "I've got this. I mean, I've got this, Your Majesty." She tried to sound confident. Sure, she and Stellan had played "The Ground is Acid" as kids, but an actual pit of acid? How had she ended up in this situation?

The queen—or maybe only an image of her—nodded. She drew her arms upward, shaking with effort.

Stepping-stones heaved from the depths, the acid sloshing over them. *Nothing you haven't done in the practice yard. Nothing you haven't seen in training.*

But the practice yard dust didn't burn blood.

She bounced to visualize the movement, and her injured heel throbbed with deep pain. She tried again, stifling a cry. Finally, seething, she admitted the obvious. "Sariva. You need to do it."

"But you're used to risking your life. I'm just…"

"Someone who came down here uninvited? Exactly." And realizing exactly what would goad Sariva into bravery, she added, "Of course, if you're too much of a delicate, useless palace lady to help, I'll figure out something."

She drew herself up to her full height, nearly five feet. "I can do it! You just watch." Her shoes slapped the stone. Of course, her toenails gleamed flower pink. A moment of contemplation, then she hopped onto the first stone and stepped carefully from one to the next. Light reflected through the dark water, casting eerie, muddy shadows on the cavern walls, strange colors writhing like smoke.

A few stones from the gem, Sariva stopped.

Edwynne grabbed her sword. Had a bigger eel appeared? "Well?"

"The next stone…it's too far. I could only make it by jumping."

Squinting at the rocks, she judged the distance. "You can make it. Sure, it looks slippery, but if you control your landing and don't panic…"

"There's a chance I won't be eaten alive by acid? No, screw this. I'm coming back." Turning around, she began picking her way across the stones again.

Edwynne took a tentative step toward the shoreline and hissed in pain. She could still move at a fast limp, but this injury would throw off her balance.

Sariva needed anger because anger seemed to make her braver. She needed something—someone—to hate.

Edwynne knew how to play that part. "If you quit now," she said evenly, "I will hold you under the acid until nothing remains of you but your skull, and then I will take that skull and use it to store boot polish and daggers and date pits. And then when people ask me, 'Edwynne, why do you have a skull?' I will tell them, 'The ancient sages have written, this is what happens to little bitches who freeze up when Almesia needs them. Thus, proclaims our Goddess on high.' And I bet you couldn't manage the jump anyway."

Sariva's glare held tears. "You're right. I can't."

Shit. She'd pushed too much, needed to try being gentler. "I didn't mean—it's not far." She lowered her voice as if coaching Tolliver through a training exercise—though Sariva, voluptuous and pouty, looked nothing like Toliver. "Bend your knees, swing your arms, and lower down when you land to stop your momentum."

"Will you pull me out if I fall?" She sounded younger. Nearly harmless.

Honestly, if she'd been about to leap over a pit of acid, Edwynne would want the same assurance. But she couldn't make the jump. Not with her foot this sore. She needed to coax Sariva into it, like goading her but in reverse. "Before you lose more than one layer of skin." She stepped across the stones, each step like a carving knife to her foot, until she stood on the one next to Sariva. Maybe just an inch more goading so Sariva couldn't accuse her of going soft. "There's some muscle in those thick thighs, right? Or is your figure just for show?" And she gave Sariva an up-and-down appraising look.

"You're despicable." But her voice had firmed up.

"Then get the stone, get over here, and slap me. I dare you. You know how to say swear words. Being able to hit someone is just the next step. I know you can do this."

She took a deep breath, shifted her weight, and made the leap effortlessly. After picking up something that glimmered in her hand, she returned, this time with no frightened pause.

"What've you got? Maybe that's the key to her prison, a magic map, or something?"

Sariva held up a ruby sphere that shone from within, casting a gentle light on her soft cheeks. "Well, stones don't usually glow."

A wave crashed, loud and powerful. *But we're nowhere near the sea!* Water, not sludge, pounded over them and dragged them both under. It felt cool as spring water and light as a breeze. A thrum vibrated like the lowest string on a castle-sized harp. Currents of rippling light met within it, like overlapping pebble circles in a clear, perfect lake.

They washed up on solid ground, clothing dry and shoes on their feet.

Sariva collapsed onto a chunk of fallen masonry, hugging the enchanted globe. Its glow pulsed against her chest. "I ought to thank you for helping me get whatever this is. Queen Oradel will be pleased, and technically, you did help."

Edwynne climbed up beside her even though she had to wedge her injured foot into a step. "I'd prefer 'Thank you, Edwynne. You saved my life, and I would have died without you and your muscles,' but I'll take it."

One single chuckle. "Fine. You weren't completely useless."

"Do you plan on coming back here?" The knights wouldn't indulge Sariva. "What else does the queen want you to do?"

Sariva's deep eyes, with those surprising amber glints, roved over her face. "Do you plan on telling anyone I've been here?"

"I don't give a shit about you, but I'll help Almesia. Next time you go into the ruins, though, remember anyone else will just knock you out and drag you to safety." Most other squires wouldn't listen to a girl. Especially not Sariva. "We figure this out, we find what the queen told you to search for, and then we're enemies again. Deal?"

"I can hardly wait." No barely concealed disdain there. Just regular, unsheathed disdain.

"You'll dye all my clothes pink, and I'll let a squirrel loose in your bedchamber. Do you promise not to lose the magic rock?"

"I can be careful." *Unlike some people*, her tone hinted.

"Then I'll see you when I must."

★

In her room, Sariva examined her garments and felt her heart—pounding, not just from the danger they'd faced. No stranger to physical activity, she could lift her brothers and chase wayward chickens, but she'd never cultivated agility. Never so much as leapt from one tree stump to another after childhood. The dark water lapping at the stones, the seemingly insurmountable gap...the handkerchief dissolving into nothing, the way acid might feel sizzling through unprotected skin, had filled her mind. It didn't matter if she could make the jump. She couldn't move, but her head had cleared, her muscles unknotted, and she realized why people might more-than-tolerate Edwynne. Under the cruelty and childishness, her steady confidence had an inexplicable soothing effect. Vered, for instance, or some youth lost in the ruins, they might feel comforted to see Edwynne striding out of the darkness, all long limbs and wild curls, a hand on her sword hilt and fire in those hazel eyes, saying something like "Unhand that woman!" or "You're going to be all right; I'm here to protect you."

Hypothetically, of course.

A knock on the door, and Melisant hurried in, aquiline features tight with concern. "Sariva—"

"What is it?"

"You've got a gazing ball message. Your family has news for you." News too urgent to convey by post.

In a chamber at the hallway's end, a large globe flashing shades of ice blue and violet lit the space. Sariva touched it and spoke her name.

A picture shimmered to life. Her mother wore an old scarf wrapped around her hair and a faded dress that had seen better days.

"Have you gotten my letters? Is everything all right?" She'd written, despite the lack of good news.

"Yes, it's just—Aziz wanted to see you. He's not been well. It's the dry air and the stress from the recent attacks." If only she'd managed to catch a wealthy woman's eye sooner. And crying made Aziz's breathing problems even worse. But how could she save her family and her country at the same time?

"Of course, we've had the village physician down to look after him," her mother continued.

"The one who says he's faking it?" She'd watched her brother wheezing, teary because "his bones hurt," and wanted to stab the physician with a crochet needle.

"We've gotten a potion to help him breathe, at least."

"Is there anything I can do?" Despite steady attendance at castle banquets and talking with Delvar about prospects, she'd managed nothing.

"Well..." Hope flickered through her half smile. "We may have had an offer for your hand. A tentative one, mind."

"Tell me more!"

"Her name is Dorenia Maddox. Her holdings are small but profitable, and she'd be all right with an interfaith ceremony."

"What's she like?"

"Preoccupied. Reclusive but respectable. And not too much older than you. I wouldn't entrust my only daughter to someone twice her age."

Sariva fidgeted with her plaits. "What did she like about me?"

"She owns a productive alpaca estate, as well as a lake and a grove of olive trees. The work apparently distracts her from her studies. I told her you were intelligent, outgoing, and could manage a household. She expressed a great deal of interest."

"I'm excited to meet her." Dorenia didn't seem to expect a whirlwind romance, thankfully. Still, Sariva hoped they would become partners and friends, that they'd feel comfortable sharing various thoughts and feelings, perhaps discuss books together on rainy winter nights. "How should I act?"

"She's rather quiet, so don't overwhelm her."

"Has she said anything concrete? Prenuptials, how much of the dowry she might waive, what I might expect to receive if she passed away? Goddess forbid, of course," she added.

"Not yet, but I have a good feeling about it. The preliminary negotiations have been rather promising." The usual weight seemed gone from her shoulders.

Aziz poked his head in. Even in the tiny picture, his face gleamed with sweat, and the interference didn't drown out the whistling sound when he breathed. "Mother, please let me talk to Sariva. I've been reading, and there's a lot of terrible things that could happen in the city. You are in good health, aren't you?" The crystal's magnifying effect exaggerated his already large eyes.

She leaned toward the crystal. "Yes, perfectly. You'd love the food here. I love the fruit. It's so fresh. How is your plush bear?"

He fidgeted and hugged the toy more closely. "He couldn't sleep all last night. I had to rub his chest."

"Tell your bear to stay in bed and not open the window too wide," Sariva instructed.

"I'll stay with him," he said, nodding.

"And he should eat even if swallowing hurts," she continued. "Whenever I see him, I let out his seams because he's grown taller, and I'd like to add some more stuffing as well." She'd do whatever she could to help him...to help her family. They all deserved better.

"I'll make him work on that. Bear misses you though." He put his toy's worn paw against the glass, and Sariva touched the crystal ball, her hand over the image. "When will you—"

The picture winked into mist.

"Please insert three gold pieces," said a sweetly automated voice.

She couldn't bear to tax their finances further. "I love you. Give Juda and Father all my love—"

Her mother's voice called out. "Sariva, remember what I told you."

"I shall!"

Brushing her hair later, Sariva sang a song from Amaldia's tragedy.

> "Roses and willow trees
>
> Spread silence over me
>
> I am strong, I shall not grieve..."

She liked the show for different reasons than others. Not because it had beautiful music or a fabulous dress transformed in front of the audience, but because its plot confirmed something she'd always known. The title character, Amaldia, sacrificed her chance at happiness with her lover to break a military blockade, rescue the country's sages, and create the Magic Mirror. She united Almesia on the strength of an oath sworn to a dead woman. It proved duty won out over love.

Maybe Queen Oradel had chosen her for this duty because she had the most to lose.

The older women, both widows, owned their own estates. Ava laid unthinking claim to leagues of desert. Lisette purchased a new dress almost weekly. Even Mattie's parents could afford to keep her at court indefinitely.

Meanwhile, Sariva only had one season to marry and marry well. A good contract would mean everything to her family. They'd be able to get medical treatment for her youngest brother, repair the old house, and hopefully even help Northern refugees.

That night, Sariva returned to her room to discover a beautiful bouquet of flowers outside her door. They glowed a luminescent blue and smelled like jasmine perfume. She felt around the crinkly waxed paper for a card, careful not to disturb the asymmetrical blossoms.

Dear Sariva,

I know it must be stressful to manage your duties with the process of searching for a bride, so I've thought of a solution. There's a couple I know—Northern, of course, and the best sort of people—who have a daughter about your age. Would you accompany me to a dinner they're hosting? I'd be happy to make your acquaintance further.

With pleasure,
Delvar

At least she had a friend and an invitation to accept. The bouquet perfumed her dreams.

The next evening, Sariva put on one of her best dresses and accompanied Delvar a short way downhill to one of the city's finest districts. They talked about theatre and books—he'd seen Amaldia's tragedy, and he answered all her eager questions about the set (modular), the costumes (sleek), and the staging (not quite in the round).

How much did you cry at the end of the first act when Rhysling died? But that seemed too personal for such a recent acquaintance.

Delvar helped her down from the carriage, his hand lingering around hers. "And—stop me if you want to, I hate to brag—afterward, the wizard helping with the special effects took me on a backstage tour."

Sariva gasped. "What was that like?" The bright gowns and coats with exaggerated detailing and shimmery fabric, the room full of wigs in long-ago styles...not to mention the dressing rooms where beautiful women made themselves even lovelier! Of course, Rhysling's actress only wore stage-knitted chainmail, spat out stage blood, carried a longsword carved of painted wood, but pretend warrior women still made her heart hiccup.

"Fantastic. Did you know when they sign something or write something in the show, it's real copies of the documents? Not blank paper like some of the downhill theatres."

The shabbier downhill theatres had their charm and strong women too. She'd loved the little playhouse in her village, with its musty curtains smelling like secrets and its one closet of props and costumes they reused for each show. She made a neutral remark. "Sounds like a lot of parchment."

A papery old woman wearing a richly colored dress opened the door. She beamed at them, her earrings sparkling. "Delvar! So good of you to pay us a visit. We found a wonderful white wine. And who's your lady companion?"

"I'm Sariva Al-Beroth. We're *friends*. I was hoping I could meet your daughter?"

"Yes, well..." A sigh, a shake of her head. "She's decided to stay at university for the weekend, Goddess knows why. My husband Itran and I will do our best to entertain you both."

They had a lovely house. While Delvar chatted with the balding old man at the dinner table and the woman—Yana—poured wine, Sariva flitted from shelf to cabinet, amazed at tiny crystal sculptures, delicate filigree candleholders, silver Goddess figurines, and a glinting geode the size of her fist, imagining using such beautiful objects to celebrate the holidays. She loved dinner too. Vivid-green soup garnished with mint leaves and a fluffy rice dish with plump dried fruit and perfectly roasted nuts.

Around when Yana brought out the main course, herb-crusted chicken breasts, the topic turned to politics.

"I swear the queen tears things down just for the sake of overturning convention. That slip of a girl pretending to be a squire, for instance. It's clear the queen let her in just so she could trot out a girl knight as an example of her *values*. I wonder how many qualified boys were turned down for the place? This disregard for the old order...one can't go discarding tradition just because it's traditional," Itran hmphed, gesturing with his wineglass.

Yana, who'd only eaten the salad, toyed with her shimmering pendant. "Young people nowadays are taken in so easily. The girl squire? I heard she started a brawl with the city guard. Right in the marketplace!"

Even at a dinner party at the other side of town. Sariva couldn't go a day without hearing Edwynne mentioned—or, even worse, seeing her.

Itran tsked. "She probably got caught stealing from a stall. And yet the university's printing handbills encouraging what they call civil disobedience. We all know the guards respect those who respect law and order. If she were my daughter...a night in lockup and a good thrashing, for one thing."

Why had she started a fight? Edwynne was impulsive, sure, but not stupid. And she'd earned her position.

Delvar chuckled, putting his arm around Sariva's chair. "Well, even though Sariva works for the queen, she's not a radical. She serves the institution of the crown, not any one leader. It's to build her résumé and attract a good wife. Isn't that correct, Sariva? You're not there to smash things."

A question. A question aimed at her. One she ought to answer, for politeness's sake. "Certainly, I wouldn't define myself as a smasher, and I do believe in the existence of government, it's just..." She sat up straighter. "I've seen the girl knight train. She's better than most of the boys; she must be. They're twice her size."

Itran's eyebrows arched. "If you say so. Darling, pass the julienned carrots?"

"This produce is fantastic," Delvar told Yana. "So fresh! Where do you shop?"

The conversation had travelled to a different topic, conversational mistakes avoided.

Except it returned to politics when Itran announced, "If we're complaining about the young people today, you know what I can't stand? Those radical Northerners at the university."

"Well, Sariva's a lovely girl. She'd be a great match for any proper young woman. She's on the side of her own people."

She ought to have appreciated Delvar's praise. Instead, anger and doubt simmered inside her. The dining room felt too warm. *My mother is one of those radical Northerners. And I'd rather side with that girl squire than with you...* She swallowed the words.

Itran kept going. "What I find the saddest is how these radical mobs are cutting young people off from their traditions. They say they're Northerners, but then they turn around and listen to blatant lies about the North. Blockade of civilians this, unequal access to food supplies that... Personally, I'm willing to die for my country."

"I'd rather not die for anything at all, personally," Sariva murmured. Everyone looked at her.

"But you *do* love your country," Yana prompted.

She loved Almesia, though Yana meant the North. "I mean, that's why I think our government should uphold our ideals."

Silence around the dinner table. Delvar cleared his throat into his napkin.

"I mean...we were charged to be agents of the Lady's will in the living world. To act in the name of justice, of compassion. How can a country claim to be sacred when it's depriving citizens of firewood in winter?"

A disapproving sniff from Itran. Yana's mouth pursed as if she'd smelled something nasty. "So, you'd advocate for us to abandon our only refuge."

She ought to have backed down. She ought to have said something like, "You're right, I don't know what I was thinking," slicing her chicken into neat bites. But when Edwynne annoyed her, she spoke freely, flashing her emotions like a glimpse of petticoat, and as she leaned forward, elbows on the table, that wildness flared in her now. "I'm just speaking for myself, but I'd say we should find allies, build coalitions. Maybe even talk to radicals protesting outside the university and disreputable girl squires. Because they're the ones defending human rights."

A long moment of utter silence. Then the couple burst out laughing.

Yana fanned herself. "She is a laugh a minute. Where'd you find her?"

"You'll grow out of it. Travel, read books, you won't be so stuck on what the populists dictate," Itran said, self-assured.

"Sariva is a diamond in the rough. I hope to see her polished." Delvar gazed at her, enigmatic, intent, amusement swimming in those strange light eyes.

"But surely you don't actually believe all that. You just want to fit in with the crowd. You young people are all so concerned about having the wrong opinion. What do you truly think?" Itran asked.

This has been a boring, uncomfortable evening.

Edwynne would empty a bowl of soup over your head!

The delicate brocade tablecloth gleamed silver. So did the fork she set down. "Delvar, I'd like to go home. I'm...not feeling well. I suppose something I ate must have disagreed with me."

His expression cooled. "Your shawl's in the coat closet."

She lacked Edwynne's ramrod bravery, but at least she'd made it through a dinner party without getting expelled.

As the carriage rolled uphill toward the palace, she gave voice to a troubling thought. "Did I embarrass you?"

He shook his head and took her hands in his. "You fascinate me, Sariva. Your optimism about human nature, flying in the face of all evidence. Some might find it naive, even ignorant, but I call it endearing. I enjoy your delicacy. Your feminine charm. And despite the bounds of propriety, I wish we could retire to the same chambers and never be parted."

"Umm." Would it be rude if she pulled her hand away?

He gripped tighter, pale eyes intense. "We've never quarreled. We enjoy each other's company. Let me solve all your problems. Marry me."

What?

Why?

This came out of nowhere.

Not nowhere. The signs had been present, and she'd ignored them. She yanked her hand from his grip. "I'm terribly sorry. You've misunderstood. I'm not comfortable with men in that way, I've informed you as much—"

"But you've seemed comfortable around me." It sounded like an accusation, his thin lips a narrow line.

"Yes. As a friend."

He drew closer and closer. Putting a hand on her shoulder. Leaning in. "I know you're concerned about your reputation, but we're alone. No one to spy, no old ladies to gossip. You don't have to refuse me. Your reputation will remain untouched."

The carriage rolled to a stop. Sariva shoved the door open and hurled herself out. She hit the road hard, scraping her knees, the palms of her hands, then heaved herself to her feet. Aside from a slight upward slant, the street appeared the same in either direction. She chose a direction at random and broke into a run.

"Sariva, come back! You're making an imprudent choice. That Edwynne girl—" He hung out the open door, calling for her to come back, for the driver to turn around. Wheels on the cobblestones. Had the driver obeyed him? She ducked behind a potted plant and stayed motionless until the sound faded.

It took almost an hour of stumbling through unfamiliar streets before the palace gates came into view. The other ladies-in-waiting had long since retired. She didn't take off her makeup or change clothes before hurling herself onto her bed and letting out silent sobs. Who would they believe, the court wizard or a teenager who'd just gotten to court? Even Ava seemed to trust Delvar.

The flowers Delvar had given her rotted in the night—choking, cloying, the sweetness from before turned filthy and overpowering. Would putting them in the compost poison the garden? When she burned them in her bees-wax candle, they went up like dry paper, despite their slimy texture. She opened both windows to get rid of the smoke. Two thoughts chased each other in spirals: *It wasn't my fault, but what could I have done?* Mother and Father had enough to worry about with her brothers: one ill and the other rambunctious. This incident needed to stay out of her next letters home.

Chapter Seven

Edwynne's foot refused to feel better. She prodded it one morning before lessons, glaring at the violent purple puncture marks on the sole, the mottled blue-and-yellow bruises spreading in tendrils around them. A thin blister nearly squished apart under her touch. "Oh, that's nasty." She tried to put her weight on it and recoiled, every texture of the floor prodding raw, peeled skin. So much for running around, even with two pairs of socks.

Luckily all the other squires had gotten their things and changed. They wouldn't see her poisoned (or infected?) wounds.

The door swung open. Edwynne flung her blanket over her foot.

Tolliver tilted his head. "Ed, what's the matter? You're going to be late. You sick or something?"

"Or something," she mumbled. He moved to sit beside her, and she made room.

A one-shouldered shrug. "Don't be embarrassed. Stars know I've done plenty of dumb shit."

Dumb shit. She'd start from there and build a good lie. "So, a while back I forgot I'd left my dagger next to my bed, and I stepped on it after a nap."

He winced. "Cuts on the bottom of your foot are the worst."

"Exactly, and I've had such a hard time keeping it clean. I think it might even be infected. But I'm just not motivated to drag myself all the way to Delvar's workshop, especially since he hates me." She could fool Tolliver, but Delvar would instantly know a ruins creature had bitten her.

"Want me to run by his workshop and see if he'll prescribe something you can take?"

"Sounds good. Sounds perfect. And you could tell the teachers I can't come to lessons because my foot's hurt, but because Delvar's treating it, I won't miss any further lessons."

He grinned. "Say no more. But you're covering for me the next time I want a day off."

As long as no one suspected her of exploring past her ruins patrol route, Edwynne didn't care. She waved him off—"Yeah, whatever"—and grabbed her pillow. Sleeping with multiple pillows, the lonely girl's answer to cuddling.

Tolliver jogged in before afternoon training, cupping a thin glass bottle filled with deep-green liquid.

"What am I supposed to do, rub it on my foot?"

"He said drink it to make your body stronger so you can fight off infections."

Edwynne uncorked the vessel and gave a dubious sniff. Ugh. It smelled even worse than the potion she'd choked down previously. Decaying leaves in the rainy season and cheap perfume. But she couldn't skip training. "Fine, bottoms up," she muttered and forced herself to swallow it. A cold, anesthetized feeling spread down her mouth and into her throat. Her tongue prickled.

"You okay?"

It took a few moments and a swig of water before she could speak. The numbness pooled in her feet, dulling the blisters' throbbing. "It's starting to work."

"Yeah, medicine does that. I bet you'll feel well enough for training."

Sure, the potion left icky green residue on her tongue, but Delvar had no reason to poison a palace squire. He just didn't care about making concoctions taste decent. Medicine with a disgusting mouthfeel would still treat her wounds. She was able to keep up at training, and she'd be able to keep up with Sariva tonight. Tolliver studied her as she laced up her boots and pulled her hair back. "You're always going out when we have free days. Without me, even! Where are you headed so secretly?"

"Best friends aren't conjoined twins. I can go places by myself."

He'd found something to poke at, and he wouldn't let go. Mischief lit his eyes. "Let me guess. Have you gotten over your dramatic vow of never loving again? Are you having secret meetings with a girl?" He leaned closer, waggling his eyebrows outrageously. "Is she pretty? What's her personality like?"

"Well..." A love affair seemed like a decent cover story. And the way Sariva's soft, glossy lips pouted when Edwynne annoyed her, the way her skin caught the evening sunlight... "She's pretty enough but stubborn. Always telling me what to do. She thinks she knows everything."

Tolliver patted her on the shoulder. "Go have a good date. She sounds like your type, and maybe this one won't break your heart."

"I'm immune to heartbreak," she declared with an expansive gesture. After Lisette's cutting words, who could hurt her? She left the squires' quarters and headed for the gates.

So what if Sariva tempted her? Poisonous plants tempted unwary bugs. Sure, Edwynne felt drawn to bossy, feminine women, but only a fool would swoon over Sariva. Derision heated her face at the idea, and she couldn't help chuckling, shaking her head at the thought. They hardly even tolerated each other! She wouldn't make such a stupid decision. She had nothing to fear.

Edwynne planned to arrive at the ruins early—scout ahead, impress Sariva with her knowledge. As she crossed the courtyard, a song drifted through the warm air.

Sariva knelt on the gravel before a low stone bench. Muttering something, she struck a match against the wall. Then she lit a candle. She held her hands like a dome around the flame, swaying with the rhythm of her slow melody.

Don't notice me. Sing even louder. Let me drink the words out of your mouth. A stone crunched under her sandal.

Sariva glanced at her, tucking a curl behind her ear, and gave a sheepish half smile. "Sorry, nearly finished, just praying for protection. Did you know we're not allowed to light candles in our quarters?"

"Yup." She'd tried it a few weeks ago, trying to worship by herself. "Couldn't you go to a temple though? The palace has a trolley station and maps."

A grand eye roll. She tossed her wealth of hair. "But odds are someone will know my parents and get in touch with them or bring up some embarrassing story from my childhood—or worse, they'll be obsessed with my parents' activism. The journey to the palace took several weeks, and I learned I can't pray around anyone over thirty. I either have to make connections to further my position or justify what my parents believe in. I've gone to temple weekly my whole life, and I just want to be alone with the Goddess for once."

What was it like being so surrounded by community, so rooted in your ancestry and your place in the world, you craved alone time like fresh air in a crowded room? Sariva had everything, and she rolled her eyes about it. *Oh,* your *parents made you learn about your heritage? You poor thing, have a petit four!*

"I'm..." *I want to leave your broken body on the flagstones. I want to shave your head and wear your perfect Northern-dark hair.* She managed to blurt out something tangential to how she felt. "Must be nice having a personal relationship with divinity. Does the Goddess fly down from the sky and grant your wishes?"

Sariva scowled. "That's not how it works! I understand you're not religious and you just showed up at Vered's party for the bread, but don't make fun of me for praying."

She stalked closer, sneering. "So your family taught you religion and even a special language to pray in. Want a round of applause? Want a medal?"

But maybe she'd let too much bitterness show. Because instead of getting angry, Sariva's face went cool and thoughtful. "You're not jealous, are you?"

"No! Why would I be? My family only goes to the star-church on holidays, and we only pray to the celestials when someone dies. I don't need to bother the sky whenever I want something." She'd never felt connected to the stars' remote brightness, never felt protected or watched over the way Tolliver and Stellan did. Prayer just meant waiting for some surge of feeling that never showed up.

"I mean, the Goddess doesn't get bothered. We're supposed to talk to her. It's like family. Like how your parents wouldn't mind if you wrote home daily."

Another thing she didn't want to think about. She fidgeted, trying to sound skeptical. "Sounds interesting."

"Want me to pray for you?"

I want to know the words so I can pray by myself. I don't want to need a translator into my own tongue. "I mean, if you insist." Did she have to admit anything more specific? She hoped not.

"What do you want me to pray for?" Sariva prompted, her tone too gentle. "I already know how obnoxious you are, so I won't judge."

Edwynne wanted to bite her. Wanted to goad her, snap at her, anything to disturb Sariva's calm dark gaze. Instead, she put her hands in her pockets and shuffled her feet. "Ask the Goddess to bring Stellan home safe." Tears threatened again. To distract herself, she kept talking. "And it wouldn't hurt if they started serving us squires better desserts either. We had fruit ices last summer, but no one can tell us if we'll get fruit ices this year. We've been getting a lot of grain cookies? It's supposed to be nutritionally balanced, but I don't want nutritionally balanced. I want fruit ices. We all do."

How much did Sariva suspect? She just turned toward the candle. "Goddess, please visit your bounty upon the squires in the form of nicer things to eat. And please guard and protect Edwynne's brother Stellan, for her sake and for Almesia's. Amen."

"That sound you were singing...what did the words mean?" Edwynne ventured, not making eye contact. She might've heard similar lyrics to a different tune at the temple.

Her round face lit up. "It's about welcoming the light of the Goddess into us and taking it wherever we go. I could teach you the tune if you want?"

Even if it came from Sariva, she wanted knowledge. She craved it even more than shining round bread. "It's not like I'm going to bow down and pray. It's just catchy."

The candlelight shone on her warm-olive skin as she smiled. It made Edwynne feel...weird. "This from the girl who pestered me about converting the instant we were introduced?"

"It's..." Shadows covered the setting sun. She wanted to take all her stupid vulnerable longing and bundle it into the river. "Quit assuming you know me. It's none of your business. I wasn't even seriously considering—"

Her expression went smooth and flat—court lady manners. "I get it. Nothing worth asking about. Not like you'd share anything with a frilly court lady whose skull you want to use to hold pencils. You're from an old Almesian family, and no one ever tells you to go to your home country. You can change religions on a whim," she said with a dramatic eye roll.

She felt further away from Sariva than ever. Why bother even asking? She possessed advantages no

Northern-born Goddess worshipper could dream of. They'd never accept her. "Forget the song. Let's just go down there. Get it over with."

Sariva blew out the candle and gazed at the smoke before tucking its stub into a little beaded purse. "I wish I could wait until I wasn't scared of whatever's down there...but let's just go now."

Edwynne walked ahead. "I studied military history, and we're searching for a statue." She glanced at the sun. They had some time.

"What do you mean?"

"After the wars, a famous knight went home and bought a cottage. All the land around it was barren because a wicked witch had lived there, but she figured out how to get around the spells and grow the most beautiful garden. They called her the Flower of Golden Ridge." Two passages led away from the courtyard, and she took a moment to choose between them. "A lot of the older boys thought the story sounded silly. Knight gets truly famous, she has offers from foreign nobles to train their armies, three different mercenary bands want her for their captain, and all she wants to do is take her paycheck and go home?"

Sariva tucked her plaits behind her ears. "Better than prioritizing bravery over common sense. My brother Juda once dislocated his shoulder jumping from a tree just because some village children dared him. I think if she wanted to go home after all those praises and accolades shoved in her face, she had a great deal of sense."

Something almost like a smile passed over her face, the way a sunbeam flickered through the cloudy water of the courtyard's abandoned fountain. "I thought so too."

She pointed down a fork in the path. Weeds sprung up through cracked stone. "This way, definitely."

In this area of the courtyard, a statue loomed over them.

Edwynne pointed. "That's absolutely her."

Sariva pursed her lips, skeptical. "How do you know?"

"Whoever carved this statue knew what they were doing. Flame-edged double cutlass with a decorated pommel? Matches the era and her rank. Impressive attention to detail." Would she wield such a grand sword someday? Would people walk under a statue of Edwynne Dovecote, patched clothes, uneven haircut, and all? She prodded at the pedestal until something depressed. With a low rumble of long disuse, a cream stone tile slid back and revealed stone steps deep into the earth. Cold air wafted up. "After you, my lady."

"You found it. You can go first."

"Sure, feed me to whatever's down there." She hurried ahead anyway: *Ha! Let it try.*

The air around them felt colder and damper, like a blanket soaked in river water. The staircase spiraled narrower. Surface sounds faded away.

Breathe, Sariva told herself, long deep breaths, just like the mind-healer taught you. In through her mouth and out through her nose, or the other way around? She settled for singing. "Amaldia, enchantress—"

"Shhh!" She had a beautiful, clear voice, but Edwynne couldn't risk the noise.

At last, Edwynne's questing fingers nudged something solid. "I think I've found a door!"

"Open it, then."

"If it's trapped or cursed, we might both die."

Sariva swallowed. "Take as long as you want."

She wrapped her hand in her tunic and tried the handle. Nothing stabbed her, but it didn't budge. "We've been learning lockpicking, but I don't have my picks with me."

She sensed Sariva's eye roll. "Did you think my plaits stayed on top of my head by themselves?"

"Just pass me the longest pin you have."

Her soft fingers pressed a hairpin into Edwynne's palm. Edwynne put her head as close to the lock as she dared and prodded around, listening for the click. "Got it!" The door swung open. They crept inside.

A few cracked magical light-globes still shed light in rusty fixtures, illuminating a large stone space. The dim glow showed moth-eaten tapestries. Edwynne pointed: *Let's go through that archway.* She moved lightly, favoring her throbbing foot.

Shifting from the corner of the room. Old leather? The covers dropping off furniture? Had they disturbed a wild animal's nest? Then more objects slipped sideways— oh, shit. Not furniture. Not leather.

The wings of a giant dragon, unfolding as it growled. It had been hibernating. And they'd just disturbed its sleep.

Beside her, Sariva froze.

"No, get down!" Edwynne yelled. She launched herself at Sariva. They crashed into a rattle of old ceremonial armor, the impact jarring her foot.

Whoosh! A gust of viciously hot flame barely missed them both before the dragon swiped at them. Edwynne rolled away, shoving Sariva to safety.

Sariva shook out her plaits. "We need to run."

Know what would have been an ideal time to retreat? Before we woke up a giant feral dragon.

"In a long, narrow passageway? We'd be even better targets."

Could she keep up with Sariva if they ran? Even the idea of falling behind humiliated her.

"So, what do we do?" Sariva asked, her eyes wide.

"Maybe we need to fight it...and what I mean is I'll fight, you hide." Edwynne shoved Sariva behind a pile of broken furniture and drew her short sword.

Instead of ducking, Sariva said, "I have an idea. Hold it off."

"What?"

"I'll explain later!"

"If I'm still alive to listen!" Fending off a threatened blow with a swing of her sword, she jumped onto another pile of rocks. They shifted under her, and she stumbled. Could she turn her fall into a dive and attack? Instead, the dragon blasted her with a gust of heat, singeing her curls and blistering her cheeks. "Sariva! Whatever you're doing, hurry up!" Her foot felt like the worst bruise she'd ever had.

No response. Did the noblewoman even have a plan? Stacks of furniture trembled as the dragon stepped closer, its big eyes fixed on Edwynne, saliva dripping from between its fangs. Like dodging a blow from a bigger squire, she'd have to move at the last possible moment.

It snarled and struck.

She rolled out of the way—but not fast enough.

The dragon's claws caught in the back of her tunic and scraped her skin. It lifted its foot and shook her. She flung her body weight one way, then the other, but couldn't get enough leverage to rip free. Another growl from its powerful throat. Its rough tail slammed into her body and knocked her from its claws. Landing, she gagged on red-hot pain.

Had Sariva fled? Edwynne searched the room. Couldn't find her. Again, the dragon's foot thudded down, and she forced herself to roll away, holding in a scream. She scrambled behind an armoire. *We're just teens! Is the queen trying to get us killed?*

"Now! Lead him here!" Sariva yelled, tossing something out from her hiding place. Edwynne couldn't figure out what. She'd fastened some velvet ropes and ceremonial metal chains, but how would those help?

A sunlit memory flashed into her mind. Camping with Stellan on the road, the way he effortlessly looped knots for—

Sariva had actually delivered.

Edwynne leapt over the snare and swallowed a scream when she landed on hard stone. The dragon's heavy foot came down, and the trap tightened around its leg, leaving it stumbling.

They both scrambled to cover.

"Could you kill it?" Sariva whispered.

"Not without ranged weapons. Besides, we're the ones who've wandered into its house. Our best bet is to flee while it's distracted."

The dragon huffed, trying to unpick the snare with its front claws.

She motioned to the door, but Sariva shook her head and pointed to a groove etched into the stone. "This looks carved by water. Follow water, right?"

"Maybe. But be careful."

"Since when did you care about me?"

A joke? Either way, Edwynne didn't answer.

As the dragon picked at the snare with its claws, Sariva tiptoed around the room, stopping at a drain. She struggled with the rusted metal, carefully prying it up. Rippling blue light—magic light—shone on her face.

The dragon snorted, its claws scratching on the floor, panting in preparation for another gust of flame.

Edwynne made a frantic hand gesture at her: *Stay quiet!* She couldn't watch. Couldn't look away either.

The dragon's gaze fixed on Sariva.

Edwynne, too far away to help, gripped her sword anyway.

Sariva froze, and the dragon shifted its weight forward, its nostrils flaring. Would it kill her? Instead, it lowered its powerful body and rested its head on its forepaws with a huff.

Edwynne exhaled.

When they left the room, Edwynne shoved a mostly intact chair under the doorknob. Such a sturdy door would at least stand up to the first gust of flame. The gemstone in Sariva's hand swirled and shifted, colors moving like ink dropped into water.

"Guess you have to admit being able to tie fancy knots is useful now," Sariva quipped, elbowing her in the side, right in her scrapes.

She couldn't even laugh without wincing. The dragon's sharp scales had left a raw patch, oozing dots of blood onto her shredded tunic. And her foot... Hopefully, the pain would fade to normal soon. Edwynne squeezed her eyes shut and focused on following Sariva, putting one foot in front of the other until they finally emerged into sunlight. Wincing, she sagged onto the chipped bricks.

Sariva frowned, fidgeting with her skirts. "I know Delvar...might not be the best option, but your cuts need treatment."

Huh, a pleasant surprise. Edwynne had expected Sariva to drag her to the wizard's musty workshop by her hair. "I thought you and Delvar were all buddy-buddy?"

She unpinned a braid and fiddled with it, tilting her painted fingernails to catch the light. "He just seemed pretty irritated when he was treating your injuries last time. Don't the knights have medics?"

If she pushed, Sariva would probably bolt, leaving her to limp along behind without an arm to lean on or money for a carriage uphill to the palace. Better drop the subject. "I can't. They'll ask questions. Ones I won't be able to answer with 'I fought with another squire,' or 'I fell off a horse.' But I'm not even seriously hurt. My foot's getting better."

Sariva raised skeptical eyebrows, her dark hair gleaming in the sunlight. "So then, why are you limping and missing a layer of skin?"

Did she need this sort of coddling? No way. Once she'd carried a knocked-off tooth off the training field, wet with blood, in her grubby palm. Boys never saw her show weakness. "I said I'm fine."

That smirk, that infuriating, superior, smug little smirk on her perfectly moisturized full lips. "Okay, then I'll race you to the tram stop."

Glaring daggers, Edwynne dragged herself to her feet. She took two hopping jog-steps before her foot refused.

Sariva rushed to her side, bolstering her so she didn't hit the pavement. "My mother spent some time as a field medic in the Northern army, and one of my brother's always sick, and the other one thinks he can jump out of trees without hurting himself. I'm entirely capable of treating your injuries."

"Did I say you weren't?" Edwynne groaned. Which, okay, she had.

Sariva's petal-soft hand slipped into hers. "Come on. Lean on me if you need to."

What would her rivals say if they saw her like this? *The little girl got hurt again; you should give me her ruins job.* Ugh.

With Sariva's shawl wrapped around her shoulders to hide the bloodstains, Edwynne hailed them a carriage to the palace. On the ride, Sariva nudged her and murmured, "I heard you beat up some city guards."

"Where did you hear it?" She'd assumed no one at the palace knew.

"Another failed dinner party. I found it boring and pretentious. Your presence wouldn't have detracted from it. This decrepit old-money couple kept talking about how much they hated you, which sounded like a story worth hearing."

"Oh." Edwynne hardly believed her ears. Sariva wished she'd been there? Sariva wanted to hear about her adventures? "These new guards weren't wearing recording crystals, and they kept rifling through everyone's things. Tolliver and I figured we'd just keep our heads down. But we got in line behind this poor old herb seller who could barely push his wheelbarrow." She told Sariva what the guards had done to him and how she'd intervened.

"And you ran in there thinking nothing bad could happen to you."

Not exactly. "They were prowling around, hoping someone would give them a reason to start shit. I figured...at least let them blunt their swords on someone who could put up a fight."

Her eyes widened. "But you were vastly outnumbered."

"Are you siding with me or with those old people?"

"You!" Sariva snapped, leaning in. "I'm just trying to figure out why you did it. I would have run and gotten help."

"They were going to hurt a defenseless old man," Edwynne explained slowly with an expansive isn't-it-obvious gesture.

She crossed her arms. "You were brave. Excuse me for trying to give you a compliment. I knew you'd just take it the wrong way."

Edwynne couldn't stifle a laugh. "Compliment taken—you're excused. I know I'm brave. I'm going to be a knight someday. Only what about you, Miss I-understand-these-ruins-kill-people-I'm-blundering-in-anyway?"

When Sariva laughed, she tried to hide it, ducking her head and covering her mouth. "That wasn't being brave, only—I didn't have any other options!"

"Exactly. I run out of options, and then I have to do something. I couldn't stop myself if I tried."

She didn't laugh out loud this time, but her whole face squinched up and her shoulders shook. "I know you're impulsive. I've seen you leap before you look."

"I'm not the one who jumped over the lake of acid."

She giggled. Not a smirk, not a sneer, but a belly laugh doubling her over. She was fascinatingly easy to rile up. "You're the one who keeps making me angry enough to do stupid shit!"

"As if you need the encouragement."

Sariva smacked her on the shoulder—a playful gesture, but it hurt like hell. She winced. Soon, at least, the carriage stopped.

Edwynne had an awful thought. "Shit. You live with Lisette, don't you?"

"We're...colleagues. We share a dorm." (Though why hesitate? Why her reserved tone, so similar to how she'd talked about Delvar?) "Why do you ask?"

Sariva would side with her fellow lady-in-waiting over a squire, right? She didn't need to tell her the humiliating, awkward truth. Maybe they wouldn't even run into Lisette. Maybe she'd be at a party. She loved being the center of attention at parties. "No real reason."

They showed their passes at a servants' entrance and slipped up a back staircase.

"One more hallway," Sariva told her. "Although I hope no one will see me sneaking you into my chambers. There would be...questions."

"I've got a reputation for kissing girls at parties. Most of the maids, a few foreign dignitaries...you're not special."

"You kiss people you hardly even know?" Sariva sounded surprised.

Edwynne tried to twist around, winced. "Are you judging me?" She wouldn't ally with someone who called her a slut.

She shook her head, plaits swinging. "I'm not. I just can't imagine kissing a stranger, that's all."

"So, have you ever kissed anyone?" Needling Sariva distracted her from how much her side hurt.

"I've kissed girls! Two girls!" She shifted under Edwynne's gaze and reconsidered. "Well, on the cheek."

"Cheek kisses are hardly a real kiss."

Sariva frowned. "What's a real kiss?"

"A real kiss is one that makes you understand why kissing is a good idea. I didn't understand what the fuss was about until I kissed a girl, but then it made sense."

Odds were someone would enjoy kissing Sariva. Of course, Edwynne would rather press her mouth to a viper. But her glossy, immaculate beauty would be fun to take apart, to smudge her painted lips and pull the pins from her hair. Would her haughty attitude disappear along with her clothing? Or would she stay cool and imperious, eyes narrowing as she effortlessly gave instructions? Edwynne pitied the poor lover stuck with such a bossy bitch. There were women with equally soft breasts and better person-alities.

"It's just...people can always be so silly about it. They sound like"—Sariva stuck her tits out—"Hello, I've just met you, but I like your face. Let's do some kissing."

Was Sariva mocking her? Edwynne refused to smile. "Have you never met someone you liked, or are you too busy, or..."

"I don't know. Bits of both, I suppose."

Up ahead, some ladies-in-waiting worked in a room with the door open. If they saw her, they'd ask too many questions.

Sariva made a wait-here gesture and crept forward. She closed the door.

One problem solved. How many more remained?

Sariva couldn't figure Edwynne out. All her propositions got proved wrong.

Her hazel eyes shone when Sariva told her about the Goddess. She had leaned in, surprisingly solemn and fo-cused. Did she genuinely want to convert? Had Sariva misjudged her all along?

No. She hated religion, only sampled prayer out of idle curiosity, and acted all snotty and affronted when Sa-riva suspected her of giving a shit.

They'd nearly died, guided each other, saved each other's lives. Did Edwynne trust her?

No, she'd rather bleed in secret than have Sariva glance at her wounds.

Did she even believe Stellan would return, or could she just not stand the thought of Sariva seeing her grief? The second seemed so like her. All hail the all-powerful Edwynne Dovecote! You'll never catch her wanting anything. She never gets sick or hurt or scared, and she thinks "feelings" are a type of dried fruit!

Sometimes she thought she glimpsed the real Edwynne—like when Edwynne had been worried for her safety against the dragon or when they'd made each other laugh on the carriage ride home. But the rest of the time, her careless, entitled attitude seemed impossible to bear.

"I'm not weak. I can manage," she'd snapped with a death glare. She kept stumbling, slowing their pace to an infuriating crawl.

Sariva couldn't help trying. "Are you sure—"

"I said I'm fine! I'm only letting you check over my injuries to humor you because you won't shut up! I'm the strongest squire in the barracks. I've never needed coddling or hand-holding, and it won't start now." She stumbled forward. Sariva instinctively moved to steady her.

"Don't even think about it."

They reached Sariva's chamber.

"Okay. Get your tunic off, and we'll see how badly you're scraped up," Sariva managed. She'd tended to plenty of wounds. Why did Edwynne's make her uneasy?

"I'm cooperating, be patient." She unlaced her tunic down the front, wiggled out of it, and tossed it aside.

Hell. The cut went up farther than she'd thought. "Your breastband too. And don't get any ideas."

"Don't flatter yourself. I'd lick the sculptures in the ruins first." With the same casual economy of movement, she took off her breastband and revealed paler skin, small handfuls of breasts, and the little rosy brown points of her nipples.

"Er," Sariva stammered. She'd seen girls in their breastbands on hot days at the swimming hole but not fully undressed.

Edwynne sat on the bed, her tone gentling. "You're right, okay? I admit it. I can't reach all of these myself. If I come into the barracks with open wounds? Even if I'm just sitting in class learning about territory wars or ghosts, my instructors will get suspicious. You helped me take down a dragon. Don't turn into a coward now."

It would have bolstered her had her fear been the problem. "Right. Bravery. I'll do my best." She went for her first-aid kit, managing a few precious seconds of avoiding the sight of a half-naked Edwynne. Finally, she had to dab on the disinfectant.

Edwynne flinched, muscles tensing. This close, she smelled like rosemary and sleepy-girl musk. "It stings!"

"What'd you expect?"

"I'm just expressing my opinion. This isn't the first time I've been patched up."

Edwynne's breathing steadied as Sariva smoothed a beeswax salve into the edges of her cuts. "How do I compare?" she tried to joke.

"You're..." Edwynne seemed distracted. "I've had worse. At least you have warm hands."

Was her tongue sticking to the roof of her mouth? Did she need to catch her breath at the touch of her own hair against her cheeks? Because Sariva felt that way.

Edwynne's shoulders shifted away from her ears. "Can I lie down?"

"Hadn't planned to wash my bedding today but go for it."

She flopped onto her belly and fidgeted a little before getting comfortable, head pillowed on her folded arms. When she stopped scowling, Edwynne actually had a pretty face. In a lanky, straggly, underfed, freckly way, of course. Her hair seemed to glow an even more outrageous shade of red, and Sariva wanted to fix it. Could Edwynne stop irritating her? Stop making her reckless? Caution flew out the window as she slung a leg over Edwynne's lower back. She dressed the wounds and wrapped bandages to hold the gauze in place. Then, ambition brewing, she seized her hairbrush.

Edwynne squirmed under her. "What are you doing?"

"Making you presentable. Unless you want to go to dinner with bits of wood splinters and dirt in your hair. Do I have to pin you down, or are you going to be polite?" She shouldn't have said it.

A smirk laden with chaos. "I'm already humoring you, but if you want to pin me down—"

Sariva covered Edwynne's mouth. A warm, wet tongue licked her palm. "Disgusting." She snatched her hand away, mentally chiding herself.

"Disgusting," Edwynne mimicked, and Sariva had to force herself not to laugh.

Slapping on several palmfuls of crème, she eventually wrangled Edwynne's loose curls into a low ponytail before angling her face toward the mirror. "There. Admit it, you're pretty."

Edwynne tilted her head one way, then the other. "What are you going to do next, wash my face for me?"

"Do you want me to?" *Do you even know how to ask for things, or can you only dare people to care for you out of spite?*

"Well, I can't be bothered," she quipped, a challenge in her eyes.

It was the closest Edwynne had come to asking Sariva for help. She'd take it. She half hauled, half dragged Edwynne to the sink and scrubbed her down, careful not to drip water on the bandages. She'd never washed another girl's face before. Edwynne complained the whole time, squinting and muttering about water up her nose. "Come on, you're actually washing my ears?"

"Yes, what a terrible fate I'm inflicting on you. It's not like you can just take the washcloth out of my hands and move a few steps away."

Edwynne made a rude gesture but didn't reach for the washcloth.

What is this? What do you want from me—whether it's a fight, a song, or medicine, why do you keep goading me into fulfilling your wishes while you whine the whole time?

Of course, if she asked, Edwynne would just say something petty and mean. Having seen Sariva's room, she possessed even more ammunition. Finally clean, Edwynne shook herself like a dog, wrinkling her nose. The petty brat had no right to such an endearing expression. "I'm late for dinner, but it's not like I can see the other squires like this. They'll know I'm injured."

"You could eat with me as my guest...if you're not too proud."

"If it's eat with you or go hungry, fine."

"I'll find something you can borrow that's not too frilly," she muttered, moving toward her closet. Fashion remained solid ground. Some searching unearthed a plain cream shirt with flowing sleeves and a green silk sash to use as a belt.

This time, Edwynne admired her reflection openly. "Thank fuck. I thought you'd stuff me into a layer cake of petticoats." And "The food better be good," she added, heading for the door. As if Sariva hadn't risked her reputation smuggling a bedraggled squire into her bedchamber. As if people, especially Ava, wouldn't ask questions.

But I might as well keep an eye on her.

The two walked into the room where all the ladies-in-waiting had gathered for dinner. Ava raised an eyebrow while Lisette did a double take. She handed her drink to a friend and hurried over to the seats Sariva and Edwynne had chosen, two armchairs with a low table in between.

"Edwynne, I asked you to leave me alone. Can't you respect my boundaries?" And, turning to Sariva, "I'm sorry, I should have warned you about her. She's impulsive, she overreacts, you can't get a word in edgewise around her. She just doesn't know what's appropriate. I suppose she browbeat you until she could resume stalking me. Even if I doubt your commitment to the cause, you don't deserve to be entangled with such a missing stair."

With every judgement, Edwynne's shoulders hunched further. She twisted her napkin as if about to rip it.

Sariva's blood ran cold with a vicious protective instinct. How dare she? "Thank you for your opinion, Lisette. I'm glad you feel comfortable sharing it with me."

"You don't need to look at me like I've spoiled your meal. I just wanted to warn you what sort of person—"

"I know exactly what sort of person Edwynne is." *And you* have spoiled my meal.

Edwynne grimly shoveled quiche into her mouth.

"Edwynne risked her life to rescue an old man from city guards. She risks her life daily to pull complete strangers out of the ruins. Even people she hates. She might not use the right jargon or go to the right seminars, but she does the right thing. And if you don't value her actions, it's your problem. Not hers."

Lisette's disdainful moue became a full-fledged pout. "You're not living your ideals right now. Criticizing my activism isn't good praxis."

"Neither is criticizing hers." Lisette seemed to have memorized the language of social change: whenever she didn't like someone, she just pulled out a stock phrase and painted them as harmful to the movement, squawking "marginalized" and "toxic" like a bird who knew the sounds of words but not their meaning.

"Never mind. Just don't say I told you so when she hurts your feelings," she announced and stormed off.

Edwynne's elbows met the table. "You didn't have to do that, you know."

"Do what?"

She gave an uncomfortable one-shouldered shrug, picking at her cuticles and the food by turns. "Pretend you like me. I'm wearing your clothes, we came in together... If you defend me, people will talk."

People would, though she couldn't afford such talk with her impending marriage. But as the words streamed from her mouth, they'd felt true. Somehow, at some point, she'd stopped hating Edwynne. "I'd have done the same for anyone. I find it difficult when Lisette's..." How to phrase this diplomatically?

The shine returned to Edwynne's eyes. She leaned in. "A judgmental bitch? I think she dropped me as a lover because I wouldn't go to lectures at the university with her. I hate theory. All those dead ancient men—give me a handbill any day."

Of course, she didn't have to act diplomatic around Edwynne. "Yes, judgmental. She keeps questioning my commitment to the cause because of my heritage, as if Northerners can only care about themselves."

Scowling, Edwynne gripped her plate. "I ought to smash a vegetable pie on her hair."

"You mustn't," which came out not the stern warning she'd intended but nearly a laugh. Imagine Lisette standing there sulking, her reddening cheeks puffed out and shoulders hunched, sauce from the vegetable pie oozing down her updo to splat on her ridiculous pink cake dress... Edwynne kept making her have thoughts she ought not to, making her attention stray from decorum and duty.

At least once they found the third magic stone and saved the queen, life would return to normal. She'd never need to spend time with Edwynne again.

The next morning, one of her potential suitors blew her off in letter form, deciding to go with another candidate. Without Delvar to introduce her to eligible maidens, she was running out of contacts. Playing the marriage mart felt like hunting for a summer job but with longer wait times and less clarity, and failure would plunge her struggling family further into debt. But a bright spot came—she and Dorenia were at the same palace press meeting.

Dorenia Maddox had a thoughtful square face and wore practical gray clothing. Sariva stared at her from the ladies-in-waiting section, hoping to catch her eye where she sat among the palace administrators. At last, Dorenia looked away from the press spokesperson at their lectern and toward Sariva.

"Hello!" she mouthed, waving, trying to keep ungainly enthusiasm from her face.

With a slight quirk of her lips, Dorenia nodded back.

The policy announcements and question and answer sessions seemed to take ages. *Stop staring at her and take notes!* She scolded herself and scrawled a few keywords in her embossed notebook.

When the meeting adjourned, some palace inhabitants descended on the reporters to answer follow-up questions, others toward the table at the end of the room laden with breakfast food: thick crusty bread, herbed butter, and sliced meats. She settled for a piece of plain bread and an apple, not wanting to risk that the dairy and meat had touched. Where had Dorenia gone?

Dorenia headed toward her. "Sariva? I've pronounced it correctly, right?"

She tried to conceal her excitement, curtsying politely. "Yes, hello. It's so good to see you, Dorenia. Can I call you Dorenia?"

"Maddox is fine, but I suppose we should be informal. I got your introductory letter. Your skill set—exactly what I'm searching for. I'd love some peace and quiet around my estate, another set of hands for the administrative duties." Her thoughtful stare pierced Sariva, light eyes intent.

Finally, an opportunity. "I'm good at facilitating peace and quiet. Perhaps we could have brunch?"

A rueful smile crossed her stolid features. "I'm booked. Maybe this weekend, on Lastday?"

"Sure!" She scrambled to flip to the schedule page in her notebook. "We can meet for lunch or dinner, maybe get off the palace grounds—"

"There's a café a few blocks south. I'll have a messenger send you the time and address."

"Sounds good. Glad we crossed paths."

"Come along, Sariva," Melisant called. "We need to review the seating for the city planning banquet."

With a shy smile and an apologetic curtsy, she dashed off. Lastdays usually meant spending time with Edwynne, exploring the ruins on the one day they could both scrounge up spare moments. But surely Edwynne wouldn't mind changing plans or missing curfew, right? She had to understand.

Later in the week, a messenger brought a package wrapped in watercolor paper to Sariva's door.

"How lovely." She examined the delicately painted flowers. "Do you know who brought it?" Maybe one of her letters had gotten through to a potential bride.

"Right!" The messenger fumbled in his pockets and triumphantly held out a tastefully calligraphed card.

From D, with anticipation. Hope to see you soon.

Not too informative. She dismissed the messenger and set about unwrapping the package. Inside, decorative paper cocooned a bracelet, a lovely silverwork cuff with flower-shaped glass beads and leaves on metal vines.

It had to be from Dorenia, right? *D* for Dorenia, who planned to meet with her and who possessed the funds for such a lavish gift.

But what if *D* stood for Delvar? What if he wanted to make up for her rejection by sending her a cursed token? The decorative paper appeared disheveled and slightly torn at the corners as if someone had unwrapped it and hastily wrapped it up again. No, ridiculous. He hadn't pursued her. Not to the point of running after her in the street and not to the point of intercepting her mail. Surely, he'd come to his senses. *Stop the paranoia and wear the bracelet.*

She slid the gift onto her wrist and clicked the lock shut. Another note from Dorenia came the next day. The meeting time and place and:

I hope you liked the gift. Been meaning to send it for a while. Kept forgetting. See why I need help?

Of course, she shouldn't have worried. She dashed off a thank-you note and sent the messenger with a note to Edwynne as well.

Hello! Splendid news. I've managed to schedule a meeting with a prospective bride on Lastday. Of course we'll have to end early and rush back to the palace, but this is important to me, and I'm sure you'll understand.

Before she could stop herself, she jotted down *Thank you for joining me for dinner* and added her elegant signature.

Thank you for joining me for dinner? Why did that feel more perilous than discussing her impending marriage? She wanted to pace, scream into a pillow, rip out the seams on an entire dress. She settled for needle felting, the stabbiest fiber art. A reply arrived within the hour.

Edwynne had pointy, cramped handwriting slanting off the scrap paper:

good to know where your priorities are. thanks loads xoxo

"Your punctuation is atrocious," she told Edwynne. "And what's this *xoxo* nonsense?"

The absent girl didn't reply.

At their usual spot, Edwynne leaned against a wall, tapping her foot. She scowled at Sariva. "So, your parents want you to marry this Dorenia woman?"

"I want to marry someone who can help my family. My personal preferences wouldn't infringe."

"But isn't Dorenia—what's the phrase—outside the faith?"

"Yes, but she's willing to convert. Or at least to let me raise children who worship the Goddess. A lot of the merchants...they think marrying into the Goddess religion will be good for business. As if we have some magical power over coin just because the first Northerners who could afford to come here all worked in trade."

Edwynne crossed her arms. "And this marriage alliance is more important than the queendom? More important than Queen Oradel?"

Sariva raised her chin. "I'm trying to protect my younger brother. I'd do anything to keep him safe."

A low blow, but it landed. Edwynne wrapped her arms around herself. "Good for you." She took the path into the ruins, her expression stony. "We don't have much time, so try to keep up."

They followed a new trail of puddles from last night's rainfall and ended up in the shadowy storage catacombs of the ancient palace, ducking their heads at stone lintels.

"Storerooms, pantries, bodyguards' quarters, and lockboxes," Edwynne muttered, peeking into one room after another.

"A lot of these have signs of age. Maybe even from Amaldia and Rhysling's time," Sariva couldn't help observing.

Edwynne's scowl deepened. "What do you see in that sad old story, anyway?"

Her love of tragedy felt too soul-deep to explain. *Horrible things happen, so why not make poetry out of them? The world is a dangerous place. And tragedies are honest: duty before love.* She settled on something less personal. "I mean, it's beautiful. She loves Rhysling so much that she hallucinates her. She never gets over her even when the war's over and she's the queen's right hand."

Edwynne snorted. "Beautiful? Did we read the same story? I thought it was depressing. I mean, the music's catchy, but—Rhysling falls in love with this Amaldia girl, and then she must sacrifice her own ship to get through the blockade like she's playing people chess. And the show presents it like Rhysling survived, only it's just Amaldia refusing treatment for a brain injury because the fever's making her hallucinate—and when she does get her skull sewn up because she can't manage supply lines while leaking spine juice, she never sees her again."

Wraiths, objectively proved, referred to imprints of strong emotions left in magic-scarred areas. But ghosts, the idea that souls could come back in some way impossible for wizards to measure—only Northerners believed in ghosts. Was anything more romantic than a haunting? "Amaldia survived a lot of assassination attempts. Maybe she just stopped talking about Rhysling's soul because she had to seem eligible after the war—"

"Right, but she lived to be eighty! She lived alone for the rest of her life. Why would you pay to see a story end like that?" Edwynne shook her head. "None of this 'her soul rests within mine' bullshit. When I see a play about pretty ladies, either they kiss each other on the lips or I get drunk and go home."

Sariva couldn't help rolling her eyes. "It's not about kissing on the lips. It's about leaving a legacy. Rhysling made her death important. Amaldia was able to unify the city-states. What she lived for survived."

"But she didn't have the life together they'd wanted. Think about it. Would you rather die for someone or spend the rest of your life with them, move in together, raise war orphans and hounds?"

"But even as a purely fictional event, it still would have been narratively satisfying! Rhysling loved Amaldia so much she was willing to literally set herself on fire. That's the ultimate act of love. Something so selfless it doesn't need follow-up." Sariva couldn't imagine being cared for so wholly, so desperately. She'd never know the kind of unflinching devotion where your life became a sword in someone else's hands. At least plays and books existed even if happy endings belonged only in fiction. She could still dream of loving someone so much it summoned their ghost.

"She still left the woman she loved to win a war alone."

"Call me a morbid Northerner, but tragedy is poignant and beautiful in a way some people just don't understand."

Squelching, heavy footsteps resounded ahead. Where two hallways met, a lumpy shadow lurched past.

Sariva extinguished her lantern. The two froze until the echoing steps faded.

"Someone else down here?" Sariva whispered.

A door behind them slammed. Before them, the floor sunk away, and murky greenish water seeped over the stone.

Edwynne tested her weight on her injured foot and grimaced. "I know we didn't hear another knight or an urban explorer. I hate it down here." She seemed on edge today, more than usual. Not Sariva's problem.

They glided through the water, inches away but nowhere close to touching. Wet shoes stamped soggy footprints as they emerged into a room that, before the civil war, magical earthquakes, and spell explosions, might have served as a feasting hall. Patches of faint sunlight drifted down from the shattered floor above, once a ceiling.

"Look at this place." Edwynne indicated the long table stretching the length of the room, the carved chairs knocked over and scattered. "I don't even think they had time to evacuate before..."

Sariva picked up a cracked plate, frowning at half an ancient seal of state painted on the faded porcelain. "Yeah."

A shriek split the air. Edwynne's hand leapt to her short sword.

Sariva fumbled the plate and barely caught it. "Did you hear—"

"Shh!" Edwynne dragged her under the table as the strange heavy footsteps echoed once more.

No...not again.

Sariva had frozen with fear the last time she saw a ghost looming toward her, mist pouring from its spectral body. Even after Delvar's rescue, she'd still felt rattled, heart beating fast, eager to drive away from the old palace toward safety and light.

The air grew colder. The fine hairs on her arms stood up. Edwynne seized her hand. She couldn't run.

"Where are they?" The piercing voice echoed as a multiheaded, many-legged figure lurched in, a ghost made of rotting corpses melded together. Some of its arms clutched spectral weapons, others clawed at the air. "Where are Amaldia's usurpers? Cursed mirror! False queen!"

Multiple ghosts from the opposing forces melted into one furious creature. Sariva shuddered. What awful spell could have forced them to combine? What could they do?

"Wait," she mouthed, squeezing Edwynne's hand.

Edwynne glared, tension in every line of her lithe body, but stayed still. Minutes passed. The merged ghost didn't leave. It roamed the room, its garbled cries growing more agitated as if something compelled it to stay.

Edwynne poked her and pointed. Sariva followed her indicating finger. Set in a high niche above a torn tapestry, a small orb shone with yellow light. Edwynne pointed again, this time at the orb, and mimed climbing.

Sariva gave her a skeptical expression and gestured to herself. *Seriously? And what am I supposed to do?*

Edwynne rolled her eyes. She pumped her arms back and forth, indicating running, and waved at the scattered furniture. *Just stay out of its reach!*

Maybe she could stay ahead of a ghost with so many limbs and heads fighting for dominance, especially with all the old furniture and chunks of fallen masonry. But she didn't want to risk it. *I hate this idea*, she conveyed via eyebrow.

Edwynne smirked and shrugged because, of course, she didn't care. She counted down on her fingers: *three, two...*

You're the worst, Sariva mouthed, but she had no choice. On *one*, they darted out from under the table. Edwynne sprinted toward the wall. Sariva hesitated.

The ghost's many heads turned toward Edwynne.

"Hey!" Sariva shouted, clapping her hands. "Over here!"

"Counterprotester," one head hissed. "Amaldia's criminals. Stop her, save the king..." The whole ghost-creature lurched in Sariva's direction with a chilling intensity, fury glowing in each pair of eyes.

She faked dodging, circling a large cluster of rubble. It hesitated for a breath but drew closer. Only the lopsided fall of rubble stood between it and Sariva.

Due to its bulk and many mashed-together limbs, it changed direction in a laborious shuffle. Edwynne, scaling the wall with deft movements, had nearly reached the niche with the orb. If she could just evade it one more time...

"*Northern!*" a masculine head roared. "*Dirty stealing Northerner!*" A chorus of shouts spread to the other heads. "*Northern bastard! Anarchist!*" The ghost lowered its stance.

Sariva wiped her sweaty palms on her skirts, preparing to sprint.

The ghost scaled the pile of rubble, screeching. It smelled like rotting meat, and flesh flaked away on its frontmost legs. An ice-cold chill seeped into the air.

I need to run, I need to help the queen—and my brothers—Goddess, someone, anyone—

"Over here!" Edwynne's voice cut through Sariva's panic. As the ghost swiped at her with a broken board, she leaned one way and darted the other, sprinting parallel to the table. At the end of the room, Edwynne climbed down as fast as she could, the tapestry ripping in her fists.

Sariva's foot caught in a hole. She sprawled forward, the rough stone scraping her palms. The ghost loomed over her, leaning down, its heads baying cruel words. She tried to get her legs back under her—she had to flee, her family depended on her!—but long skirts tangled her limbs.

The ghost reached into her chest.

Ice-cold mist poured down her throat and into her lungs, closing around her heart. Strength drained from her body like she'd gotten heatstroke and gone a week without sleep all at once. Even breathing felt difficult.

I should beg for my life, but my body just wants to lie here...

"Fuck off!" Edwynne yelled, charging the ghost. She slammed the glowing orb into an exposed patch of skin. It tried to dive away, but she lunged after it. Its legs thrashed and tripped under it as its many heads keened in pain. Then its form wavered. It gusted away on a scream.

Edwynne knelt. Her calloused hands tested Sariva's forehead. "Stars, you're freezing!"

"I'm...f-f-fine," she attempted. Why did Edwynne's touch feel so soothingly heated? She almost wanted to lean into those bony hands the way stray cats leaned into sunbeams.

"You're not. Let me help you out into the sunlight; you need fresh air."

Time passed in glimpses. Edwynne's boots splashing in the murky water. Her long fingers slapping Sariva's cheek. The chapped, irate slash of her mouth. Damp stone. Slightly less damp stone. "You idiot! Don't die on me. If you do, I'll kill you. I'll carve your bones out to use as bookends."

"And you'll..." What had she threatened last time? "Use my skull to hold pencils?"

A laugh burst from her, almost a sob. "Glad you're aware of it."

They made it up to ground level. Edwynne dumped Sariva onto a low bench, the orb in her hand glowing bold yellow. Flashes of light danced in its swirl.

She stuffed the orb in a pocket, stalked closer, and grabbed Sariva's chin. Her pointy-chinned sulky face felt too close, her hands too warm and rough. The lighter flecks in her eyes didn't show in this light. They seemed deeper and more solemn. "Are you all right?"

Sariva batted ineffectually at her hand. "What do you think you're doing?"

"You're the one who's all fussy about safety. I'm just checking for head wounds."

"Fine. Check away." Her voice sounded thin and hoarse.

Edwynne sifted through Sariva's long hair and tilted her face this way and that with a contemplative scowl. "No blood. Can I see the back of your neck? Lift up your braid?"

"What's the magic word?" she managed through chattering teeth. River gulls yelled overhead.

Her scowl reached new heights of displeasure. "I hate you. Let me guess, please?"

"Say please." This time her teeth barely chattered. Needling Edwynne felt normal, the furthest thing from bloated corpses.

"Please," she echoed almost politely. Her face had an oddly open, expectant quality as if the sunset had pacified her.

"And your tongue's still in your head." She didn't feel so chilled now.

"Don't press your luck." But she almost smiled as Sariva leaned forward, letting her hair tumble over her face.

Edwynne's fingertips trailed over the nape of her neck, parting her hair, gathering up the long strands to examine her scalp from one angle, then another. Her hands went all the way up Sariva's braid. She lifted it to peer underneath.

Married women—married Northern women—covered their hair. "Your hair is part of your body," Mother had lectured as Sariva watched her wrap her thick, graying plaits with a silk scarf. "You need to be demure with it in the eyes of the Goddess and your betrothed, just as you might with any other part."

At thirteen, at fifteen, Sariva had rolled her eyes. "It's only hair. It's not my knees or anything. Some people even shave their heads."

But at seventeen, shivering as her stockings dried in the spring evening, she understood. She felt Edwynne examining her hair, Edwynne's touch lingering on her scalp. Perhaps she'd start covering when she got engaged.

At last, Edwynne relinquished her braid. "Head seems all right. Think you can make it to the castle?"

"But a private carriage. Not a shared one. And we can't bring the gems to the queen tonight either. I need time."

Edwynne withdrew, the familiar hard-edged scowl slamming over her features. "To prepare for your big important noble meeting. Trust me, I wouldn't dare forget. I'll get you to the carriage stop, but I'm taking a public trolley. You can make your own way home."

Sariva tried to salvage the conversation as they limped out of the ruins, forced to lean on each other. "Edwynne, don't—"

"For once in your life, leave it," Edwynne snapped. "I get it. Your own priorities are more important than saving the queen." And, on another attempt, "My patience—don't test it. None left." She hailed a carriage for Sariva with a piercing whistle, opened the door, and shoved her in.

"Like you had any," Sariva grumbled. And, to the driver, "Palace Hill, please."

Edwynne made a rude gesture to the window as the carriage rolled away.

She knows nothing about my priorities or where I'd rather be. She only sees the duty binding me. She doesn't care about anything else... Adults in the real world, from historical military geniuses down to teenage interns, had to struggle and make sacrifices. If Edwynne didn't recognize that, the problem lay within her. But they still needed to work together.

Chapter Eight

After hurriedly changing into clean, dry clothes and braiding her hair once more, Sariva passed through the sitting room.

"Lady Cypress, can you do a service for me?" Lisette called.

Sariva tried to not sound skeptical. "What is it?" Despite her opinions, she ought to aid her coworker for the good of the palace.

"I'm buying a new dress, and my allowance is two hundred florins." She mentioned the huge sum so casually.

"And you'd like me to help figure out what you ought to wear?" Perhaps Lisette had noticed her dressmaking talents.

"No, I thought you could come help me bargain."

Had she misheard? "Pardon?"

"Well, because you're Northern." When Sariva didn't reply, Lisette evidently took this as a lack of understanding because she hurried to explain. "You're good with money. You could help me get a better deal on fabric. And I'm doing a lot to stop the political abuses in the North. I sign petitions, I've got a handcrafted scarf made by a refugee nomad artisan, and I never buy anything from occupied areas. What have you been doing for the nomad refugees lately? Come to think of it, I haven't heard you condemn the Northern government's abuses at all."

Sariva stared at her blankly until she realized Lisette expected an answer. "Let me see if I understand," she began. "You want me to take action against people in a country I've never been to and don't have citizenship in, where politicians I can't vote against make policies in a language I don't speak."

"They're your people," Lisette replied with a shrug, poised between offhand and affronted. "If my country did war crimes, I'd take action. You have to be politically engaged about the issues."

"And the form you want my engagement to take is...helping you bargain for a dress even though I'm not great at numbers or math?"

Lisette sighed. "Listen, I know you're desperate to wear your tacky symbol and pretend you're oppressed even though your country has a giant army and your people are rich. I get it. You have such a hard life. But could you at least stop pretending I'm traumatizing you? It's only shopping."

"She's right," Fabiola, one of Lisette's friends, added. "I mean, the least you could do is condemn the human rights abuses in the North. But you're just here flaunting your privilege."

Lisette jabbed a finger at Sariva's Goddess pendant. "And you know what? The queen wouldn't let you wear divisive jewelry. You know who else wears religious pendants? Nationalists." She held out a hand.

What did she expect Sariva to say? *You're right, I must flee my oppressive culture, and wearing something incompatible with activist politics burns my skin! Get it off! Aaaah!*

She'd hoped for friends here. People who cared if she couldn't find something to eat, who would cover for her when she had to go to religious services. At least reading tragedies had taught her to survive alone and friendless. "I've an appointment," she blurted, pushing past them both.

"You're only defensive because it's true!" Lisette called after her, and Fabiola giggled.

She wouldn't let them see her cry.

At least the meeting went well. She remembered every encouraging thing Dorenia said to scrawl into her letters home later. She started with "I'm so glad you're wearing the bracelet I got you. I didn't know if you would like it," as soon as Sariva hurried in. She continued with reassuring earnest statements like "I'm interested in getting to know you better," and "Having you around would make my life better," and " I want to get in touch with your family to work out arrangements."

Sariva just sat there, openmouthed with joy, stammering bits of sentences like "Of course!" and "Absolutely!" The best part was learning that Aziz could come stay in Dorenia's house outside the city and have specialists examine him.

Of course her parents would approve the match. Dorenia fit every criterion for an impeccable bride.

Ha! She couldn't wait to tell Edwynne, wipe away the squire's smug smile with a flash of her engagement ring. *I'm an asset to my family and my community, and you're not.* What would she say? What face would she make? As Dorenia walked her back to the palace, Sariva kept turning different images over in her mind.

"It's been a pleasure," Dorenia told her with a firm handclasp.

Would she kiss her? Sariva tried not to flinch and exhaled when she leaned no closer. "Of course, likewise," she told Dorenia, offering the cheek kiss etiquette suggested.

As they went their separate ways, she imagined a gate opening into possibility, giving her family a better future.

From her room, she could almost glimpse the squire dormitory on the other side of the palace grounds, a low building hidden between trees. Or maybe she couldn't quite see it. But perhaps she glimpsed the silhouette of the single-story dark shape where Edwynne folded her narrow body into a sparse bottom bunk.

Is she awake too? Is she cross that we fought?

No, of course not. She can't stand me. Why would she care?

A few days later, the three magical orbs glowed softly in Sariva's workbag. The pit of acid, the angry dragon (who'd chewed through the snare by now, judging from her knowledge of dragons), and the ghost mob. She and Edwynne didn't make the best team, but they had refrained from killing each other.

But why had the witch turned on her friend after serving the queen for years? Sariva supposed they would find out.

A hand rapped on Sariva's window. She hurried to unlatch it.

Edwynne heaved herself over the windowsill and tumbled in. "Anyone could have seen me climbing up the trellis. I feel ridiculous." She wore a green tunic and loose brown leggings—for training, sleeping in, or both? Edwynne seemed the type to carelessly go to bed in her clothes.

Sariva slung her workbag over her shoulder. "It's not like we can move Queen Oradel to a different building. Besides, anyone who saw you climbing up to a lady-in-waiting's window would guess you were headed for Lisette." She meant to tap into Edwynne's hatred of Lisette and prompt her to make some funny, cutting remark like "I would rather lick a ghost" or "I want to make her hair into a mop."

Edwynne just shrugged and grunted.

While the other ladies-in-waiting were enjoying a leisurely brunch, Edwynne and Sariva made their way to the queen's bedchamber. Sariva reached for the doorknob, but Edwynne shushed her. "There's someone inside!"

The door swung open, and the voices emanated more clearly.

Not him, not again.

Sariva seized Edwynne by her wrists, hauled her inside the nearest closet, and yanked the door shut.

Edwynne opened her mouth, indignant, and Sariva slammed her hand over the other girl's face. She should have expected Edwynne's warm, wet tongue prodding her fingers as if testing for gaps.

They glared at each other in mutual disgust.

Delvar's voice filtered in from the hallway. "Glad you called me up. I know she was agitated earlier, but after I performed some healing magics, she's resting easier."

"She seemed so upset," Ava agreed. "Since the palace's last day off, it's like she's sleepwalking. Or sleepfighting. Battling some invisible enemy. I just wish we knew the nature of her curse."

"Believe me, I'm spending every spare moment figuring out how I might be able to resolve this matter."

As their voices faded, Sariva peeled her sweaty hand from Edwynne's mouth.

"What was that about?" Edwynne demanded in a whisper.

"I didn't want him to detect the magical items. The queen told me to keep my mission a secret, remember?"

Edwynne frowned but didn't press the issue. With the hallway safely empty, they went into the queen's room.

Queen Oradel slept propped up on pillows. When Sariva and Edwynne entered, her eyes flew open.

Sariva curtsied. "Hello, Your Majesty. Umm, how do you feel?"

Her face creased in disappointment. "Mmm."

Sariva held out the glowing orbs: soft pink, bold yellow, shifting blue. She, Sariva Al-Beroth, was about to rescue the queen and make Almesia a better place. Oh, Edwynne helped too, but the queen had trusted *her*. She'd acted with courage and seen the plan through. "Do you know what these are?"

With glacial slowness, her expression unchanging, Oradel nodded.

Edwynne bounced on her toes. "Pieces of your soul, right? At least, pieces of you. Maybe of your power. So, because of these, you were able to talk to us."

Oradel's gaze scanned from Edwynne to Sariva and back. "Yes. I hid them." And eventually, "But I don't want them back. I don't want to be myself."

Sariva felt like she'd been drenched with ice water. She groped for words but could only manage a miserable "What?" One of the orbs fell from her limp fingers and into her shoe.

"You can't bring me back. He came and took me somewhere beautiful. Everything I do here matters, whether I'm weeding my garden, cooking a simple stew for dinner, or helping the neighbors till their fields. I don't want to fight against injustice. It's endless. Let me stay in this beautiful world. Let me stay here in my little cottage where no one wants to storm the palace and wring my neck. And so many people want me dead. Let me be nobody. Let my enemies consider me harmless... I'm so tired of being the one to save you all."

Except the queen's voice didn't come from her unmoving mouth. It came from the beautiful tapestry hanging on the wall as if from far away. Had another part of her soul been magically trapped inside the work of art?

"Are you inside the tapestry? Who put you there? How do we get you out?" Sariva blurted, tripping over her words.

The queen's body screamed, shrill and agonized as a ruins ghost, and spasmed, arching off the bed as her limbs jerked wildly.

"What's happening?" Sariva cried.

Edwynne turned to her, just as frantic. "What's happening? You mean, what did *you* do?"

"I didn't do anything! What are you supposed to do when someone has a fit?"

"Turn her onto her side so she doesn't throw up and choke? Or bite her tongue? Or choke on her tongue? I'm not a medic!" Edwynne spluttered.

Sariva gently rolled the thrashing woman over. "Oh, Goddess, I'm so sorry."

The door exploded open in a burst of magic.

In swept Delvar, a squadron of the castle guard on his heels. "Treachery," he breathed, clutching his chest in theatrical horror. "I knew I was right to be suspicious."

A guard levelled his sword at Sariva and Edwynne. "What should we do, sir?"

Delvar had a grimly, square-jawed expression. "I'll need to find out who they've been radicalized into working for. But, in the meantime, get those dangerous magical artifacts away from those untrained young girls!"

Two guards rushed to Sariva and pried two orbs from her numb, unresisting hands. But the orbs weren't dangerous. Delvar had lied to them, to everyone at the palace, just the way he'd lied about being her friend. *What's going on?* lay on the tip of her tongue, yet she knew asking questions wouldn't help.

"Where's the third orb?" Delvar asked.

She prayed Edwynne wouldn't give her away. "What third orb?"

Delvar shook his head at her, smirking. "And I was so worried! Of course you don't understand magic." Then he ran to the queen's side. He stroked the air and murmured something. After a few moments, she lay still.

Another guard tried to wrangle a furiously struggling Edwynne. "You need to cooperate, miss," he kept saying, and exasperated, "Miss, you've committed high treason! Harming me won't help your case!"

Edwynne went motionless, allowing him to tie her hands behind her back. "High treason?" she echoed, eyes wide with disbelief.

The two guards on Sariva yanked her wrists behind her back and fastened a knot. Rough rope cut into her skin. She didn't like how the awkward position thrust her breasts out or how Delvar's gaze slid up and down her body.

"Delvar's wards told him the queen was in danger," a guard announced.

"Don't fucking touch her," Edwynne growled, thrashing. She flung her body weight one way, then the other. Sariva's heart leapt into her throat.

"I'd expect better of you," he said darkly. "Stellan's squire, the best of all the Queensguard. After the palace has shown your family so much charity. Well, never mind. We'll find the truth eventually. Take them to the dungeon."

The guards marched them down the hallway and past the other ladies-in-waiting, who had evidently gathered to check on the commotion. Sariva's foot hurt from having the small magic rock inside her shoe.

"What's going on, Court Wizard?" Lisette asked.

He had a grim expression. "These two were involved in an assassination plot against the queen. They snuck dangerous magical objects into her room."

Lisette gasped, although her eyes shone with excitement. "I knew it! Those Northerners can't be trusted. I'll have to tell everyone in the palace."

Sariva hated her delighted expression, a contrast to all those who knew the truth. "Lisette, you're an absolute bitch," she called over her shoulder.

Lisette turned to another lady-in-waiting. "Did you hear what she called me? How dare she! I just knew she wasn't meant to be one of us."

Meanwhile, Edwynne gave Sariva a slow, admiring nod. Sariva felt a fragment of relief because whatever happened, they were in this impossible situation together.

At least for now.

Edwynne's captors headed off the main staircase on the ground floor, but the guards holding Sariva continued down. Delvar strode ahead.

"Should we have her brought to your workshop?" a guard asked.

At last, he shook his head, his thin features toying with a smile. "No, I have a meeting with the sultan about a possible alliance between Almesia and the North. I think it'll go well, seeing as how we already agree on a lot. Civilized countries need to stand together against the wrong sort of people, and their army can help advance Almesia's interests abroad. And it'll solve their demographic problems when we send all the wayward Northerners home."

"Yes, sir," another guard agreed.

Delvar turned to Sariva. "You plan on helping me, right? I did this for you. I plan on strengthening ties between the North and Almesia and passing laws so that no one talks badly about the North or its sultan. You deserve better than the way your colleagues treated you."

What would Edwynne say? Sariva took a deep, deliberate breath, her jaw tight. "I didn't ask for any of this."

He drew back with a wounded gasp. "I'm just trying to help you. Your people, your family. Unless, of course, you want my enmity?"

He controlled the queen, the city guard, and perhaps the castle guard as well. Killing Queen Oradel? Overthrowing the government? Whatever his goal, Sariva needed to stay on his good side enough to survive. "No," she murmured, lowering her eyes. "I... You have my best interest at heart."

"Good girl." He patted her on the head. "Maybe just an hour or so in the dungeon. You've been quite rude to me, you know."

Sariva's heart sank as the guards herded her away. A few seldom-trod winding hallways later, they shoved her into a dimly lit old cell and slammed the door. Did they remain outside? She couldn't tell. The thick walls muffled everything.

Dust motes swirled in a lonely sunbeam. She cracked her wrists, fingertips exploring the knot. The orb oscillated faintly in her shoe. Hmm. Not too complicated. Give her some time and a bit of rough stone, and she could get her hands free. She had nothing but time.

Sometime later, the door creaked open. Edwynne stumbled through. A guttural moan came from her throat as her lanky frame folded to the ground.

Sariva rushed forward to prop her up. "Edwynne!"

A blotchy bruise covered half her face, one eye swollen and her nose bloodied. She hunched forward, guarding her stomach, and when she tried to stand, her injured leg buckled. She went down like a sack of potatoes in Sariva's arms.

"Are you seriously hurt? Let me untie your hands for you, come on," Sariva stammered. Rolling Edwynne over coated her hands in tacky drying blood. A shallow head wound? Or something more serious? She tugged at the rope until it loosened, until she could slip it off Edwynne's uncharacteristically still hands, dotted with smudges of blood and little faded freckles.

Edwynne just slumped across Sariva's lap, her pale eyelids fluttering.

Sariva grabbed her shoulders and shook her. "Edwynne. Ed!" Of course she hated Edwynne. But losing her one ally, the one source who could back up her story—it felt like someone taking a sharpened spoon to her chest. Hollowing her out until nothing remained.

A hand reached up. Edwynne batted at her cheek, barely a slap. "Don't cry, your eyelash paint will smudge." She lay in Sariva's lap, half-lidded eyes glowing hazel in the single beam of sunlight.

Sariva's throat tightened. She could barely force words out. "I didn't think you cared about makeup."

Edwynne shifted as if seeking a comfortable position. "Yeah, well..."

"Well, what?"

"You do." With a groan of effort, she sat up and dragged herself a few feet away from Sariva. "Fuck. I feel awful. Of all the days to get cramps! I'm not even due to bleed for two more weeks. Got any more salve?"

Sariva shrugged, helpless, but couldn't stop herself from smiling a little. "Still in my room. But what happened to you? You look awful."

A bitter smirk twisted her fine-boned features. "Some of the squires sided with Delvar, and they wanted revenge on me for all the times I kicked their asses in the practice yard. Now they know they can beat me as long as I've got both hands tied behind my back and a stomachache. Hope the accomplishment stays with them." She folded her cloak into a pillow and leaned against the wall with a sigh.

What should they do? No solution seemed perfect. Escaping would put their families and anyone suspected of helping them in danger. The new guards would hurt innocent people searching for them.

Staying would mean certain death. She'd choose a chance, even a slim one, any day.

But how could they escape? They sat behind a thick, locked door with multiple guards stationed right outside, and other guards had taken Edwynne's short sword and dagger.

Sariva interlaced her fingers behind her head. Something poked her fingers, an answer. "Edwynne," she murmured. "Do you think you could pick the lock?" Next steps could wait.

"It seems complicated. If I had something to use, it might be worth a try."

She yanked her jeweled hairpins from her plaits and held them forth in offering. Edwynne hesitated, her gaze darting from the glinting pins to Sariva's face. Finally, after a few moments, she snatched them up and headed for the door.

Please let this work!

Time passed. The single sunbeam shifted across the dirty floor. Sariva moved the orb from her shoe to an inner pocket. Minutes or hours later, Edwynne ran a hand through her curls. "Got it. Seems like they only left two or three guards outside."

"Seems like you have a plan."

"Whoever the city guard side with, the Queensguard wouldn't betray Oradel. And they have safe houses in the city. I visited one with Stellan. We'll go there and plan our next move, tell people about what's happening to the queen. Backup plan, one of Vered's activist friends who does direct action can hide us."

Sariva cracked a smile. "We're not Vered's favorite people."

Edwynne played with the rope, wrapping it around her hands and letting it fall. "She'll acknowledge we're not throwing bread at each other anymore."

It sounded solid, but... "What about weapons? Unless you can defeat armed men barehanded."

She grinned, snapping the rope between her fists. "Oh, I'm armed."

She locked eyes with Sariva, counted to three, and nudged the door open.

Chapter Nine

Edwynne should have felt afraid. Ought to have trembled. The older squires had surely expected it, leering and grabbing her as if they could intimidate her. But she'd locked every feeling deep inside her mind.

The way she'd felt when Sariva touched her face and called her Ed? Locked away. Irrelevant.

She charged through the door.

The closest guard managed a syllable of warning before she leapt onto his back, slung the rope around his neck, and pulled taut. Locking her legs around him, she yanked both ends of the rope one-handed. As the other guard swiped at her, she grabbed the first guard's sword and dropped to the ground, letting him collapse, gasping for air.

Inside the dungeon, Sariva rattled off a frantic plea to the Goddess.

The other guard swung again. She dove behind his companion and, when he moved closer, pressed the blade to the prone man's throat.

The guard on the floor went motionless.

The other frowned, skeptical, drawing closer. "You wouldn't kill him. A nice girl like you? Palace-trained?

Queensguard? Just put down the sword. Delvar can keep you alive if you cooperate. After all, he found a use for your brother."

He's lying, part of her mind shrieked. *Don't let him fool you. Don't wuss out.* But a small, scared part of her, not wanting to believe the palace could turn against her, whispered, "My brother?" She lowered the sword just a hair. Then further.

Sariva made a noise, half whimper, half groan. "Edwynne, no."

But Sariva didn't have a well-connected family who could bribe the government. She either escaped or died.

Hands inching away from his weapon, he took another step. "I saw him just the other day. He's been cooperating. He's Delvar's chief of security or—"

She shoved the prone guard against the wall, then leapt forward. Her foot connected with the other guard's crotch in a flying kick. When he crashed to the ground, she kicked him in the nose and knelt to grab him by his hair. "You're lying!"

He grimaced. "You crazy girl. You're the one who committed treason. I'm just saying who I saw at the briefing. He stood right at Delvar's side! And if you know I'm making shit up, why are you so scared?"

Before he could comment on her shaking hands, she slammed his face into the ground. Blood trickled from his nose. He went limp.

"Oh, Goddess." Sariva crept out, face pale as if about to vomit. "Did you kill them?"

"I doubt I hit them hard enough." But she didn't want to check.

Running footsteps approached.

"What do we do?" Sariva whispered.

Make a break for it? Drag the guards into the cell? They didn't have time.

One of the ladies-in-waiting came around the corner. Edwynne pointed the sword at her. "What do you want?"

Sariva let out a deep breath. "Oh, good, it's you."

"Paveya," the chubby middle-aged woman said by way of introduction, her dark eyes grim. "You must flee. I can't do much to help, but here's some food and nondescript clothes for the journey. The wizard plans on executing at least one of you."

Sariva wrung her hands. "What's going on? You have to explain. Is the queen still alive?

"There are larger forces at work. The less you know, the better."

Sariva raised her eyebrows. "But we don't know anything."

"Take my white gelding from the stables."

"At least tell us where you want us to go."

"Izalena's cottage. Follow the river out of the city and go north through the hills. The horse will know the way."

If they could get to Izalena, if they could somehow evade the city guard and the wizard's men, if their escape went unnoticed for long enough, they had a chance. They got changed and locked the guards in their cell.

Sariva seemed like a different person in plain clothing with no makeup. Her bracelet's clasp had gotten stuck, but Edwynne had suggested hiding it under a scarf.

"Won't the guards catch us at the gates?" she asked, jogging to keep up with Edwynne.

"Most people don't know of his plan or your status as prisoners, and I gave the wizard's men a parcel of treats laced with sleeping powder," Parveya responded.

A stranger offering food was something to be suspicious of. But a respectable woman? Ladies-in-waiting could get away with it.

When they reached the stables, a different guard eyed them warily. "You sure you want these ragamuffins to take your horse?"

"These new stable workers have permission to exercise him for me," she explained to the main groom. "With all the tumult in the castle, I won't be able to take him out for at least a week."

As they walked, Paveya kept up a constant chatter, pretending to be garrulous and empty-headed. However, when they went through concealed places, she gave directions: which route to use, which road to take.

"Won't you be in danger?" Sariva whispered back.

"You have enough to worry about. I'm a canny old woman, and you two are practically children. Eat the food I packed for you and put on the cloaks if it rains."

They rode out of the castle and into a surreal ordinary day. People ate at cafés, strolled along the sidewalk, and walked small hounds. Edwynne had a white-knuckled grip on the horse's mane.

Behind Edwynne, Sariva cast an anxious gaze around. Every time she breathed, her breasts and belly brushed the tense muscles of Edwynne's back. They could have done with a bigger horse. "People are perceiving us."

"They will be if you keep acting so jumpy," Edwynne hissed back. "Your boss said people don't know—"

"She's not my boss. My boss is the queen."

"—so calm down."

Her momentary silence seemed too deliberate. Right away she pondered in a murmur, "What the guard said about your brother."

The response came automatically. "He was lying to try and distract me. Now be quiet and let me navigate. You don't know these roads."

"Can I put my hands around your waist though?"

Edwynne cast a baleful glare back: Was Sariva mocking her? But her expression had an innocent cast. Even more so barefaced.

"Fine." Sariva hugged her around the waist, her manicured hands clasping just below Edwynne's breastband.

Pain clenched inside her. "Move your hands, my stomach hurts. And quit grabbing me so tightly."

Edwynne sensed Sariva roll her eyes, but she gripped the back of Edwynne's cloak instead. Even then, Edwynne couldn't manage a full breath. Something caught between her ribs. Her head pounded.

They wound between the large houses near the castle and went into the hills. The series of wooded hills and valleys functioned as a natural barrier protecting the castle and its environs to the point where a youth with a crossbow could hold off an army here. But it made for slow and difficult progress.

A raindrop fell onto Edwynne's hair. Then another. Lightning crackled across the sky. She tried to smile. "Guess we should put on the cloaks."

Outside the city walls, they were on uneven, stony ground, picking their way through scrubby trees. The rain came down as if they stood beneath a waterfall.

A man's voice rang out. "There! I see them!"

Edwynne's breath caught as pain lanced her chest. Recognizing the voice, she turned around. A group of men in armor rode toward them. At their head galloped—

Her brother. Alive.

Her brother, alive, riding at the head of a squadron of Delvar's men.

Heart sinking, she turned to Sariva. "Take the horse, find somewhere to hide. If I don't catch up—"

"Edwynne, no. I won't let you risk your life to—"

"What am I supposed to do, risk yours?" she shot back, leaping from the horse. "I can't protect both of us. Screw that." And she slapped the gelding's flank. Sariva, not the best rider, couldn't keep it from rushing away.

With hatred in his eyes, her brother dismounted.

"Stellan." Her voice cracked, sounding too young, too emotional. "What is this? What are you doing?"

Face stern, he reached for his sword. "I'm doing what's best for the country."

Before Edwynne could reply, he swept her legs out from under her with a low kick, and she fell. Forced to roll to her feet, she barely dodged his next punch. Stellan could predict her every move. She ducked back and forth, fists up to protect her head. Should she punch him in the chest bindings? Gouge out his eyes?

She could kill a stranger to protect herself, but her own brother?

Stellan caught her by the waist and threw her into a tree. The impact knocked the breath out of her. Everything blurred. If she lived, she'd have bruises, maybe broken ribs.

"Delvar wants us. Break her legs if you have to," one of the men on horseback called.

She dragged herself to her feet, using the olive tree's low branches for support. Moving made her eyes water. The back of her throat convulsed. Sariva would run, right? She had no reason to linger. She hated Edwynne. They hated each other.

"If you insist," Stellan replied.

He spun his Queensguard longsword in a lazy silver arc. Hilt over thumb, the way he'd once shown Edwynne.

Her borrowed sword felt too light. She dropped at the last second, letting the branches shield her, and rolled out of the way of his next attack.

"Stellan." He didn't answer. Like it wasn't even his name anymore. "Stell—"

Grunting with effort, he swung again.

Edwynne blocked the blade's momentum with her own. Then, jittery with furious terror, she lowered her short sword. "Do it."

Stellan just stared at her.

"Do it! Cut my head off. Slit my throat. Because if you can, I don't want to live in a world where the only family I have left does shit like this!" Birds in the trees took off at her shout. *If he kills me...* She closed her eyes.

He yanked her into a rough one-armed hug, sheathing his sword, barrel chest shaking with something like laughter. "Edwynne, kid, I could have killed you."

"You didn't. You wouldn't." She hugged him back, breathing him in: herbal aftershave and oiled leather. For a moment, the world made sense.

"He's not going to kill her!" one guard called.

Another's armor jangled as he moved. "Ah, shit, the magic wore off."

Stellan's dark eyes went serious. "Run. I'll keep them from coming after you." He shoved her away, taking up his sword.

She stumbled, turning back. "I can't leave you here!" One Queensguard knight on foot against a whole group of city guards? What if he lost?

"Just go! That's an order. One knight to another." He might as well have said he believed in her. That he trusted her to do what needed to be done, no matter what.

Edwynne ran.

Crossbow bolts zinged past her. One nicked her shoulder, and she struggled not to cry out. Metal crashed against metal. She hurt all over, but what hurt worse was knowing she'd found Stellan only to lose him again, and she'd left him to his fate.

At last, she reached the copse where Sariva and the horse hid.

Sariva grabbed her shirt collar and yanked her to eye level. "How do they let someone so profoundly stupid be a squire? You could have died."

"But it was Stellan. My own brother," she shot back, pulling away, fists clenching.

Biting her full lower lip, somehow perfect even without makeup, she glanced over her shoulder. "And he held off the other soldiers?"

She couldn't talk about her selfless, impossible brother. Not when he still fought for all their lives. "He's buying us time. And we can't waste it. We need to move."

As they scrambled onto the horse, Sariva gasped. "Edwynne, your back."

"Just a scratch. Arrow didn't even stick." So why did her head spin?

Raindrops fell like stones. Edwynne's wet clothes clung to her skin, to her wounds. She squinted through the mist at the wiggly lines of wavering trees and swallowed hard, wishing she had a plain biscuit or a bit of cool water with lemon. Her mouth tasted like dry grass and soapy hair. Could she dismount for a minute to be sick behind a tree? Something wet caught in her throat. She choked on it, managing to cough up the soggy lump.

Sariva tugged on Edwynne's sleeve, forcing her to turn around. Then her eyes widened. "You were shot in the shoulder. Why are you bleeding from your mouth?"

The words took a moment to sink in. She swiped at her mouth. Bright red stained her sleeve. "Oh," Edwynne said stupidly, swallowing what tasted like coins. "Why-why'm I..." Her head held the words, but her sluggish, overheated body wouldn't respond. Gripping the reins, holding on to the horse with her thighs, talking to Sariva...it all felt impossible. Her stomach lurched again. So did the world.

"Ed, don't you dare."

The world went gray. She toppled off the horse.

Chapter Ten

Blurting out unladylike language, Sariva climbed from the horse and shook Edwynne's limp body. She didn't respond.

Thunder split the sky. The horse startled. Sariva lunged for its bridle and missed. With a frightened whinny, it wrenched away and bolted down the path. The only color in Edwynne's ashen face came from the blood on her lips. She lay motionless, shallow breaths barely moving her chest.

If they followed this road, they'd eventually come to the witch's cottage, right? Or would moving Edwynne worsen her condition?

Either way, she couldn't just sit here and wait to be captured. Not when whoever came for them would treat Edwynne worse than the provincial village doctor had treated Aziz. And certainly not when she still had the orb, which they could perhaps use to save Oradel.

She slipped her arms under Edwynne's and tugged.

It was slow, miserable going, the rain heavy enough to smother her if she tilted her face upward, the ground slippery and sucking under her thin shoes.

A noise caught her attention, distant barking. "We'll find them! They can't have gone far!"

I might not have Edwynne's strength. But I won't give up without a fight.

Sariva pushed at the foliage, searching for shelter. A cave, even a few trees leaning together, a large hollow tree. Anything. *Goddess, please help me!* There had to be some path she hadn't noticed.

Lights winked through the thick rain. Some distance off, she could just make out the shape of a cottage, a candle glowing in the window.

If she could reach safety before their pursuers found their tracks…

With renewed strength, she tugged Edwynne forward as the dog's baying grew louder. At last, she tripped over the doormat and pounded on the cottage's door. "Help! My friend is hurt!"

No reply, but had the searchers heard her?

She took the risk again, throwing her weight against the door. "Please, we need help!"

When it opened, she tumbled forward.

"What's all this so late at night? An old woman needs her rest, you know." The middle-aged woman peering down at her had a kind, ordinary face, and Sariva wanted to weep.

"We were traveling, and bandits attacked our caravan. They took our horse, and we're not dressed for the weather. Please, my friend is ill." The lie came easily. She tried not to sob too hard.

She beamed at them. "Ah, you're the girls I was told to expect. Come inside and we can wait out the storm."

Sariva kept up with Izalena, who carried tall, gangly Edwynne like a sack of potatoes. "She wouldn't injure herself for attention. She gets plenty of exercise, eats fruits and vegetables. You've got to help her, please."

Her wry smile didn't reach her eyes. "Sounds like you've had a hard time with healers."

She breathed out, shaking. "Yes."

Izalena went into a small, cozy room at the side of the cottage and laid Edwynne on a low cot. Edwynne instantly curled into a ball, guarding her stomach. Outside, trees thrashed in the howling wind, but the bundles of dried herbs hanging from the rafters—she recognized lavender and mugwort— barely rustled. "Has she been injured lately? Poisoned?"

"Something in the ruins bit her." She unlaced Edwynne's boot, slipped down her sock, and found only a healing scab beneath. Someone must have given her a potion to get rid of infection, but who?

"Delvar must have slipped her something under the guise of a draught for the wound." Her midnight eyes cold, she pressed a rag soaked with something into Sariva's hands. "Make your friend suck on this while I prepare an antivenom. We have a long night ahead of us."

Cradling the rag so it wouldn't drip, Sariva sat resolute on the edge of the bed. "Are we friends, Ed?" she murmured, stroking Edwynne's clenched jaw until it relaxed a fraction and then prying open the firm line of her chapped lips. Luckily, Sariva's olive skin didn't show a blush, but her cheeks still heated. She dabbed the cloth onto Edwynne's tongue. Awake, would Edwynne permit such a liberty? She'd tossed her shirt aside so Sariva could treat the scrapes on her back...

Izalena swept back in cradling a wooden bowl with several little bottles and cloth bags in her apron. "Good, you managed to give her the potion. I notice you're quite protective of her. She seems to trust you."

"I mean—" Automatic protests jostled for priority: She hates me, we can't stand each other, she'd never let me take such liberties when conscious. But none of those felt true. Not since Edwynne had attacked the guards to protect her. Not since Sariva had stood up for her against Lisette or since they laughed together on the public trolley. Maybe not even since she'd panicked surrounded by acid and Edwynne had goaded her into moving with stupid threats. "We make a good team," she finished at last, tugging the blanket over Edwynne's still form.

"I know what you mean. Oradel and I made a good team too. You still have a piece of her soul, don't you?"

"Yes. Do you want to see?"

Izalena nodded solemnly. When Sariva handed her the small glowing orb, she let out a shaky breath while cradling the orb like a firefly in her hands. "I'll give you something to keep this safe. Perhaps the sort of thigh holster I use for miniature potion bottles." Half turning away, she whispered to the orb, "Oh, Delly, sweetheart. Where did we go wrong? What have you done?"

Sariva didn't catch what she murmured next, only that Izalena brought the orb to her lips as if to kiss it. Instead of completing the gesture, she hesitated, staring at it for a long moment.

Sariva cleared her throat. "Edwynne still needs help, right?"

Izalena flinched as if guilty. She handed the orb back at once. "Yes, of course."

Hours later, Sariva warmed her still-trembling hands on a mug of tea. After hours of watching Edwynne writhe and flinch and cough up blood, Izalena said she was out of danger for now. But the exhausted, limp figure beside her seemed so still, so silent compared to the Edwynne she'd seen dancing through battle on her first day at the castle.

Normally, she'd rein her feelings under control by embroidering or painting her face, but the trundle bed in the corner beckoned like a cool pond during summer, and she eyed it longingly for only a moment before making her decision. Sleep now, she decided, pulling the plumpest feather-filled pillow over her head. Worry tomorrow.

Although Sariva wanted to sleep forever, Izalena rose early.

Sariva woke to the sound of her singing a folk song in another room, her voice creaky and wavering but alight with life nevertheless. *Life goes on; you still have to get up and eat breakfast.* Drifting into the cottage's kitchen brought a pleasant surprise: The table boasted a splendid brunch.

The lemonade was invigoratingly cool amidst the humid morning. She ate rice pudding with tiny red berries before deciding to try the cake.

She cut one bite, tasted it, and nearly wept. Tabernacle cake, just the sort her parents used to bring out after services. She and the other children would hover like vultures, then dive on it the instant the priest finished his blessing. It reminded her of the last letter she'd ever received from her grandparents in the old country.

When would she be able to go home?

And her parents—did they truly think she tried to kill the queen? Or what if Delvar told everyone she'd died in a botched escape attempt? They'd try to keep Aziz from the shock, but if some of the boys at school told him or one of the shoddier nurses let it slip...

Sariva shook her head. She couldn't go to his bedside or even send a letter. She had to concentrate on the battles she could still fight.

A rough brown dress, unevenly dyed and crookedly stitched, lay next to the water barrel. It appeared exactly her size. With a sigh of resignation, she peeled off her be-draggled yet well-made servants' clothing and pulled on the rough-woven dress. She ought to wake Edwynne.

Edwynne's dreams usually tangled through strange im-ages: mixed-up legends, beasts from old manuscripts. But in this dream, she leaned against a sturdy warmth at her back, safety permeating her limbs, and a softness smelling like wildflowers she couldn't name.

Cold fingers grabbed her shoulder.

Bunk prank! Last time they'd tied her up with boot laces. Was it the cellar for her and Tolliver this time? Well, let them try! She awoke, shrieking and lashing out.

Sariva, hazy in the morning sunlight, stumbled back-ward with a yelp of surprise. She wore a brown dress tight over her bust and waist, her hair down and loose.

"Why'd you wake me?"

"Is that any way to—do you remember anything from last night?"

It felt hazy. Like she'd gotten too drunk. "I...threw up?"

Affronted, she flung her arms in the air. "Yes, to say the least! Delvar poisoned you. You could have died. Izalena and I were up half the night tending to you, and when she said you'd make it, I practically collapsed from sheer exhaustion." She rubbed her red-rimmed eyes, the skin underneath puffy: Had she been crying? Why?

Edwynne turned her confusion into a joke. "So, you do care about me." She expected a return to normal, an insult or a sarcastic comment in return.

Instead Sariva paused, fidgeting. She chewed her lower lip. Finally, she mumbled, "You ought to come see our host. Izalena said you'd met."

Huh.

Outside, lush green vines tangled with a canopy of olive and lemon trees, and jasmine blossoms grew from sigil-painted terra-cotta pots. A woman with waist-length hair and perfect dark skin emerged from the trees. "Good morning to you both."

Edwynne beamed. "Izalena! Figured you weren't a traitor. Sariva said you saved my life."

Izalena quirked an eyebrow. "Sariva said you chugged a glass of poison. What was that like?"

"Tasted like grass."

She chuckled. "Sounds consistent."

Sariva stepped forward. "Miss Izalena—I'm not sure how to correctly address a witch—we've been running for our lives, the palace wizard and guards are trying to kill us, and the queen is sending me mysterious messages in my dreams. A ghost tried to eat my soul. I understand if you can't help us, but please tell us what's going on."

"It's...complicated. But I'll tell you all I can." A bent tree uncurled itself to form a chair, and she sat. "Delvar, the queen, and I were students at the academy. She studied city-craft: politics, economics, and law. I studied magic. Delvar, both. But Delvar fell in with the wrong sort of crowd. He went from someone who didn't care about politics to someone terrified of political change, even dropped out of school to study with some bizarre fringe sorcerers. I tried to make him see the error of his ways, but it always turned into arguments with him calling me brainwashed. When he said he wanted to get his life back on track and asked if he could visit the castle...I wanted to forgive him for old times' sake."

If Tolliver ran into the squires' dorm saying he'd killed someone, Edwynne would offer to bury the body. "What happened next?"

She sighed, shoulders drooping. "It turns out he'd been part of a plot to steal the queen's soul and mind-control her into being a puppet ruler. I caught him sneaking into Oradel's bedroom at night and fought him with all my strength and all my magic, but he managed to pin the deed on me and convinced his pet guards to chase me out."

"And the orbs?"

"Oradel agreed I should hide the lost pieces of her soul until someone she trusted could return them. We thought the ruins would be the last place anyone would want to search."

"But Delvar put part of her in the tapestry before we could return the pieces, right?" Sariva asked.

She hesitated. "From this far outside the city? I have no idea. I only know they couldn't be returned. We need to sneak back into the palace and break the spell before it's too late."

We! Finally, an adult on their side, one they could trust.

"Edwynne, get changed. Sariva, find something to cover your hair. I'll disguise myself as an old woman, and we'll set off."

For some reason, Sariva still couldn't get her bracelet off.

"Maybe the clasp's rusted shut, or maybe it's charmed. You could get Izalena to take it off with magic," Edwynne suggested.

"Probably. But it's a gift from my intended, and I don't want her to see me without it. Besides, she wouldn't give me something dangerous. I'd have Izalena check if I wanted to waste our time." The bracelet reminded her that safe, normal life awaited at the end of this adventure. She'd reunite with her family and keep them safe.

Edwynne rolled her eyes but didn't protest. Instead, she handed Sariva a shawl to cover the bracelet.

Izalena examined both girls. "One more thing." She reached into the birdbath, pulled out a scabbard, and handed to Edwynne.

"What's this?" Edwynne said, unsheathing the blade.

"A gift," she said cryptically.

Edwynne had seen and handled hundreds of swords. She'd gone with the other squires to the museum at Legacy Fortress, where they crowded around the display cases of ancient weapons and elbowed one another as their breath fogged the glass. This sword was plain and useful. Meant to be wielded, not admired. "Short sword, shallowly fullered. Steel loop hilt. It's light for its length but incredibly well balanced!"

Izalena smiled. "You've missed something."

Edwynne traced the symbols carved onto the blade. "Is this magical?"

"It makes the hair on my arms stand up. Right here." Sariva breathed, demonstrating.

"It has an aura of protection. You can use it to block magical attacks on the battlefield."

"Wait. Battle magic? How old is this sword?"

"It dates back to the wars."

Edwynne tilted the blade to catch sunlight. "Damn," she replied with feeling.

"With it, you'll be able to dispel any magical attack a wizard might send at you and lead the charge to fight them on even ground. Now we can return to the city."

Sariva bit her lip, uncertain. "Begging your pardon, but...how? You don't seem to have any horses."

"It's possible for a mage to summon magic from many things. Some work with emotions, others with forces of nature. My specialty has always been my garden...with a side of wind!" Her fingers danced through the air as if she played an invisible lyre. A breeze whooshed through the clearing, then a whirlwind, which solidified into a power-ful silver drafthorse. The horse bent his graceful head and sniffed a grapevine.

"The wind horse doesn't take well to being sum-moned for long, but I can convince him to carry us back."

Edwynne shrugged. A wind horse? Sure, she'd try anything once. She could even ride a camel, and those were spiteful beasts with teeth like tombstones. When she patted the horse's flank, it seemed solid enough, so she hoisted herself up.

Sariva hung back, so Edwynne gave her a disdainful eyebrow raise. "What, are you a coward?"

She glared. "No." Grumbling under her breath, she scrambled onto the horse behind Edwynne. Despite everything unexpected, at least she could still goad Sariva into taking action.

"What about you?" she asked Izalena.

"I can fly."

With another gesture, the horse started moving. Powerful muscles shifted as the wind horse took a sharp turn. Up ahead, an ancient fallen tree blocked the path.

He jumped, but the impact never came. They were flying over the treetops, yet the horse ran as if on solid ground. Wow! She'd never climbed higher than the palace watchtowers.

"We're so high up," Sariva's voice wavered.

"You know you can hold on to me, right?" Sariva had saved her life. Least she could do.

"I don't need to... Fine." She wrapped her soft arms around Edwynne, chin tickling her shoulder. Her perfume—or maybe the soap she'd used, or maybe just her own scent—smelled like chamomile and roses.

The wind swirled around them both as powerful hooves tore over the clouds. Sariva's shriek turned into laughter, and Edwynne found her own delighted scream curling into a harmony.

The witch flew beside them, her arms outstretched like a bird. Her fringed shawl billowed around her. At last, the wind horse touched down between two trees. Sariva and Edwynne hurried for the city gates, and Izalena walked beside them, leading the horse.

People streamed into the city. Even amidst the strange magical weather and traitorous schemes, ordinary life had to continue, including market day.

Edwynne gestured. *Come on.*

Izalena took a step forward and froze. She clutched her head, stumbling.

The girls exchanged frantic glances.

Sariva took off her scarf and draped it over the witch's head. "It's just the humidity. Come over to this bench, Auntie, dear."

They helped her to a nearby bench under a tree's spreading branches.

"What's wrong?" Sariva asked.

"Delvar placed an antimagic barrier around the main city. If I try to get more than a block inside, I could suffer a brain bleed. Even if I make it unscathed, he might deduce your survival from my presence when I trip the barrier. The two of you will have to finish this alone."

Edwynne patted Sariva on the shoulder. "Come on. We'll reach the palace before dark for sure." She hurried toward the gate.

But Sariva didn't follow. When Edwynne glanced back, she trembled all over.

"Well. That explains a great deal," Izalena murmured.

Sariva blinked at her, smoothing her arms up and down as if trying to banish a strange sensation. "What does?"

"You must have magic. Oh, not enough to need training but enough to recover from a ghost attack within an evening or know when someone's trying to speak mind-to-mind with you. Don't worry."

Edwynne glanced over her shoulder. The guard now conversed with another guard, and both turned to point at the witch. "We need to hurry. Can I try and drag her through the barrier?"

"Her magic isn't sufficient for something like that to harm her, so it's worth experimenting. I'll return to my cottage and see if I have anything to help break the barrier. In the meantime, stick together, and be brave, both of you!" Izalena rushed off.

The guards followed, armor clanking.

Edwynne and Sariva joined the line of people streaming into the city. Sariva made up answers to the guards' questions, sprinkling them with nonsense so specific it had to be true: "I need to buy a goat because my father's goat fell off a ridge, and my friend needs a package of sesame seeds so her mother can make a replica of the city from candy."

As people poured through the city walls, Sariva wobbled and had to lean against Edwynne to stay standing.

"I know you. You're a stubborn bitch. No falling over screaming for you," Edwynne whispered, linking her arm through Sariva's. She wanted to ask, "How does it feel to find out you're not who you thought you were?"

Sariva's muscles strained as her mouth opened and closed like a fish. "You're nearly there," Edwynne told her, squeezing her hand.

Sariva took one more step. Her shoulders sagged, and she exhaled. "I think we're through. Thanks, Edwynne."

When Sariva smiled at her like that, it felt strange. "Now we need to put as much distance between ourselves and Izalena as possible."

They sprinted through the tangled streets. The wind flung Edwynne's curls into her face, and dead leaves rattled on the cobblestones. At last, Sariva slumped against a wall. "I can't run anymore."

"Then let's rest. Can you answer something for me?" Edwynne knew she shouldn't pry, but she wanted to.

Sariva tucked a sweaty braid behind the delicate shell of her ear. "Depends on the question."

"When I'd been poisoned"—maybe she'd be better off not asking, but she needed to know—"were you sleeping in the bed with me? I thought I—" *Felt your hand in mine, your arm flung over my back, breathed in your hair, smelled your skin...* "I just thought maybe you were there."

Her words came out almost gentle. "What, did you think I wanted to let you die? Izalena needed an extra pair of hands to hold damp cloths and make you drink. And then, I would've fallen asleep anywhere, but it's a tiny cottage. She only had one bed. Excuse me if I didn't want to sleep on the floor after the day we'd had."

Edwynne ought to have left it alone. But she couldn't resist teasing Sariva. "And is it proper to sleep with one woman when you're engaged to another?"

The Sariva of a few days earlier might have taken it as an insult. "Are you calling me unfaithful?" or "And what does that mean, pray tell?"

But here and now, Sariva just smiled ruefully. "Not proper at all. But I needed a rest. And you were warm."

Edwynne shoved Sariva, who elbowed her in return. Resuming their bickering felt like falling asleep in one's own bed after months of travel, stretching out on the old familiar mattress, and curling up under the weight of a quilt someone beloved had stitched.

Distant music floated through the air, along with the smell of fried food and freshly trodden grass. "There's a festival uptown. We'll be harder to catch in the crowd."

"That's nearly the most reasonable idea I've ever heard you suggest."

Wandering past the food stands, they talked about how fried pickles were an easy food to cook badly and how you had to be a complete fool not to like leek medallions. If they could just ignore the overwhelming odds against them, everything would be all right.

Music flowed through the air. A vivid tune strummed on a lute and a singer's tipsy voice shouting lyrics with the crowd. A woman in a ruffled skirt swirled past, twirling a wooden hoop about her waist. Sariva darted out of the way. Two boys playing with wooden swords yelled as they sprinted across the path, knocking Sariva into Edwynne, who caught her by the elbow.

"Stick close. I'm not running after you if I lose you in the crowd."

Edwynne read only smug victory in Sariva's expression. "Fine? You want me to stick close? Then let's hold hands."

Though taller, Edwynne slowed—unconsciously?—so Sariva could keep up. Whenever drunk students careened by, Edwynne used her body as a barricade. Sariva had only suggested holding hands as a dare, but she didn't dislike it.

Would they be able to spend time together once everything returned to normal? Once Sariva moved to her betrothed's country home? Time moved too quickly. Their enemies did too.

"Maybe we could listen to the music for a minute. We'll seem suspicious if we rush, right?"

Edwynne didn't let go, her hand warm and sweaty around Sariva's, fingers interlaced like no one could pry them apart. They made their way to a bench.

Edwynne picked up a free news broadsheet and held it out for Sariva to see. "Can you believe this? It says the queen's been attacked by assassins, and now she's appointed Delvar as interim advisor. What rubbish... People should do something!"

Sariva's shoulders hunched. How had he gathered so much power? "I mean, we were taken in. I was, at least. Until he's in power and shows his true colors, no one will know what he wants, and then it'll be too late."

"Let's not assume the worst. Izalena said we'd be able to work things out." She tossed the news broadsheet to the ground and stepped on it, then tugged Sariva to her feet.

Sariva wouldn't let herself be pulled, her voice a frantic whisper. "How are you so confident? Just because the guards are off our trail right now. When I think of my family, my brothers, what Delvar might do to them—"

A one-shouldered shrug. "Hey, you're not the only one with siblings."

"Edwynne, it's not funny, I'm—" *Scared*, she wanted to say. *It terrified me when I thought I'd lose you. How are you so casual?*

Edwynne tugged Sariva off-balance and slammed a warm hand over her mouth. Should she lick or bite Edwynne's long fingers? Give her a taste of her own medicine?

Fear swam in Edwynne's wide hazel eyes, and instead Sariva gently uncurled her fingers and surrounded them with her own. She had little scrapes on her knuckles and oval fingernails bitten short. "Oh, Ed. Are you scared too?"

"No." Angry tears choked her voice. "Not for myself. But Stellan—he's my only family, all I have left."

"And you could have died." Selfishly, she feared losing Edwynne as much as losing her brothers.

Edwynne nodded, jaw muscles tight in her little pointy chin. "And I could have died! Me! I've never even caught a cold. That stupid wizard, what the fuck!"

Some ways away, two slumped, sweaty guards trudged out from behind a food stall. Sariva heard them talking to each other.

"So, we're searching for two women, one fat and olive skinned, and the other tall with curly red hair."

"Can't we just go enjoy the music?"

"This is important. They're probably committing treason."

"Let's just get this over with so we can say we checked everywhere. Why would radicalized teenage assassins be dancing at a festival, anyway?"

Sariva's muscles stiffened. They'd been found. "We ought to find a hiding place," she whispered.

Edwynne pointed. "Under the blanket!"

An abandoned picnic blanket lay on the grass. They scrambled underneath.

In the darkness of their temporary shelter, Edwynne's muscles tensed, her eyes wide with fear. How had Sariva ever found Edwynne intimidating or frightening? Blinking back tears, a muscle twitching in her pointy jaw, she reminded Sariva not of a fearsome wild animal but of a feral young thing without its pack, stranded in the rain and hissing at rescuers. *For all her grace, all her strength, she's no older than me.*

Sariva, lowering herself to the grass, tugged Edwynne's arm. "Here." It felt like a selfish, short-sighted plan, but the guards weren't searching for a young couple, for two people making one shape.

Grumbling indistinctly, Edwynne slumped over her and went boneless. Not unconscious, just exhausted, her shoulders shaking as if she fought back tears. Her knees and elbows poked into Sariva.

I'm here, she wanted to say. *I've got you; I'm not going anywhere.* But she couldn't lie. She settled for "Breathe, Ed," as she tucked a frizzy ringlet behind the other girl's ear.

Edwynne took a deep, trembling breath, her thin, chapped lips parted. She let it out and gulped in more air.

What would kissing Edwynne feel like? Did she kiss as an end in itself, or would she rather skip right to the main production? She kissed, yes, but had she ever *been* kissed, coaxed into staying still and feeling, the way she hardly moved with Sariva's fingers tangled in her hair?

Had anyone ever wanted to look after Edwynne like this instead of just letting the powerful knight-to-be ravish them?

Sariva knew better than to wonder.

"The assassins aren't in this area. Maybe they split up," a nearby guard called.

His colleague swore. "Fuck it, we've searched the whole area, and we've got people stationed at all the public transit stations. Let's go back to HQ."

"Are you—" Sariva began.

Edwynne scowled, pulling away. "Fine. I'm fine. Let's go." Trying to stand, she tripped over her feet, then the blanket. The color left her face. Even the golden hour couldn't put it back.

"Maybe we should try for the palace tomorrow. We've been on our feet all day. I'm so tired." She gave an exaggerated yawn.

"Well, if you're tired... I know some of Vered's older activist friends have safe houses. I guess we could rest there." Of course she'd never admit fatigue herself.

They left the crowds and music, dodging families cooking on open fires and kids playing ball. Something lingered in Sariva's thoughts though. Why had Edwynne called Stellan her only family?

They left the festival through a back alley. Here, the streets wound uphill, and the roof of one building often met the porch of the next.

Outside, boarded-up windows and a padlocked door made the building appear deserted. "Are you sure?" Sariva whispered, avoiding the streetlight.

Edwynne nodded, slipping up to the door and knocking. Something moved behind the wood. The door creaked open.

"Edwynne? Sariva?" Vered peered between them, dumbstruck. "We thought you'd been killed! Used as scapegoats for Delvar's assassination of the queen!" She opened the door a little wider. Inside, people sat at tables and on the floor, drinking, eating, or going over maps of the city.

"She hasn't been assassinated. It's more complicated than you've been told."

Vered's gaze flitted over them again, and Sariva realized how close together she and Edwynne stood. "Seems like that's not the only complicated thing. Come inside, both of you."

"Is there somewhere I can sleep? I'd like to turn in for the night."

Thud! A slip of a girl with light sandy skin slammed the window open and tumbled in. Her hair had fallen from its pins to form a disheveled mass of fraying silk about her worried face.

Vered ran to her. "What is it, what's wrong?"

The girl struggled to catch her breath. "I ran all the way here from the quarter gate. They're searching every building for those two." She pointed to Sariva and Edwynne.

"Right, party's over," Vered yelled, climbing onto a table. "Apprentices, back to your workshops. Students, back to the university. If you've got family or friends who can protect you, hightail it to them. Otherwise, lock down your squats until we can regroup."

Edwynne shook her head. "We're the ones who should leave. I don't want to put you or anyone in danger."

"Fuck that," the girl who'd climbed in the window told her. "You two risked everything to be here. And you're the ones who can save the queen. Even if some of us get thrown in the cells, we're not abandoning you."

"This place functioned as a smuggler's den prewar. There's a secret staircase."

As everyone else trickled out of doors and windows, whispering hurried goodbyes and running in separate directions, Vered ushered them to a closet. A little spiral staircase, the ceiling low enough to force them onto hands and knees, ran upward.

"Hey, at least we're not in a small tunnel like this underground," Sariva offered.

Edwynne actually smiled.

"Are you all right?" Edwynne asked once they were in the hidden hallway.

"I am, I promise." *I could be better than all right, but I care too much about you to ask.*

"If you're sure."

Edwynne placed a hand on her shoulder, a steadying gesture. Impulsively, Sariva turned it into a hug. She closed her eyes and leaned against Edwynne's bosom. How did she smell? It wasn't something one could put words to. It was just good. As soon as she could, she regained control of herself and hurried the rest of the way to the room.

There were a few blankets in the sparse chamber, and they arranged beds for themselves. Sariva carefully made hers as far away from Edwynne's as possible.

Chapter Eleven

Past occupants had left sleeping bags and pillows in the attic. The bedding smelled musty and sweaty but not moldy. Edwynne curled into a ball and tried to sleep.

But Sariva couldn't stay still, and in the small space, every noise she made seemed loud. She arranged her bedding, rearranged it, sighed, got to her feet, and began pacing under the highest point of the slanted roof. She'd stop eventually, right?

She didn't.

After a while, Edwynne couldn't bear it anymore. "Okay, fess up. What's wrong?"

Sariva sat down. She hugged herself, her loose hair streaming over her shoulders. "There's a holiday starting tonight. One of the minor ones, a lot of temples don't even celebrate it, but it's the death anniversary of a certain sage my father admires. We always pray for wisdom and eat pastries." She wound a curl around her finger, biting her lip. "And now my family probably thinks something horrific happened to me. They'll be in no mood to celebrate, and I might never see them again."

The need to know more pulled at her. "What's the celebration like?"

"Father puts on different hats and reads some tales the sage wrote. He even does voices. All the kids laugh even if they don't understand the morals, though of course no one in our family thinks his voices are funny. But he keeps doing the voices anyway. It's ridiculous."

What was it like to spend so much time with your birth parents that you got tired of the ways they tried to make you laugh? To roll your eyes at someone you loved, knowing they'd still be there for you? Edwynne hungered for those ordinary moments. Wanting carved a deep hole inside her, deeper even than the palace ruins. "I think it's ridiculous that you don't appreciate your family," she muttered, jaw clenching.

"I mean, everyone gets annoyed at their parents sometimes. And I miss them. I want to go home, I just—"

She wanted to go home? She *could* go home. It wasn't fair. Edwynne leapt to her feet. "You have parents to get annoyed at! You grew up with them. You spend so much time with your parents, your community, that you can even laugh at them and say you want space. I don't have a future among my own people. I'm nobody. They put my parents in a plague pit, and I don't even know which one." Just an anonymous field with grass growing over the remnants of burned corpses among miles and miles of anonymous fields. Only the wind and rain visited such places. Her breath caught.

Slow, amazed realization dawned on Sariva's face. "Ed, you're—"

Edwynne cut her off again. She wanted to laugh and scream at the same time, but making too much noise might endanger them, so she slammed her hands into her thighs. "One of you! Yes!" Even in a whisper, her voice shook. "Why do you think I asked you about religion when we first met?"

"If I'd known you were Northern—" Sariva spluttered.

Bullshit. Edwynne didn't want to listen. "Even if I wasn't Northern, you shouldn't have decided I was mocking you. Being nasty is no way to treat someone who genuinely wants to convert. You'd just met me, and you decided who I was!"

Sariva curled her mouth in a sneer. "Like you didn't do that? You didn't see a person; you saw a noble. You decided I would break your heart."

"Because everyone has!" She couldn't raise her voice, but she wanted to. "My so-called family lied to me my entire life. My brother helped them, and now he's marrying someone who hates me, and I dated Lisette... As soon as I met you, I wanted you to like me. I wanted you to like me so fucking bad." Handing Sariva her heart on a platter struck her as objectively stupid, but she couldn't stop. She just kept projectile vomiting words. "I wanted you to like me. And then when I realized I couldn't have that because somehow I'd fucked it up just by existing, I wanted to make you hate me with your whole heart. Because then at least you'd know I was there." Now she'd fucked things up with Sariva again. Stupid, impulsive Edwynne, always bombarding people with her over-the-top emotions. Choking back a sob, she buried her head in her arms, resisting the urge to rock back and forth.

A gentle touch rested on her shoulder. "Hey, Ed?"

She'd liked it when Sariva had called her Ed in the dungeon, her touch careful, her voice filled with soft concern. But she shouldn't get addicted to having someone care.

"I..." Sariva fell silent for a few seconds as if searching for words. She moved closer to the point where Edwynne could feel Sariva's breath in her curls. "I don't hate you," Sariva said at last. "And I know I should at least try to be indifferent toward you or try to care about you a normal amount because I'm supposed to get married, but I could never ignore you even if it meant starting a fight at a dinner party. Whatever I feel for you, I keep feeling it. My Ed, my knight, I opposite-of-hate you so much more than I should."

Someone cared about her. She licked dry lips as she blinked up into Sariva's moonlit gaze, the attic seeming much smaller and warmer than before, like a secret hideout in the darkness. "My parents—my birth parents—named me Elyanit."

"It means star. Is that what you'd like me to call you?"

"Yeah." Her voice cracked as she rubbed her eyes. Edwynne was just the female version of Edwyn, but Elyanit had a meaning all its own.

Sariva pulled her into a pillowy hug. "Little star," she murmured, cradling Edwynne as she shattered. She touched Edwynne's nose with something recognizable as a handkerchief. "Blow. You're getting all snotty."

Edwynne did. "You've been so nice to me lately."

"Maybe I realized being mean to you was a mistake."

"Because I'm Northern?"

"Because even though you hated me, you risked your life to protect me. You kept my secrets, followed me into dangerous places when no one else would, and saved my life so many times. If I didn't have to go through with this arranged marriage..." She seemed solemn.

Edwynne hardly dared to breathe. "Yeah?"

She felt, more than heard, Sariva's whispered out-pouring. "Then I'd love you. Ed, if I wasn't, if I didn't—"

Edwynne uncurled herself from the hug, her face tilted upward. "Who's to say you will? We might die to-morrow. You should do as you please with me. I opposite-of-hate you too."

Sariva, a thoughtful gleam in her eyes, tapped her on the nose. "You're always trying to get me riled up, always trying to make me do something I know I shouldn't. But it works. I want to do so many terrible, unladylike things to you."

"We have time," Edwynne said.

Then Sariva pulled her against her body. "Open your mouth, little star."

Edwynne instantly obeyed. A sparkly, soothing blankness filled her mind.

Women usually thought that because Edwynne liked to wear boy clothes and spar, she'd take a more masculine role in bed. No one had ever tried bossing her around, but she adored it to the point where if Sariva had kissed Ed-wynne while they stood, her knees would have buckled. Even seated, she felt like swooning.

As Sariva's touch trailed over her shoulders and lower, she made a very undignified *eep* noise. She'd never gotten so flustered. "You don't kiss like a fine lady," she stammered.

"What do I kiss like?" Her adorably smug expression suggested that she knew the answer and just wanted to hear Edwynne say it.

Instead of sitting back and waiting to be kissed or pulling away constantly to offer critique, she expected Edwynne to bend to her will. "Someone who cares about what I want. Someone who wants me."

Sariva smirked and claimed her mouth once more.

Much later that night, as Edwynne slipped into sleep, Sariva said, "Ed, Elyanit. You know I still have to get married, right?"

"Right," Edwynne mumbled, rolling away from her and fumbling for her shirt. Of course Sariva couldn't stay with her. She couldn't be kept. She hated that, no "opposite" necessary.

All too soon, light came in through the small, dusty window.

"Coffee and naan?" Vered's friend Nyssa called from the foot of the stairs. Better not to die on an empty stomach.

"So, what's the plan?" Edwynne asked as they hurried through the quiet early morning streets.

"Back at the stables, before we escaped the palace, Ava slipped this into my hand."

"Key to...the back gate?"

"Servants' entrance."

"Clever."

They turned their cloaks inside out to show the duller-colored lining and pulled the hoods low over their faces. Following the orb's glowing pulse, they hurried through the city. There were fewer guards than yesterday, so perhaps they assumed Sariva and Edwynne had left the city and stayed out.

"Have you got a pass?" a guard asked, barely seeming to care about the answer.

Sariva burst into tears. "I left it with my apron in the cupboard... I was going to get a bonus today for shining the silver. Mum and Dad will be so vexed with me. Oh, stars, this is awful—turn out your pockets, Vi, perhaps you've at least got yours..."

Picking up on the deception, Edwynne began to methodically pat down her own clothing. She hoped her blank face made her appear dull-witted rather than like the bad liar she was.

"Everyone else will be here soon, and I can't have you clogging up the queue. They just hired me on for the coronation, and I'll lose my money if there's enough of a complaint. Go on, you can show your pass to me on the way out. And make sure to tie it around your neck with a bit of string or something!"

Instead of going to the housekeeper to fetch their instructions, they snuck down side hallways, following the orb. But when they emerged from a servants' staircase, a rushing noise filled the air.

Wind roared up, pushing them both back. Edwynne grabbed the banister. The narrow spiral stairs would break her neck if she fell!

Sariva tried to stand her ground, but the force knocked her off-balance. "Edwynne!" she yelled.

Edwynne's muscles strained. She had to hold on to the banister! As Sariva tumbled toward her, she hooked her arm around the other girl's waist, catching her at the last possible second.

The wind died down, and Sariva shivered. "What was that?"

"Not what," a male voice drawled. "Who." The air shimmered, picking out appearing details—gold embroidery on a fine cloak and a staff topped with an egg-shaped emerald. Delvar stood in the narrow hallway, his posture untroubled. Slowly, his mouth widened into a smile.

"Sariva, get back!" Edwynne shouted. She drew the magical sword, ready to attack.

"Finally, I was concerned I'd have to send you a formal invitation."

Did he think he could mock her and get away with it? She charged toward him, rage boiling in her belly, and moved to attack.

His pale eyes narrowed as he made a single gesture. The stones below her feet seethed and changed into a mass of carnivorous vines. They jabbed at the gaps in her clothing, stabbing into flesh.

She swung at the vine seizing her ankle. Another bit into her wrist. With a swirl of her blade, she changed her target. The first vine ricocheted up, locking around her neck.

"Now for the orb." He stalked toward Sariva.

Edwynne drew her enchanted sword. "If you hurt her—"

"Hurt her? Like this?"

Pricks of lightning jumped from Sariva's bracelet, sizzling and crackling over her body, jolting her as she sank to the floor. No wonder she hadn't been able to remove the bracelet. Delvar must have tampered with it somehow, enchanting it.

"I hope we won't need another such display," Delvar said casually.

Sariva pushed herself up to her hands and knees. Slowly, she stood, whispering, "We won't."

Reluctantly, Edwynne sheathed her sword. How could she protect Sariva without a weapon? "You don't need to hurt her. I'm the one who planned all this."

Delvar raised an eyebrow. "Is that so?"

"Of course. I mean, Sariva's from Northern nobility. Does she seem the type to plan something like this? I'm a ruins guard, so I knew the layout. I knew that things had changed, that someone had crept into the ruins to store objects, maybe treasure. I'm stronger and taller than her. I told her if she didn't go along with me, I'd make her regret it."

Sariva nodded eagerly. "I only fled the palace because I thought you'd kill me, and I don't know what your enemies have planned. I was only along for the ride because I knew I couldn't get the stones without that girl's help. You don't know how horrific it's been having to pretend I tolerate her. She clings to me, cries on me, faints in bad weather, and whines about my need to marry well. Having her as an overbearing friend, talking my ears, off is worse than having her as an enemy."

Did Sariva's words convey a willingness to go along with the improvised plan, or did she actually resent Edwynne? Edwynne couldn't tell. But Sariva cared about her, right?

Delvar glanced between the pair, lips pursed. "Only along for the ride, hmm? I want to believe you, but my men who were chasing you through the city said you seemed to be in cahoots like best friends on an outing. How do I know you weren't conspiring with this Edwynne the whole time?"

"And I'm sorry for refusing your advances earlier. I know you have my best interests and those of my people at heart. I just... I didn't know what your intentions were."

"My...intentions?"

She nodded, dark eyelashes fluttering. In the sunlight, her eyes were deep wells of innocence. "I believed you merely planned to use me and discard me. That all you had planned was a few moments of fun. But now I realize you're much more thoughtful than I was led to expect, and you have some larger plan in mind. Something much...greater. You want to save the Northern civilization, so I should get over myself and help you."

Delvar beamed. "Splendid. I had a feeling you'd see reason eventually." He held out his hand, and Sariva took it. He made a spell-working gesture at Edwynne with his other hand.

Cramps like buzzing needles seized Edwynne's feet and ankles, the circulation cut off. She tumbled to the floor. Her numb arms buckled under her, and her chin bounced off the tiles so hard her head rang.

"What should we do with this ruffian?" Delvar asked.

A dainty sigh. "Whatever you wish. It's none of my business whether she lives or dies."

Edwynne tried to protest, but Delvar made another gesture and magically clamped her jaw shut. Invisible fists slammed into her stomach.

Sariva walked away without looking back. Edwynne could barely stand when a trio of guards—yes, the ones she'd pummeled during her last escape attempt—hauled her to her feet.

"Good to have you back," one of them muttered. "Now walk, you bitch. And don't think we've forgotten what you did to us!"

Whatever happens to me, Sariva is safe.

Chapter Twelve

Would Delvar punish Sariva for her past defiance? Had he already killed her family? Sariva expected corpses. Instead, Delvar led her to a sitting room where a servant poured them both chilled mint tea.

Once the servant had departed, he regarded her. "First things first: the last of the orbs?"

Sariva winced inwardly. Of course it would come down to this. Inside a skirt pocket, the magical sphere shifted like a trapped bird thrashing in terror, the fragment of Oradel's soul fluttering frantically against her own magic. But if she wanted Delvar to let his guard down, she had no choice.

"I have it right here." She drew it forth and handed it over, hoping no twitch or tremor would betray her nervousness.

He turned it back and forth, a smile spreading over his features, and whispered, "Finally."

Sariva couldn't stand to watch him gloat. "How were you able to track us? I thought the bracelet came from Dorenia..."

He chuckled, tucking the orb away in the leather bag he carried. "Of course it did. I only bribed the messenger.

I know you're too well bred to take gifts from men who don't make their honorable intentions clear."

She fiddled with the ornate cuff. "It's a bit tight. Could I remove it?"

"Of course...after the wedding. I just don't want anything happening to you since my enemies are still at large in the city. You could be in danger."

I already am.

"But enough about me. I'd love to tell you more about what I'm doing to help the North."

Did he plan on committing war crimes?

"For instance, it's going to be illegal to criticize your people. Disapproving of the sultan? It's the same as acting unfairly to all the Northerners who've decided to move here. I won't have anyone smearing or legislating against our ally abroad. And I'll send as many knights there as I can."

Yes, probably war crimes.

"Oh, Delvar." She sipped her tasteless, unsweetened tea and tried to regulate her breathing. "You have no idea... I'm so pleased to hear you care. And you want to marry me too? Why me?"

He shrugged with a lopsided smile, a gesture that could have been endearing, almost boyish. "I'm no expert at talking to women. None of them ever want to hear about magical theories or economics, what's truly meaningful in life. But you listen—you appreciate me. I find the willingness to listen more attractive than conventional beauty. And the international alliance wouldn't hurt."

"Well, I've always thought that I could be moved, so to speak, by the right man." She beamed sweetly at him as if the idea didn't make her queasy. Anything could happen between now and the wedding, she reminded herself, and I have nothing to gain by angering him. She stayed silent for a moment, but he seemed to be waiting on her to continue. "After all, isn't it well known how women are attracted to money and power?"

Sariva slipped true sentiments under the masks of honeyed words, telling him what she sensed he wanted to hear. Each absurd lie felt like sipping poison, as if the words ate away at the lining of her throat and left a blood-sour taste in her mouth. She thought of the terrifying cruelty she'd heard about in family legends.

"That's wonderful, Sariva. Having you at my side—someone who used to be a 'progressive'—will do so much to legitimize my rule."

"Anything to preserve the institutions of government."

"I have plans for our wedding and the coronation."

"You can get so much organized on such short notice?" She gasped, wide eyed. Surely, he couldn't.

"Ordinarily, no. But I've got a foreign army and my own private army. People are apt to listen to me." He took a folder of papers from his bag and slid it toward her. "I know you have an eye for aesthetic and symbolism. How could I improve this? And be honest with me. Don't just say it's perfect. The queen hired you for your skills after all."

"For a start, I guess you could make some announcements the first day in office. Find the queen's least popular policy and immediately undo it." And hopefully he wouldn't make it into office.

"The first thing I can tell you from experience is"—she took a deep breath—"when you host the palace press conferences, offer the reporters food before they can interrogate you. They'll be in a more charitable mood. And even though the sultan legislates public executions, it's one of his most unpopular policies. Kill your political enemies quietly. Maybe even make it seem like they killed one other."

"And the coronation?"

She continued to read over the papers and provide suggestions. Hire a local children's chorus in addition to professional musicians. Give wedding favors to the commoners even if you can't get enough cake to go round. "And have you asked your guests for a list of dietary needs? It wouldn't exactly serve international relations if a diplomat collapsed from allergies."

"This is genius, Sariva. We have publicists but no event planners. I know it's not the most traditional, but will you help me plan the wedding and coronation? The people will adore you... I know I do." He leaned across the table and brushed a loose curl behind her ear without a by-your-leave.

Get close to him. Find the queen. Strike when the time came.

If she lived long enough.

She bit her full lower lip. She knew people found her mouth attractive. "I was wondering...if something happens to me, will you still take care of my family? They need me. One of my younger brothers was born with an incurable disease."

"Of course, darling. Say the word."

Would her parents be too proud to accept help from someone against everything they stood for? Not for their son's sake.

His sudden, rough kiss stole her breath. He gripped her chin like a fisherman prying out a hook, and his beard scratched her cheek. Sariva squeezed her eyes shut and held her breath. If marrying this man she hated kept her younger brothers safe, she'd do it. Duty over happiness, as always.

At last, he pulled back and touched her face, a parody of gentleness. "I'm so glad we could come to this arrangement."

Sariva nodded. She couldn't resist trying to get more information out of him. "But what about the radical Northerners? I mean, there are a lot of them, especially at the university."

Delvar chuckled. "Don't worry. While you were out of my reach with that horrible witch, I found their hideouts and placed them under an extra-strength mind control spell. I'm even going to invite them to the wedding, and I doubt they'll be any trouble. It's not as if someone could shock them all out of it at once. My guards will be monitoring the crowd for any disturbances."

"I'm glad you care about my safety so much." And she forced herself to kiss his cheek.

★

I have time. Sariva paced the candlelit room in her flowing white nightgown. *I may have nothing else, but I have time.*

Delvar believed it wouldn't be proper for them to share a bed before the wedding, so he'd retreated to a room with a shared wall. For all his magic and power, no mortal could organize a coronation and a wedding overnight.

She had time to rescue her friends, her country. But did she have anything else? Doubtlessly, she'd given away where Vered and the others were by staying at their hideout with the tracking bracelet. Stellan had been killed in battle. Izalena, if she still lived, was imprisoned or in exile. Even if magic powers lurked within her own sewing-calloused hands, what good was a completely untrained minor magical gift?

And Edwynne—

No, she couldn't think about that. In both history and the stage adaptation, Amaldia had said "fuck it" to forgetting her lover after sacrificing her. She'd caught madness or encephalitis rather than accept that she'd ordered Rhysling to her death and hallucinated the swordswoman standing just off her shoulder for most of the war's remainder. Such an unflinching woman could shatter her own mind without losing skills.

But Sariva was no genius or prodigy or strategist. What skills did she even have to lose? She had some training in communications and courtly manners, good penmanship, and the ability to sew a garment without a pattern but nothing more. She wouldn't investigate Edwynne's situation. She certainly couldn't ask Delvar to spare her life.

And let's say I did manage to conjure a mental Edwynne. What would she tell me? "Stab Delvar and run, you idiot?" *I've never even killed a chicken! How would I know where to stab? Of course, she'd mock me when I couldn't get the dagger through his ribs.*

She clapped her hands over her mouth to muffle a laugh or sob.

As she shook with the effort of silence, a voice came from the other side of the wall. Its faintly tinny sound indicated that Delvar had commandeered a crystal ball. "Working with the Northerners? What are you thinking? Delvar, I hate this. They'll just gabble about their gross female supremacy deity and steal from us when our backs are turned. I mean, they're not Almesian. How does helping a bunch of lying, cheating, superstitious backwater crazies help us make Almesia into a country for, well, Almesians?"

Delvar sighed. "First things first, the public relations potential is astounding. Let's say people call us exclusionary, accuse us of wanting to kick out everyone from cultures that don't have their priorities straight. Instead of pretending we want some idiots who live in nasty tents, we just say 'Look at the Northerners! We're being nice to them. When minorities care about achievement, we treat them well.'"

"But why the Northerners?"

Sariva scooted toward the wall as quietly as she could.

"Because we can control them. They're so scared of losing their little scrap of land they'll bow to anyone who helps them defend it against the savages. When we've gotten rid of their enemies, we can sweep in and convert them. Either way, having them all in one place presents a lot of solutions to our potential problem up north."

"Sure would save us a lot of hard work. But, in the meantime, at least we can bribe them to keep them from causing trouble. You know how they are, willing to sell out their own child for a handful of coins. Willing to buy someone else's for even cheaper. Is that what you did with your lover?"

"Sariva? Absolutely. For a Northern girl, she's surprisingly attractive."

"Until she turns to the side."

Delvar gave a nasal chuckle. "I'll have someone cast an illusion spell on that misshapen nose of hers. Until then, well, I can conceive an heir from behind. And I'll keep her in silk thread and gemstone Goddess pendants for the rest of her life. She wouldn't raise a finger against me."

"I bet a girl like her has a lot of powerful connections up North."

"Mmm. She downplays it, but of course, she'll be able to make allies for me. No one who worships the Goddess is really Almesian. Eventually, the truth will come out."

"Let's say things go wrong though," the other voice argued. "This Sariva girl's been a radical in the past, and she wasn't part of the original agenda. I'm concerned you're letting her curves sway your judgment, Delvar. What's your contingency plan?"

He scoffed as if not believing that he'd need one. "She's five feet tall. No combat training, no magic. Worst comes to worst, I get rid of her, and we find someone to blame it on."

"That's my boy. Get in touch again if you want to add anything to the coronation plans, all right?"

"Will do. And send me the draft of Oradel's speech by tomorrow morning."

They exchanged pleasantries before Delvar closed the magical connection. Sariva sat on the floor next to her bed, not daring to move. If only she could go back to her early days at the palace when she only had to worry about Lisette passive-aggressively doubting her activist credentials and Edwynne putting a pond frog in her shoe. *People think Lisette's side is worse, but no one will ever hate us as unthinkingly, as casually as Delvar and his ilk.*

The next day, two attendants helped Sariva into a heavy, ornate gown and contoured her nose smaller. Crinolines swayed under the tiered skirt with every movement.

"Are you sure you wouldn't like His Regency to make your nose smaller with magic?" one attendant asked. "He's so generous he even enchanted mine. It hardly hurts besides the nosebleeds."

"No, thank you." She wanted to still recognize herself in the mirror. After today, she wouldn't recognize Almesia in the news.

★

The actual transfer of power happened simply. The queen stood on a second-floor balcony, unrolled a scroll, and read her speech in measured tones. Below, Delvar's guards held a struggling, shouting tide of people back from the elites' seating section where finely dressed people sat in neat rows.

Someone must recognize the wrongness of the situation—someone must stop it! Her gaze fixed on the courtyard entrance beyond the barred gates.

Amaldia would have turned Delvar's supporters against him with false promises, manipulated a stranger into killing him in his sleep.

Rhysling would cleave the gates in two and the guards' heads from their shoulders.

Izalena could fly in on a horse made from magic. The Queensguard might—

Oradel finished her speech to a polite smattering of applause.

Someone below screamed. The guards pushed the crowd farther back, staves and swords at the ready.

"What's going on?" she asked Delvar, who was seated beside her.

"Someone tried to climb the fence. Of course, the guards will make an example of him."

A rock sailed over the fence and crashed into the courtyard cobblestones between two chairs. One man near the impact leapt from his seat and another screamed.

Delvar beckoned Oradel to his side, and the guards on the balcony followed.

"Sir, we'd better get you all inside," one murmured. "The protests might get violent. There's a panic room—"

"Considering the magical weapons I've equipped the men with, I'm sure there's no need. We'll just stay inside."

And this way he didn't have to puppet Oradel into approximating concern.

When the party had safely made it inside, Delvar reached for her hand. "My poor girl. You're shaking." He pulled her body flush against his.

"I suppose so. I'm not used to violence." She tried to avoid breathing his scent. "May I go to my room and change out of this dress? I only want to lie down, and you must need to defend the palace with your magic. I'm scared I'll get in the way. You're so brave to help fight those protestors," she added, her tone breathy with innocence.

"Of course." He kissed her hair and squeezed her before relinquishing his grip. "Don't worry. By the time the coronation is over, I'll be able to tap into the energies of the Magic Mirror. I'll be so much more powerful. You'll never have to face this kind of chaos under my rule."

Of course the guards drove the protestors back. Of course they had carts at the ready to imprison the unconscious and wounded in repurposed warehouses and used the palace's hunting hounds to track down many who'd escaped.

How ridiculous to think someone would come to save her! Happy endings weren't real. Sariva read tragedies to prepare herself for the inevitable, and in the story of her own life, she didn't play a protagonist. A minor character like her, with no plans or useful skills, would be lucky to survive.

★

Queensguard soldiers were only supposed to be taken prisoner in wartime. Scrolls of law codices allowed a captured soldier to write home for ransom and receive medical treatment for any life-threatening injuries, as well as making sure they got fed regularly.

Based on the pattern of light through the oubliette's grating, Edwynne had spent six days in the lowest level of the dungeons, maybe a week, and eaten fewer than six meals. Mostly she slept. When she couldn't sleep any longer, she did push-ups, swore at the guards who occasionally patrolled above, and planned out elaborate menus.

She wrapped her arms around her empty stomach. Did Delvar plan to execute her? Sure, the constitution prohibited it, but she suspected Delvar didn't care about laws.

An uneven gap stretched between two stones. She leaned over to pick out the dirt and moss with her bitten-down fingernails. One particular pebble seemed wedged firmly into the mud. Tilting her head, Edwynne dug her fingernail in deeper, trying to wiggle it free.

The grate overhead rattled. A faint sunbeam trembled on the dungeon floor.

"Psst!" A concealed face shadowed the grating.

She put up her middle finger at the stranger. "Fuck off."

Instead of getting angry, the stranger drew back. "You seriously don't know me?"

"Tolliver?"

"Got it in one." He pulled back his hood for a moment, allowing her a better glimpse. "Don't worry, Edwynne. We're going to rescue you."

"What?"

"Me, some of the other squires, and a few of the youngest knights too. People who knew Stellan. For his sake, we won't let you die here."

Just as Sariva hadn't given up on saving the queendom, neither had her friends. Edwynne scrambled to her feet and leaned against the wall for stability. "Tell me the plan." She'd written Stellan off already. Hearing his death confirmed shouldn't hurt. She shouldn't need to fight back tears.

Tolliver fidgeted, his posture shifting.

Edwynne closed her eyes for a moment and took a deep breath. "You do have a plan, don't you?"

He leaned down and pressed his face to the grate. "Everyone figured you'd be kept in the new dungeons, the ones on ground level, and not the old ones, which flood when it rains. But we're figuring something out."

Edwynne wrinkled her nose. "What's your plan?"

He set his mouth in a grim line. "We're going to fight our way in and then fight our way out."

"You idiot. You're going to die."

He shrugged. "Yeah, well. Stellan will probably come back as a ghost and slaughter us if we don't at least try. What was it you said you hated about Amaldia in the play? That she played people chess? Well, we're not going to play people chess with you."

She closed her eyes for a moment and took a few deep breaths. Stone dust drifted through the sunbeam. "There's something important I need you to do first."

Tolliver nodded, seeming serious and only a little worried. "All right. What is it?"

"Izalena gave me an enchanted sword, and it can cut through magical protection. Without it, we'll have no chance against the wizard. You and the others need to sneak into the armory and steal it. Get it to whoever's in charge of fighting back." She described the sword's appearance and gave her best guesses as to where in the armory it was stored.

"I know the sword's important, but you're important too. And...Edwynne?"

"Don't say it. Not if it's some stupid soppy shit," she warned. "We're going to see each other again, and we'll both be fine."

"Edwynne Dovecote"—he tapped the grate—"I've been counting. You owe me five shkal and a bag of dried apricots."

She couldn't help smiling. "You stole that dried fruit from me."

Tolliver glanced over his shoulder. "Someone's coming. I'd better run."

In his absence, there was only the beam of shattered sunlight, creeping endlessly across the dirty floor.

★

The next evening, Delvar hosted a dinner party. The "happy couple" had just descended the grand main staircase when a flying Mattie collided with her waist. Teary-eyed, she pulled on the fabric of Sariva's skirt. "Sariva, please, you've got to help."

Sariva wanted nothing more than to drop to her knees and embrace the bedraggled little girl. She noticed Mattie's half-undone plaits and the stains on her blouse. Instead, she looked down at her, sensing the wizard's gaze like a nearby stench. "What's the matter?"

"Ava, she's heard they brought Stellan's armor, maybe his body. She's in the dungeon, and I went down to visit her, and she's just staring at the wall. I can't make her eat porridge or anything. She's going to die down there, and no one will tell me what's going on. But she couldn't have done treason, she couldn't! She's in the old, ruined palace dungeons. The ones not legal to use anymore. The ones with water and mosquitos. You have to help her! You're not going to marry him, are you?"

Delvar's arm swept around her. "Come now, milady. Surely you're not consorting with the sister of a traitor?"

The young girl's gaze met Sariva's. "Don't let him use magic on me; I don't want to fall ill—Sariva, please, tell him not to hurt me! Or tell him to let Ava go free. You have to do something!"

By betraying kindness, she'd break her charade, and if the wizard saw her as a threat, he'd kill her quietly and blame the traitors or destroy her will and turn her into a magical puppet.

Some guards sprinted up, and Delvar turned on them. "How dare you allow this girl out of her rooms! She's the relative of traitors." Though he didn't raise his voice, it still held palpable anger.

"Apologies. She's so small it's hard to keep an eye on her," one guard stammered.

Delvar raised an eyebrow. "Would you like to be small? I can do that."

At his glower and upraised hand, they hurried away, dragging a weeping Mattie by the arms.

"My apologies. I'm having her sent to a boarding school once Ava's sentenced, so it won't happen again," he told Sariva.

"Of course. I appreciate peace and quiet." She could find no other words and changed the subject. "So, you mentioned the dinner tonight would be attended by your supporters. Can you fill me in on who that includes? Their names, their preferences, if I should avoid any specific topics. I've learned from my mistakes at other parties, and I want to help by being a good hostess."

"Don't worry. You know everything you need to about them." He gestured at the double doors into the dining room. They slid open.

Delvar was right. She recognized everyone in the room.

"Sariva, hello!" Vered, dressed head to toe in conservative dark colors, hurried toward them. Her prayer shawl bore a pattern of Northern flags. "I'm so glad you're joining our cause. Delvar is such a brilliant man, and the North does so much for human rights now that I've considered—"

Delvar snapped his fingers.

Vered's smile froze. Everyone at the table stilled too.

He turned to Sariva. "Well? What do you think?"

How could he control this many people so seamlessly?

"It's a bit of a shock," she admitted. Even an ally of his would betray surprise. "How did this happen?"

"Well, they were on the front lines of the protests against the queen handing over her rulership, most in garments or jewelry betraying Northern heritage, so I found them easily. As for the spell, of course, it's more complex than the one I used for Oradel. It's not like I'm wearing their souls. They're trapped in a thought loop, my magic linked into their own willpower and cognitive dissonance."

What if something breaks it? she wanted to ask, but that seemed too obvious a ploy. Instead, she merely smiled. "That's fascinating. You know so much about magic."

He snapped his fingers again, and Vered unfroze. "— the complexity of the situation. I'm glad you two are here. Now we can eat, and maybe you can give input about what to do with the radicals at the university. It's such a shame to watch them turn their backs on their heritage."

Sariva sat down between Vered and a friend of her father's, a distinguished man who'd written books extolling the vibrancy of Goddess worship in diaspora. Now he nodded in unison with everyone else whenever Delvar spoke.

The elegantly plated dishes of fish, vegetables, and potatoes cut into decorative shapes tasted like plain salt, lacking texture in her mouth. She wanted to wipe her sweaty palms on her gown, but the beaded skirt prevented it. Delvar chatted with his guests, flattering each in turn and making jokes to amuse himself. "Of course you know how to manage money," he quipped. "Can't wait to get my hands on those secrets. At least you don't live off the government the way Plains folk do. Wish they could take a few pages out of your book! Do they think the government is their parents? I mean, it's not like they have family structures!"

Everyone laughed in chorus, eyes bulging, tendons ghoulishly straining in their necks. The crystal chandeliers overhead cast fractured patterns of light on every waxen face as the laughter died down and talk returned to a polite murmur.

"So, how do you plan on celebrating your wedding?" Vered asked.

Her wedding? It still seemed like a nightmare. "That's a good question." She fumbled for her wineglass. It tumbled from her sweaty palms and shattered on the marble floor, impossibly loud. Deep-claret wine spilled over the tiles.

Sariva tore her attention away from the glass and back to Vered, who stared at her, eyes wide and face pale.

"Sariva?" Her frantic gaze darted around the ballroom, searching for exits. "What am I doing here? I was at the protests."

Delvar shoved his chair back. "Damn it. This spell operates under its own power, but reapplying it takes so much energy."

"No!" Vered shrieked. She sprung to her feet and stumbled on her long skirts as she bolted for the doors. "Sariva, help me!"

Everyone else continued to eat and talk in normal calm tones.

Sariva took the only action available. She picked up her serrated knife and cut into the fish, her attention completely focused on slicing it.

Vered tugged at the magically sealed doors, screaming, until Delvar caught up to her.

"No! Let me go! You can't—" Her cries fell silent. Moments later, Delvar escorted a smiling, complacent Vered back to her seat.

The attendants brought out the dessert course, a pomegranate and citrus fruit salad and a glazed lemon cake. Afterward, everyone wished Delvar and Sariva well with exclamations like "I'm so excited for your wedding!" and "I can't wait to see your bride's beautiful dress!" before guards escorted them to their quarters in the palace.

Sariva swallowed while prodding a half-eaten orange slice with her fork. "What was that all about? Vered acted so strangely. Did I mess up your magic?"

He groaned and ran a hand through his thinning hair. "The spell's almost perfect. Like I said, it runs on their own energy, but a sudden shock can disturb the balance. Even though renewing the enchantment doesn't tire me, it's a complex process."

A way to break the spell—to free her allies! She felt dizzy with hope.

"But we'll still be able to have them at my wedding, right? I'd assume you'd be able to keep things peaceful with all the guards you hired, plus it will send the right message to those who don't support us yet."

He puffed up, taking it as a challenge. "Of course! Protestors and outsiders won't be able to create a disturbance. I'm sure of it."

But what if the disturbance comes from me? She could do something surprising with her wedding dress, perhaps alter it to reveal another gown underneath, and have a speech prepared in the chaos. Though no genius or warrior, she knew how to modify a dress.

★

Early the next day, Delvar took her on a carriage ride into the city. Some streets appeared peaceful, but others had been attacked by the guards: empty storefronts, broken windows, and boarded-up doors. On a few corners, people had set up tributes to the missing or dead with pillar candles, fabric flowers, cards and leaves, and even, in one case, a battered teddy bear.

Delvar hurried her past that one, telling her, "The protestors are just trying to manipulate the narrative by highlighting the bystanders who deserve sympathy. Besides, we have a fundraising brunch to attend."

She signed autographs and tried on tiaras. They ate little flower-shaped pastries at an airy café. Could she leave a note on the bill begging for help? No, of course Delvar would pay for their food. And even if she snuck away to the privy and wrote a letter home on the wastepaper, doubtlessly he had agents watching her family. She'd have to stick to the dress scheme and hope it worked.

Smiling and nodding, even when she wanted to scream and throw her drink in some old bigot's face, got her through the morning and afternoon. Finally, they rode back to the palace. She expected the worst to be over, at least for the time being.

As they passed the river, Delvar took her hand. "Look out the window, Sariva."

She expected to see the old palace cordoned off, maybe a team of wizards marching through the rubble, burning ghosts to nothingness. Instead, as their carriage ran along the riverbank, two of Delvar's new guards hoisted a limp form out of the river. A person? No, a corpse from the way its head and arms dangled.

"Stop the carriage," Delvar told the driver. He rolled down the window on his side and called out, "How'd it work, Jax?"

Sariva turned her attention to her hands, her fingers flexing so her nail polish sparkled. Why would Delvar show her such a morbid scene? She wouldn't ogle some poor corpse.

The guard lowered the body's legs to the ground and hurried over, long strides over the stone pathway. "Just as you said. We suspect she tried cutting through the wire with some debris, but once your illusion spell took hold, all the fight went out of her."

A faint smile crossed Delvar's thin lips. "I wonder what she wanted? I suppose we'll never know."

Sariva dug her fingernails into her palm. "What's this? Who was she?" Part of her knew already, a gnawing, hollow feeling below her ribs, yet still, she prayed. *Goddess, let me be wrong. Let her be safe.*

"I forgot to tell you, but you're safe now. No one will force you to do anything you don't want to," Delvar said. And to the guard, "Show my lady. Hold up its head."

The guard gripped a hunk of the corpse's sodden curls and hauled its gaunt form to full height. River water darkened red hair to chestnut, and a pale, bloated face stared unblinkingly.

Edwynne had gone to her death to prove Sariva's innocence.

Sariva wanted to scream, but noise died in her locked-up throat. She couldn't even swallow.

"Now you're safe," Delvar repeated.

"I understand. I've just never seen a dead body before." Her voice shook. People didn't die like that in books: swollen limbs stiff and floppy at the same time, patches painting their skin like bruises, pink foam trickling from their eyes and nose.

She wanted to run to Edwynne, hold her, bite anyone who moved to take her away. She wanted to scream.

If only Edwynne were here to slap her across the face. "Get it together," she'd whisper harshly. "Going into hysterics like a little girl will only make things worse."

Sariva took a deep breath, tearing her gaze away from the corpse. She couldn't go into hysterics. She had to stay calm and at least try to kill Delvar. But how was that possible if even the Queensguard couldn't overcome his forces, if even Edwynne hadn't survived to fight another day?

She spent the rest of the day lying on her bed. "I'm so sorry, I've got a migrane," she groaned when Delvar came to invite her to dinner.

He fetched a healing enchantment, which she gratefully accepted before pouring down the sink.

Whether she curled up beneath the covers and prayed for sleep to take her or stared at the ceiling until her eyes watered, she envisioned the pale, puffy corpse of a formerly vibrant woman. The half-assembled dress stood like a headless ghost at the end of the room. It wouldn't leave Sariva alone either. Did she even have a chance with this absurd scheme?

"Does it matter if I have a chance?" she murmured.

But as a follower of the Goddess, she had a responsibility, and it would feel unbearable to watch Delvar obtain power, knowing she hadn't even attempted to stop him.

Even if she didn't stand a chance, she could still try. Making an attempt would certainly feel better than just waiting for the inevitable. She got out of bed, went to her sewing kit, and threaded a needle. She'd throw herself into the project, making neat stitches and combining fabrics until her hands went numb with pain. Perhaps she lacked hope, but stubbornness? Pettiness? Spite?

She could still manage those.

Chapter Thirteen

Magical interrogation, Edwynne knew, was as dangerous as dueling a dragon. Some people died right away. They'd start jittering and blood would pour from their nose, and within moments, their eyes were as dead as a doll's, and they never spoke another word. It was why mage trainees were watched carefully and why the Queensguard squires had never seen it demonstrated. What was he doing to her? She only knew that her skull clenched like a vise as strange lights flickered.

Delvar let go. Edwynne's head slammed against the padded restraints; for a moment, her vision went black. After the vivid recollection, the dungeon seemed even dimmer and colder. She snatched a breath. Risked another. Her chest felt unbearably tight.

What has he uncovered? Her thoughts swam.

"Write that down, will you?" Delvar asked, turning to his apprentice. "I've gotten a lot of information I can use against the Queensguard should they try to unseat me and fail. Knights aren't so different from ordinary men after all."

Edwynne squeezed her eyes shut, holding her breath until she could trust herself to exhale normally. That was the first betrayal: her mind's need to survive. His power had pinned her against the walls of her soul. When she could have shattered, she yielded instead, giving in a breath before extinction.

Except this was a duel, just like any other. She imagined constructing a siege tower of unimportant moments, arming it with boredom and irrelevance.

On the outside, she gasped for air, writhed in her chains. Her gaze took in the walls and the looming faces, everything shrinking and growing like a warped reflection.

The wizard's apprentice leaned forward on his stool. Without conscious thought, she could read his face and bearing: a weedy worm eager to avenge his low status through the suffering of a powerful girl. He wanted to see blood. Not just the trickle dripping from her nose and oozing down her lips; he wanted to see her flayed alive in her own mind, begging for a release from pain.

And Delvar...

She could examine a whole battle with a glance, cataloguing enemies and allies in a flash of impression. His sharp face seemed composed in grim austerity.

He just wanted to win.

Except he wouldn't. Not while she lived.

Her whole body tensed. She gathered jagged shards of breath, readying herself for whatever assault might strike next. "If you've so much as touched Sariva, I swear to the stars—"

"Let me guess, you want her for yourself? How pathetic." The apprentice loomed his face closer. "You're just an unwashed brat with ambitions above her station.

There's no way a beautiful woman would be interested in someone like you."

Gritting her teeth, she refused to reply. Her silence seemed to anger him.

"Did you hear me? I know you're stupid, not deaf! Well, girl? What do you think?"

The moment his face came too close, she was ready. Her teeth snapped. She bit down on his nose. Wild jackals bringing down earthquake-heavy prey could not have gripped with stronger jaws. Magic scythed through her body.

If there's no trained healer, if there's no time to dull the pain, squires learned to bite down on a rag and breathe. She tried to breathe.

Pressure shoved into her stomach and knocked the air from her body. Her mouth fell open, and she struggled not to gag.

"Master Delvar, I want her dead." The apprentice pressed a handkerchief to his nose, and his voice was nasal and furious with startled tears. "I want her dead now!" He stomped his foot.

Delvar glanced at her. She flinched, expecting instant pain. Instead, he studied her, his cold regard as subtle as smoke.

Edwynne didn't blink.

Delvar turned away abruptly and stalked across the room. With quick, efficient movements, he gathered up his tools for scrying. "She's of no further use to us. I may as well figure out a way to dispose of her."

★

In the hours before dawn, a cart rattled through the streets. Edwynne sat in the back like a parcel. When she struggled, the wire binding her limbs made her bleed. Delvar had wrapped her up, chuckled at her anger, and watched as some guards loaded her into a cart.

She managed to spit out her gag. "Where are you taking me?"

"We'll be there soon enough," one guard said before taking a swig from his flask. Another chuckled darkly.

"Hey, Delvar, are you going to tell me anything?"

He sat in the front of the cart, facing forward, and didn't seem to notice her. One of the guards reached back and cracked her across the jaw with a meaty hand.

Fine, she wouldn't ask questions. He couldn't be planning to leave her out for wild beasts, right? Nothing big came this close to the city.

At last, they reached the river, and she began to realize his plan. The recent rains had swelled the banks, sweeping objects like fallen trees and roof shingles downstream on the current. Even a strong swimmer might get caught up in debris and drown. The barbed wire tying her hands meant she didn't stand a chance.

The cart stopped with a sudden jerk. The wire pulled taut, and she held in a scream.

"There," the first guard said. "That ought to do for you."

Then the magical net tightened around her. Her own desperate breathing filled her ears. The sharp strands wrapped so tightly around her that her chest had no room to expand. She struggled, trying to bring up her hands; her knuckles smarted and bled.

"Any last words?"

A desperate fizzy haze filled her mind. Angry people made mistakes, she remembered Stellan telling her. Angry people made mistakes—

The wire was right against her face. She pretended she was trying to gnaw through it. Instead, she sliced the tip of her tongue and spat a nice messy mouthful of blood right into his face.

His contempt turned to rage in the pale dawn light. "I thought I'd be merciful and kill you quickly, but the plan's changed."

"Where should we put her?" a guard asked.

"Under the pier, on the riverbank. She'll drown once the water rises."

The guards hauled Edywnne out of the cart; the more she thrashed, the tighter the net dug into her skin.

"Who knows," Delvar added, his tone contemplative, "she may live long enough to hear the cheering crowds. It'll certainly give me something to smile about during the wedding." With a flick of his fingers, the ends of the net wrapped around one of the wooden poles.

He left her there, left her hating him, the force of her hatred pouring from her tearless eyes as he sauntered off merrily.

Drowning is more of a threat than the cold. The instant she submerged, her body pleaded for air. Except she knew how to swim, knew how to wait. She held her breath until her sharp cocoon bobbed to the surface again.

First test passed. She wanted to savor her victory by laughing or smiling, but she saved her air, knowing she'd need it.

Edwynne could have been severed from her body in an instant at any point during their journey. Instead she was spider-wrapped to the decaying timbers of an abandoned dock. Time dripped past. If she took the stingiest gulps of humid air, she could steal a few more moments of life even though no one had passed by in the pale light of the morning.

A dream called to her, soft and sweet.

"Elyanit. Our Elya, our little girl. Wake up, darling."

Brightly colored images danced before her eyes.

In a Northern temple, sun shone through stained-glass windows, coloring a grand white marble statue of the abstracted Goddess. A man with laughing eyes and a graying beard draped a green-and-silver prayer shawl around her shoulders. "Your coming-of-age ceremony, Elya! I'm so proud of you." His gaze held the same honey-brown light as hers. Could this be her father?

Then the scene changed.

She stood in a small, cozy kitchen much like Vered's. A woman with wild red hair, just like her own, held a mixing bowl, floury handprints on her apron. Drawings made by young children in school adorned the walls. "Eldest daughter, it's time I show you how to make Grandmother's tabernacle cake. Our guests will be here soon for the holiday."

"The guests?" Edwynne—Elyanit—blinked at her mother.

She laughed, shaking out her curls. "Of course! Don't you remember? Your aunts and uncles and cousins, and your friends from temple, and even your girlfriend."

She showed Elyanit how to measure the ingredients with her fingers and mix the batter until all the lumps came out. Generations before her had cooked the old family recipe, no matter what country they lived in, and they sang old songs together, laughing when they forgot the words.

The warm kitchen seemed hardly large enough for them both, especially when Elyanit's youngest siblings, the five-year-old fraternal twins, rushed in. "Elya! Mommy!" the little girl squealed, hugging her around the legs. "Are you making cake?"

The boy, gangly and freckled, stood on his tiptoes. He tried to dip his finger into the bowl, aiming to sneak a lick of the batter.

Her chest tightened. Maybe from emotions. Why couldn't she catch a full breath?

"Not yet, darling," Mother told him. "The guests will be here soon."

And soon, Elyanit's younger siblings came home from school. They rushed through the front door, laughing and jostling, shoving back and forth, before they opened their book bags to show pictures they'd drawn and assignments they'd turned in. Then came her grandparents, smiling down at her. "You look just like your mother, darling," her grandmother said. "You're beautiful just like I was at your age."

Her grandfather ruffled her hair. "Let's finish our strategy game. I'm so proud to have such a clever granddaughter."

Elyanit's head spun as she stumbled in front of the open door. She gasped, but breath eluded her.

Her friends from temple hurried in and surrounded her. "Elya, it's so good to see you! Are you okay?"

Vision blurring, she glanced from one face to the next. Didn't her mother say her girlfriend would arrive soon? "Where is she?"

One friend put her hand to Elyanit's forehead. "You're so pale. Maybe you should go upstairs and lie down for a little. We can start prayers and do our festival skit after you've gotten some rest."

Her mother nodded. "Once you feel better, you can put on the prayer shawl your grandmother made for you and your heirloom necklace. We wouldn't dream of excluding you. I need an ally when it comes to not laughing at your father's ridiculous jokes."

Elyanit blinked. She'd heard that before. Who'd mentioned a father trying to be funny on a holiday? Black eyes. Soft curls. A solemn round face.

Sariva.

Sariva, who'd been captured by the evil wizard. Who was counting on a knight to save her.

She stared into the faces of her loving family. The parents who'd always treasured her, the grandparents who'd joyfully passed down her traditions, the younger siblings who idealized her. Her home, her place in the world. Everything tragedy had stolen from her. Everything she'd ever wanted. But Delvar had spun this illusion, perilous as anything in the catacombs, and she couldn't stay as her air ran out. She couldn't live in dreams of what might have been. She tried to memorize her mother's face, taking in every freckle, every line. "I'm sorry, everyone. But this isn't real."

Edwynne strained against the magical wires and broke the surface, gasping for air. Cold water weighted her limbs, replacing the warmth of the kitchen. Wet rags clung to her clammy skin as her empty stomach clenched. Hot tears poured down her face to mingle with the river water flowing just below her nose. Even without her birth family, she had people who loved her, people to live for. Stellan had been willing to sacrifice himself so she could escape. Tolliver too. Vered and the others doted on her, Mattie admired her, and she'd never find out if Sariva truly loved her if she died today. Maybe she lacked the ready-made community some people were born with, but she'd made her own.

She would protect the people she loved. Or die for them. It felt worthwhile either way.

A pulse of tide sent her nose under the current. She held her breath until it passed. The feeling of iron bands encircled her chest.

"-wynne?"

Were people searching for her, calling her name? If only she could see their identities. Getting their attention would be risky. If they weren't interested in rescuing her, she would be wasting her air, shortening her life. But letting herself relinquish hope meant even more certain death. Maybe the chance of success was slimmer than a fingernail, but she had to keep trying, even as the current roiled around her. She was a Queensguard squire with the good fight in her bones. She tensed her muscles and pushed against the string. "Help! Help! I'm trapped down here!"

Footsteps rushed toward her; people shouted. Someone pulled on the string as if reeling in a fish, moving her closer to the shore.

"Don't panic," a familiar voice told her when her ears were above the water. "Try to hold your breath, all right? I wish you wouldn't keep getting into scrapes like this!"

As Tolliver hauled her out of the water, she bit her tongue to muffle a scream. The wire's sharp edges bit into her skin, pointed barbs piercing through her unprotected forearms and legs. When at last she was on solid ground, the pressure barely let up. Even breathing hurt. It was as if she'd tumbled into a field of cacti.

"Right, I'm just going to figure out how to untangle you." He clumsily pulled on something. Acting by instinct, she tried to thrash away. A sharp point scraped her face. She smelled blood.

"Squire Dovecote, hold your position." She'd heard that voice, those words, so many times while crouching in a grove of olive trees, surrounded by the scent of goats and rain, waiting for bandits to crunch by on the gravel road. Pausing before a stone passageway as a scout crept into the red rock to figure out if the noise up ahead had been made by a wild beast or just a lost cat. And training exercises. Always training exercises.

Edwynne lifted her head from the cobblestones. "Stellan..."

A raw scab covered his snub nose, and he knelt, favoring his right leg. But he was alive. He brushed her hand through a gap in the net. "You're going to be all right, Edwynne. Tolliver, don't try to pull the net off all at once; it's tangled with her hair and clothes, so let's cut the wires we can see before doing anything."

Stellan explained how he'd used his superior reflexes to surprise and overpower the other knights, how he'd snuck into the city and met up with Tolliver and the other knights still loyal to the queen. She watched his open, friendly face and the glints of gold in his dark eyes as he talked, the way his rough hands gestured in excitement. Elyanit, raised only by her biological family, would never have met Stellan. She almost pitied that other version of herself. The instant Tolliver finished cutting the wires, she fell into her brother's arms, breathing him in.

He exhaled against the impact and tousled her soaked curls. "Glad you're alive too."

"Come on, you need to eat something," Tolliver told her.

"Want wine," she mumbled.

"No, not wine. Food." He prodded spoonfuls of date paste and crumbled bits of cliff-berry biscuit between her lips.

For a moment, with her best friend looking after her and her brother's arm around her shoulders, everything seemed all right. She shook her shivering limbs and rubbed her fingers to make sure she could still feel. "What have I missed?"

"They arrested loads of people during the raid, but no one who knew what was going on. The wizard's furious, of course. We're holed up at a nearby tavern; it's not the sort of place guards would dare go. Everyone will be happy to see you. Can you walk?" Tolliver asked.

"I can stumble."

Tolliver patted her on the back. "Right. If we see anyone we don't recognize, say something drunk and pretend you're about to throw up in the gutter."

At thirteen, she'd shot up like a mint plant, which made her as tall as Stellan. Normally, she found this hilarious. Now she wished she was still small enough for him to carry her easily, the way he did with Mattie, because the exhaustion only worsened her shivers.

After she slung her arms over their shoulders, Edwynne lurched along. If only Sariva had been able to escape and come with them! A hug from Sariva would get the chill out of her limbs, and Sariva would no doubt have brought something luxurious to the search party like hot chocolate or an embroidered shawl. Edwynne would murder a mug of sweet chocolate in one greedy swill and bury her face into the lilac-scented weave.

"How's Sariva? Has she been rescued?"

Her mentor and her friend seemed unsure who should speak. Finally, Tolliver said, "She's joined forces with the wizard. She rode through the streets with him, smiling and waving, while his private army beat protestors to the ground, and she's going to marry him. They even signed press releases together."

There was no way Sariva's gambit could have evolved into such an all-encompassing, genuine something. "But I know she's planning to betray him. We made eye contact about it."

Tolliver squinched his face up, clearly puzzled. "You what?"

"I can tell what she's thinking sometimes. And it was my idea to pretend that I was responsible for everything. She wouldn't betray me, I know it." Perhaps it sounded foolish out loud, but Edwynne still believed.

"Sure. She's just pretending to advocate for laws making it illegal to criticize the North. She just pretended to authorize your execution. Face it, Edwynne, your taste in women has failed you again."

As they headed away from the river in the cold light of dawn, her brother and best friend half carrying her, Edwynne stayed silent.

"Right, we're here at last."

Everyone knew a sailor had died in a brawl at the Wayward Caravan, and they brewed the wine in a barrel on the roof. But when you were doing disreputable deeds, it came in handy to have disreputable allies.

"Where's Vered?" Edwynne asked, searching the dark, smoky tavern. "Where's everyone?" She recognized only a couple friends from the university or the artists' quarter.

Stellan thinned his mouth into a frown. "There was a protest at the queen's abdication ceremony, and a lot of people were captured. Seemed like a horrible situation, according to those who'd escaped."

Would her friends face death too? She needed to act.

One of the queen's ministers stood on a table giving a speech.

"But is it ethical for us to rise up in open rebellion against a leader?" another interrupted. "I mean, Queen Oradel made a speech handing over her authority to him, and the Magic Mirror shows he has the same amount of support as her. Even if his beliefs are wrong, he's followed all the rules."

"He only got magically appointed because he half killed the queen," Edwynne said loudly. Everyone turned to stare at her, and that only solidified her determination. "She stuffed her soul into some gemstones for safety, and he's wearing them like a necklace. Just thinking about it makes me sick."

"You mean the Magic Mirror didn't choose him, and neither did a majority of the people?" the first minister asked.

Edwynne scowled at the ridiculous suggestion. "Of course not. I think I'm the only one who knows what really happened." She ended up sitting on a knife-nicked table in the cheap riverside tavern, sipping cold mulled wine and telling the story of the past month. She could have spun it as a tale of her own knightly heroism. But she wasn't a storyteller, and any inflation of already wild events would probably come off as false. Instead, she tried to remember as many specific facts as possible and speak calmly without varnishing the truth, the way Sariva doubtlessly would.

At last, the politicians sat back with grim frowns. "So he's controlling the queen like a magical puppet? That would explain a great deal of things," one murmured.

The other hit the table. "Damn. I knew something seemed off about that resignation speech."

Edwynne nodded. "The queen's whole plan was to stop him from doing that, but she didn't count on the number of backup plans he had."

"Look what I found," Vered's friend Nyssa said, leading an unexpected guest. Mattie clung to the woman's hand.

Stellan ran up to her and hugged her. "What are you doing here, little one?"

She shook her head. "The wizard wanted to swap me for ransom money, and he's got Ava chained up in the dungeons, but I took some jewelry from the false bottom in my trunk and bribed a servant to sneak me out within a load of guests' laundry. Ava said if I ever found myself in trouble, I should go to the Queensguard."

Stellan nodded. "All right. Things could be worse. Hopefully, he plans to ransom Ava as well or at least use her as leverage, especially now that you're out of his grasp."

"Will Ava be all right?"

"She's brave and clever, just like you."

It wasn't a yes, but perhaps Ava was stronger and more resilient than Edwynne had expected.

"Anyway, if he was willing to use subterfuge and paperwork like any normal politician," continued the minister, "I'd probably say we shouldn't kill him. But he's willing to murder to attain his ends. People with so much magic, let alone so much ego, make awful rulers. He'll probably kill anyone who questions his rule. I say we save the queen and get rid of him before he goes after us."

Edwynne couldn't agree more. "And even though he's chosen the weapons, we still ought to fight."

With that, the conversation turned to battle plans.

"When a guard comes around, I'll ask if they want extra flavoring or a new flavor, and those jugs will be spiked. Poison, a sleeping powder, whatever I can get," said a woman who sold drinks on the street.

"I'll offer to dance for them, a veil-removing dance. In honor of the coronation," a dancer from the docks said. Their feet were tapping under the table, already thinking of a melody. "Then I'll sort of poke them with my hairpin. It's drugged too."

Edwynne nudged them. "Make sure you don't stab yourself!"

"What can I do?" one boy asked.

Stellan leaned down and regarded him. "Well, what's your task?"

He fidgeted. "I wash the guards' breeches. Nothing important."

"That's something," Edwynne said. "An army can't fight naked. You could make the clothes uncomfortable or make them smaller—"

He beamed up at her. "Stars, that's brilliant!"

The knights and squires suggested ideas so everyone could contribute. Although it was still early in the day, several students ordered big glasses of pomegranate wine and toasted each idea.

But people wondered if they could really succeed.

"So, they'll use dust-spell vapor? Oh stars, people have died from inhaling it," she overheard a woman say, her voice shaking with nerves.

Across the room, the students were drinking more and more with each toast. "To not having to present our masterworks if we die at the guards' hands," a skinny youth cried out, raising their cup. A boy laughed in grim agreement and touched his own glass to theirs. At the next table, one knight was polishing the same patch of breastplate repeatedly, his face expressionless.

"Shopkeepers, street performers, artists, university students, and half the Queensguard. Against most of the city militia plus mercenaries." Tolliver, sliding in next to her, sounded morose. "Edwynne, I'm positive we've studied battles with worse odds, but I can't remember them."

"Well, we're prepared to risk our lives, and they're just in it for the pay, right?" In the North, they dunked converts in the freezing ocean. Being able to die for a cause meant being able to live for it.

"Most of them genuinely support Delvar, aside from being well trained and well armed."

Edwynne shook her head while touching the enchanted sword Stellan had reunited her with. "People will be on our side. They're just too scared to make the first move."

Tolliver shifted in his seat. "And if no one joins us? Delvar's always been shitty to people from abroad, but people say he's done some good things for the academies."

"Some of them will. And maybe that's all we need." She leaned in, elbows on the table. "Don't people always read about the Mage Wars and wish they could have done something to save Amaldia's life or that they could have stopped the Deepwitch before she killed off the royals of two countries and started so much bloodshed?"

Tolliver just shrugged.

She poked him. "We absolutely used to play at rescuing the last of the ancient queens from the Slaughter Banquet."

"But that was kid stuff."

Edwynne kept going. She didn't believe him. "So many people want to be heroes. They want to be able to say they changed the world for the better. That's what we're offering. Don't you think we'll get at least a few takers?"

"Maybe," he said unconvincingly.

Stellan, at the other end of the table, sighed and rested his head on his hands. "Maybe I shouldn't be doing this," he mumbled to a fellow knight. "I mean, we're out-numbered with so many comrades locked up. He's proba-bly mind-controlled some of them like he did me. Do we even have a chance?"

Did he really mean that? They couldn't just give up. She jumped to her feet. "Hey, Stellan."

He raised his head. "Yes?"

"How does the wizard Delvar turn a doorknob?"

"I don't know."

"He holds it and waits for the world to revolve around him."

A few people laughed, but many seemed confused.

Maybe she should have just let the matter drop.

Then Tolliver stood. "What's the difference between the wizard Delvar and a public privy?" He didn't wait for a response. "One of them is disgusting and you don't want to go near it, and the other one is a public privy."

This time more guests got the joke, even a few of the knights.

Stellan slammed his fist on the table. "Stars curse it, these kids have a point. We can't act like we've already lost."

Another knight clapped him on the shoulder. "And it means we should hold fast to hope. We have the stars on our side—"

"And the Northern Goddess," Edwynne added firmly. Maybe Sariva prayed for them at this very moment.

"Right. That's more than enough to celebrate." He raised his sword. "Win or lose, we'll show the world that the people of Almesia won't just roll over for a tyrant, and that's worth a toast!"

Those who could do so toasted, even with water; those without anything raised their fists and slammed them on the table.

It amazed Edwynne how the mood had turned from funeral to festival.

Someone went to a nearby shop and bought pistachio marzipan, candied pink dragonfruit, and sticky honey pastry. The bartender pulled a special bottle of pineapple wine from a hidden cabinet as people sang old revolutionary songs. If one voice faltered into frightened sobs, another would take up and strengthen the tune. And Edwynne, Tolliver, and Nyssa made sure everyone had enough to eat.

She'd struck a match in a dark dungeon and discovered a room full of candles waiting to be lit.

Chapter Fourteen

A bevy of twittering maids dragged Sariva out of bed when the sun was just venturing past the horizon. Slender hands hauled her upright and removed her nightgown.

Sariva stood as still as a doll, watching the girl in the mirror transform from bedraggled sleeper to bride-to-be. She shivered with exhaustion.

"Arms up," one of the new maids told her, and "Turn your head," and so forth.

Compliance came easily. They piled layers of clothing on her body: undergarments, corset (stifling) and petticoat (enormous), and finally, the rustling sculpture of her gown. The weight of shimmering damask weighed her down even more.

People manipulated her doll-like body as she watched from afar, putting her into a carraige and pulling it through the streets. She remembered waving although layers of snow seemed to insulate her body from the rain and the warm summer breeze. Her wedding would take place on a custom-built stage in one of the city's largest plazas with a boutique commandeered to serve as staging area.

Delvar pushed open the double doors without even a gesture. Around his neck were the three gems of the sleeping queen's soul: soft pink, bold yellow, and magnetic blue, surrounded by a buzz of static, presumably signifying a protection enchantment. He squeezed her shoulder. "My beautiful bride. Shall we go see our people?"

Anger pierced the dull cloud around her mind. His people? When he hated so many of them and had beat many into compliance with his guards and spells? Absolutely not. For Edwynne's sake, for everyone's sake, she had to at least attempt disrupting his plans.

If she enraged Delvar and then failed to escape him, if her failure led to a mysterious death from unknown causes on her wedding night, at least people would know who killed her. Maybe it would inspire them.

Besides, a tragic heroine rarely survived.

Edwynne kept touching the brim of her velvet cap to make sure it was pulled far enough over her eyes, the enchanted sword concealed at her hip under her tunic. Many former Queensguard members and assorted rebels in similar disguises were scattered around the crowd. Hopefully, the newly hired guards wouldn't expect attacks from such a well-disciplined force.

The guards' presence was thicker than they'd anticipated. Who knew he'd hired this many mercenaries off the books?

Many of the city's prominent citizens had been bribed or intimidated into making long-winded speeches. One merchant clasped his skeletal hands atop the podium.

"The truth is, no man has stood up against foreign influence the way Delvar has. And this man and this woman are proof that anyone can rise from humble beginnings to serve their country!"

He bowed, and Sariva glided forward. Even from a distance, Edwynne could tell gemstones and beads coated the silky fabric of her glittering dress. The crowd went wild with applause at her dreamy appearance. Delvar, seemingly irritated she was getting more applause than he had, scowled, and the clapping died down.

Is Sariva really going to marry this man, legitimize his rule just to survive? Lies like these tear my heart. I want to skewer her vows on the point of my sword.

Today, Delvar wore indigo robes embroidered in gold sigils. He, too, made a speech.

Edwynne glanced at Stellan. "The people sitting in front of the stage look unarmed. They might flee. We could cut them down if they don't."

Stellan shook his head, his expression tight. "Out of the question."

"Why?" But then she saw why.

The temple priest hired to perform the ceremony ascended the platform. His glazed expression showed that he, too, was under an enchantment. Sariva felt more alone than ever, but at least she wouldn't die alone. She felt the silent throng's regard.

In a roped-off section below the platform, the city's activists sat in neat rows, unblinking.

One of the head guards hurried up to Delvar. "My lord, there's been a problem. Our scouts who are watching the crowd think there might be some Queensguard operatives scattered amongst the guests. No one high ranking, but they might pose a threat."

Sariva caught her breath. The Queensguard. Edwynne's teachers. Stellan's friends. She hadn't hoped they would help her, but she'd kept working, not because she thought she stood a chance but because it was her duty to try. Her stubborn refusal to give up had paid off.

Delvar dismissed the guard. "They won't." He went to the edge of the stage and dropped the spell in an amplified voice. Only the people seated nearby could hear when he said, "Followers, I need you to protect me. Do as you were instructed."

The ensorcelled people got up from their chairs. Some pulled batons or swords from under the seats while others drew daggers from their clothing, and they formed neat rows in front of the platform. Vered limped behind the rest with a stumble as she took her place in line.

Delvar seemed satisfied. "All right. Take my hand as we practiced."

The temple priest started a droning chant as they glided forward.

One step, then two, and she ripped away from Delvar's grasp to pull the hidden string in the bodice of her dress. Sariva twirled, swift and graceful. As she spun, a new garment unfolded over the old. It swallowed up her fine wedding dress as if the fancy gown had never existed. Her skirts shaded to the colors of the Northern and Almesian flags in faded tatters. Two indigo handprints sparkling with gold, the color of Delvar's robes, stood out on her waist. She wore a sash of white fabric flowers that seemed wilted.

Dressed like the flag but bearing Delvar's mark. The message was clear. *This is what Delvar has done to me. This is what he may do to all of us.*

A ripple went through the lines in front of the stage as people lowered their weapons and exchanged confused murmurs.

Delvar grabbed her arm hard enough to bruise. "Why are you doing this? I can protect you. I can protect your people."

Armed men had emerged to fight Delvar's guards. If she could distract him, keep him from renewing the spell on his human shield, they stood a chance. "What makes you think we can't protect ourselves?" she shot back.

"Well, historically—"

"Things haven't been great for us. I know." After all, the North had functioned as a refuge at first. "But when someone tries to snuff us out, we make them fight for every drop of blood."

"You have more in common with someone like me than with the Plains folk or the Islanders. You're highly educated. I'm your natural ally." As he regained his affronted dignity, his hands swirled in spellcasting motions.

What would Edwynne say to goad him? The words came easily. "My parents came to this country broke as shit. Your people have been here so long you're just Almesian. I don't think we have much in common after all."

Exasperation broke his focus. "Sariva, darling—"

"You plan to assault me from the back because my nose is an eyesore and then call me darling? You're a fucking coward. Go eat a knife." Edwynne had first provoked her into saying swear words. Now, she loved the way they tasted in her mouth.

Delvar opened his mouth, affronted, and the guards faltered as their battle lines broke. Activists, Queensguard soldiers, and even ordinary people wielding improvised weapons like heavy book bags and canned fruit swarmed them from all directions.

"If this isn't your fight, go home," a Queensguard soldier yelled.

An Islander woman laughed. "If that rich Northern bitch in her fancy ball gown is staying to die with us, seems like it's everyone's fight."

Being called a rich bitch didn't delight her. But the sight of people taking up arms and defending themselves against Delvar's mercenaries, side by side with Northern students from the university, thrilled her, and she had nothing to lose by setting the record straight.

She shouted from the platform, trusting the amplifying spell to pick up her words, "I'm not rich. My family's house is falling into a swamp, and we can't pay doctors. I made this dress myself!"

The Islander woman gave her an approving nod. "Nice work, bitch with no money. Can you make me one?"

"Maybe! If we both live!"

Meanwhile, Delvar frantically tried to reweave his spell.

"For the queen!" one woman yelled. She wrenched a wooden flagpole from its moorings and hoisted it like a spear.

"For our freedom!" cried a food vendor, raising his skillet.

Delvar made an abrupt gesture and flung something at Sariva. Her legs locked where she stood. A dull cold spread through her body, starting at her rib cage and trickling outward. Her heart fluttered weakly. The chaotic scene blurred. Reaching for her magic, she touched only ice.

A lithe figure armed with a gleaming sword pushed through the melee. Their voice rang out. "Queensguard, to me!" When a guard took a swipe at them, they danced back, cap tumbling from their head. Close-cropped auburn curls shone in the sun.

It couldn't be. Fear and exhaustion had driven her to hallucinate. She wouldn't dare hope.

Another guard lunged, and the figure waited until the last moment before rolling through his legs, coming up to slash at his back. "Hang on, Sariva!" Edwynne called.

Sariva could deny the truth no longer. Edwynne had survived.

Edwynne's blade glinted, a streak of silver light—but the wizard and his followers called up creatures to swarm her. Shadows oozed over the cobblestones like smoke and oil. One accomplice barked a string of harsh syllables. His hand clenched into a claw, and he yanked upwards. Cracks splintered in the earth. A wailing mass of merged ghosts seeped up, carrying the cold air of the catacombs.

Edwynne smirked. She twirled her blade and rushed forward to meet them. The first time Sariva saw her, she'd marveled at her skill. Now she was even stronger and more magnificent.

Sariva wanted to cheer like a wild thing. Even magically frozen, she managed a little squeak.

"Down," Delvar yelled, pointing to Edwynne. Her legs tumbled from under her. She crashed forward, skidding on her palms. The enchanted sword fell from her grip. Its light went dull.

At the wizard's urging, the shadows and ghosts swept forward, driving the knights back. They pressed closer to each other with worried expressions and weapons in defensive positions. Wizards and wraiths alike charged toward Edwynne. She struggled furiously, and her frightened eyes met Sariva's.

She remembered Edwynne's arms around her, Edwynne stroking her hair to check for injuries, Edwynne sprawled smirking and indolent on her bed, and the ice evaporated. Energy fizzed through her body. Her power sprung up like a geyser, dissolving Edwynne's bonds.

Just as one of the ghosts lunged for her, Edwynne rolled out of the way, grabbed the sword, and leapt to her feet. She dispatched the howling creature with a single stroke. Her smirk seemed to say *Who's next?* as she ran toward the assembled wizards and their flunkies.

The effortless speed and agility she'd once demonstrated in the training yard shone even stronger now. She weaved in and out of the monsters, her blade flashing, giving the other knights room to maneuver. A wild grin spread over Sariva's face. "Come on, Ed!"

Edwynne glanced back at her fellow knights and nodded. They charged as one.

Within minutes, many of Delvar's allies had been killed or captured or, if they were sensible, had fled in the direction of some far distant country. Many people who had arrived to see a royal wedding found themselves pressed into service carrying the wounded. Sariva hung back in her impractical gown, searching for Edwynne as Delvar spat curses at her from a few paces away.

"Anyone with some medical knowledge, come over by the food stalls," Stellan yelled. "We'll use these benches to stabilize those who can't safely be removed to a hospital."

On the dais, several knights knelt to bind Delvar's hands. He struggled and swore at them. "It's too late. You may have stopped me from becoming king, but our queen lies on her deathbed still. One good thing will come out of all this, at least. She'll die and take her policies with her before anyone can take the magical barrier around the city down."

Of course, Edwynne looked awful in a shabby salmon velvet suit, too loose at the shoulders and too tight across the chest and thighs, with the breeches rolled up wrong. Her hair drooped in different directions (she'd tried to pin it up under the hat, a lopsided travesty), and a split lip oozed blood onto her bizarrely pointy freckle-spattered chin.

"You," Edwynne bellowed, elbowing people out of the way.

Sariva scrambled down from the platform just in time for Edwynne to collide with her at full speed. She smelled like sweat and leather.

"I thought you were dead," Sariva managed.

Edwynne laughed. She tried to wipe the blood away but only smeared it across her face. "You think you can get rid of me? I'd haunt you if I died."

Their foreheads touched, and their breath mingled. For the first time in ages, Sariva felt thawed. "I know."

"But I saw you," Delvar spat. "They dredged the river for your rotting corpse."

Edwynne regarded him evenly, one sun-warm arm slung over Sariva's shoulders. "Your crossbow-happy guards killed a lot of people. Someone let my brother dye their dead friend's hair and wrap the body with enchanted wire."

And after long enough underwater, one gangly woman might resemble another.

"Right. How do we fix the queen?" a knight asked, leaning beside Delvar.

He laughed. "The spell is stuck, and I'll never help you undo it."

At this, Edwynne lifted her head. "Never? You mean that? Maybe if you begged for your life—" She sprinted across the platform.

Stellan, his concussed reflexes slow, gave a hoarse warning shout at the same time as Edwynne's little knife touched the wizard's throat.

But it was Sariva who gasped at how cold the blade was, who raised a hand to her throat and dropped to her knees with a soft, awful thump.

The wizard laughed. He sounded older, tired. "That magic bracelet isn't just a tracker. You can't lay a finger on me, no matter how much you would like to."

A moment passed between the two girls: Edwynne questioning, and Sariva grim and tight-lipped.

Edwynne smacked him across the face, and Sariva didn't even wince. "Then fix it, get the queen out of the tapestry; you started this whole mess when you thought that colonialism would fix the economy!"

Sariva hoisted up her ragged dress, alight with realization. "What if it goes both ways? The connection. I could draw on his power, circumvent the queen's prohibitions, talk to her as mage to mage."

"It's a terrible idea, and you'd probably die," Delvar said, shaking his head.

If Delvar wanted her to avoid it, she'd throw herself into the plan. "Come on, everyone! We have to get to the queen before it's too late!"

Along with Stellan and Vered, they commandeered a carriage and rushed back to the palace. The Queensguard had managed to fight off the guards stationed there. Wearing their green-and-white uniforms, they flung doors open for the group. They'd also released the political prisoners, including a bedraggled Ava, who flung herself into Stellan's arms. Edwynne didn't even scowl at her.

As they sprinted through the corridors, Edwynne tugged at Sariva's threadbare sleeve. "So, you're really going to send your mind out of your body to search for Queen Oradel? Are you sure about this? I mean, what if you send out the part of your mind that reminds the rest of you to breathe?"

"If that happens, I can just come back, right?"

"Sure." But she didn't sound certain.

When they entered the queen's bedroom, she sat bolt upright in bed, gasping for air.

Sariva had an idea. "Give her the orbs."

Edwynne placed them in her hands. They began to glow, and her breathing calmed. Her closed eyelids moved.

"Can she hear us?" Edwynne asked.

"Of course. They're parts of her soul. Now I just need to find the rest of her," Sariva told everyone.

They'd heard Oradel's voice coming from the tapestry. It stood to reason her missing fragments still lurked within the fabric.

Sariva knelt before the pastoral scene painted and embroidered onto cotton cloth. She took a deep deliberate breath, clasped her hands in her lap, and reached out with her mind. A breeze brushed over her face, carrying the scents of wild roses and fresh-cut herbs. Birds she didn't recognize chirped in the distance. But how could she reach this place in the tapestry? A solid stone wall stood in her way.

All right. If there was no path, she'd make one. "Can someone get my workbag? The one with the wool roving, not the one with the linen squares." To get inside the image, she'd need a door, one she could grasp and open. Embroidery—especially thread painting or satin stitch, especially three-dimensional—would take more time than she wanted to risk. The queen only took shallow breaths while she hardly blinked.

"What color bag is it?" Ava asked.

"I've seen it." Edwynne leapt to her feet and hurried down the corridor.

Sariva decided she'd use the tan and dark brown for the door. She had enough of both left over from past projects. A simple little door like the one on the cottage past the archway of roses should suffice.

Edwynne rushed back. She laid the bag by Sariva. "What are you going to do with wool? Isn't it for, I don't know, spinning into sweaters?"

"No. Needle felting." She found the skein of light-brown roving, ripped off several little pieces, and began to arrange them into the shape of a door. One layer crosswise, another lengthwise, a third across again.

"The tapestry's cotton, and cotton takes wool easily. Then I'll have something I can touch."

Hmm. The wool beneath her hands remained still, inert. No wind brushed across her hand. What had she missed? Maybe she'd try felting it and then enchanting it. Of course she stabbed herself rummaging for the felting tool when the barbed tips caught her skin.

The wool door shifted, taking on the texture of wood grain. "Right, that's a start. Pass me the dark brown?"

"Got it." Edwynne pressed the soft fiber into her injured hand.

She laid down thin lines in dark brown, and the magic pulled at her hair, her clothes. The world lurched under her.

Words came from a long distance away.

"Sariva. Listen to me." Edwynne's voice steadied her. "You can control this."

Sariva nodded. With the sheer force of her will, she pulled the magic under her control, tightening it like the warp on a loom. *I know who I am, and I outrank you.*

She felted on a little ball of wool to serve as a doorknob, then stitched it to the tapestry. With every motion of her needle, the door expanded. It went from the size of her palm to taller than a person, big enough to step through. So she did.

Sariva landed on a path of hard-packed dirt in a summer forest, her workbag slung over her shoulder. She followed the path through the woodland into a clearing where herbs and flowers grew in exuberant bunches around a modest cottage. Gathering clouds hinted at rain on the horizon. She went under the rose archway, four-petaled blossoms fluttering white in the breeze, and up the steps to the cottage. Then she knocked because, even in an illusory magical setting, good manners still applied.

The door swung open and revealed Oradel. She didn't appear as her real-world self but as a young woman barely older than Sariva, a local assistant councilor still.

"How are you? It's so good to have a visitor. I know it's a long walk from the neighboring cottages. My wife's away, and I haven't gone into the village for a few days. I'm running low on beeswax, but it just seems simpler to wait until market day when I have plans with some friends."

Did she perceive this illusion as her real life? Sariva didn't know what to say as Oradel ushered her inside.

"I've got some tisane brewing. The blueberries are from this spring's harvest, and I picked the mint this morning. Would you like a cup?"

As if prompted by her words, the kettle whistled.

"Your wife?" Sariva ventured.

Oradel smiled dreamily. "Yes, Izalena and I have been together for a long time, ever since I decided not to go into politics." She poured the water into two delicate cups and added heaping spoonfuls of dried fruit and herbs. "Now, you seem familiar. Have we met, perhaps in the village? Do you want sugar or honey?"

She'd risk it, perhaps rip the bandage off as well. "My name is Sariva Al-Beroth. I'm a lady-in-waiting at the palace."

A teacup tumbled from Oradel's hands and shattered on the ground. Her dark eyes blazed with fury. "No. I'm not coming back, and I'm not taking up my post. Do you have any idea what a shit place the world is? It's full of hatred. Full of despair. I stop one hurtful law from being passed, and my enemies draft a thousand more. I offer one child food and another school full say they're starving. At least here I can accomplish things. I don't have to step outside to a city full of my failures. I don't want to fight anymore."

A thin thread tugged at Sariva and made her feel unbalanced. She knew something was pulling at her from far away. For a moment, a phantom hand hovered on her shoulder—

Sariva, Delvar's done something! Oradel's having a seizure. Your body's shaking. Where the hell are you?

Laughter, somewhere. Like a jackal in the mountains.

Sariva closed her eyes for a moment. She opened her hands and let go of the thread and the needle she held in the real world.

The world coalesced around her, autumn cool. Rain would come later, the pressure of distant clouds against her skin.

"All right," she said.

"What?"

"All right," Sariva repeated. The floor was solid under her feet. "If you stay, so will I. I'm a lady-in-waiting. I'm supposed to help the queen."

"I expected you to drag me back kicking and screaming. Why are you humoring me?"

"If you want to rest, no one should have to spend all their time fighting, right? Let me help you sweep the floor."

Somewhere, Sariva sensed a thunderstorm. *Beat-flash. Beat-flash.* She counted the pauses. It was moving away as her heartbeat receded. She had promised to remain.

Oradel seemed calmer now. She moved about the cottage while humming a Plains song, and she began chopping ruby beets for soup.

"Izalena—" Sariva started, curious despite herself.

She smiled ruefully. "Has never given any signs she returns my feelings, though I've been pining after her since first year at the university."

Sariva finished picking up the teacup pieces. "Well, that's interesting," she replied, purposefully ambiguous. Perhaps she could tempt Oradel?

She scoffed and chopped the beets harder. "Don't waste your time. On the off chance she might love me, I'd try to persuade her to come here. The outside world is falling apart. Even if I die, I'm done trying and failing to change the world by myself."

Time was running out. How long before she had no body to return to? How could she persuade Oradel the real world was worth fighting for? She needed to think.

A distant voice echoed in her ears. *Sariva, you idiot, what are you doing? Teaching Her Majesty embroidery?*

Edwynne had meant it as a joke. But the more Sariva thought about it, the more it sounded like a plan. Sitting at the kitchen table, she conjured an old project from her workbag, a large embroidery piece she'd been working on with family and friends at home, then spread the fabric out.

"What's that?" Oradel asked with mild disinterest.

"It's a tapestry. Everyone is supposed to do a section."

"It doesn't look like a project you can complete by yourself."

"Sure, so we could say we'll never finish it. We could even tell other people not to waste their time sewing. After all, no one person can complete it, so what's the point?"

"How does the tapestry look if we do that?" Oradel asked.

"Let's find out." Sariva waved a hand to magically manipulate the thread. Some sparse colors crawled over the fabric.

Oradel shook her head. "With all those empty patches, I'm not even sure what the design is supposed to be. Seems like almost everyone slacked off. It reminds me of how many people let Almesia down. They take the easy route instead of supporting what's right, or—even worse than not caring—they're cruel on purpose. It's like instead of sewing their sections of the tapestry, they go in with a pair of scissors."

"So, there's a passage from the books of the Goddess." The familiar words came to her without thought. "*You are not obligated to complete the work, but neither are you obliged to desist from it.'* I like to think of it as meaning"—she wound a piece of string around her fingers, trying to figure out exactly what she meant—"it's not your job to teach people they're supposed to care about others. It's not your job to make sure everyone does their piece of the tapestry or to make up for their failures. You just have to do your part so the people depending on you can manage theirs."

Oradel looked like she was listening.

"What I mean is, it's not up to anyone to fix the whole world. Not even a queen. But maybe you can save one person's world, or a piece of it, and that's what spreads."

Power built in her with every word, magic bright as the moon. She spread her hands over the fabric and let the world change, piece by piece.

Thread crawled over the fabric, sparse patches of undyed muslin filling themselves in.

"Look at that. One stitch at a time, one tiny stitch!" Color spread, trickling out stitch by stich at first, then covering whole swathes in an instant.

The tapestry had seemed blank and hopeless. Now, it became a vibrant world. Blue spread across the sky. Trees reached their leaves out, birds stretched their wings, and bright flowers bloomed.

Only two squares of the picture remained to be stitched. Sariva held out a needle. "Do you want to try?"

The queen took the needle and gazed at it. "I think I get it. Even if our side is doomed to lose, I'm sure as stars not going to let the bastards have an easy victory."

Oradel, skilled in diplomacy, not sewing, had clumsy and overlarge stitches, sometimes even uneven. But they blended beautifully into the pattern. When she stabbed her finger and cursed under her breath and wiped the blood on the cloth, even that seemed to blend.

With practiced movements, Sariva filled in her own square, a Northern wildflower blooming in seemingly forbidding ground, delicate petals adding color to the many-shaded world.

She looked outside again, sensing distant signals from her body. A thunderstorm rumbled like soft heartbeats.

"Right then." Oradel said, rising. She seemed determined and queenly, more mature than ever. "Let's go put up a fight."

They gathered up the tapestry in bright messy folds. Leaving the cottage behind them, they ran into the untamed summer rain and gave all of themselves to the storm.

Sariva awoke as Edwynne pounded on her chest and then tried to blow air into her lungs. "Hey—easy now!" Sariva managed in a weak and raspy voice.

Edwynne breathed out. "Thank the Goddess, you made it."

When Edwynne's lips met hers, she kissed back. For one bright, splendid moment, the world was perfect and theirs.

"She's all right?" someone asked.

"They're both fine," Stellan answered.

Sariva sat up. Her body ached as if every limb had fallen asleep, and her head swam as if she had heatstroke. But she didn't miss the warning expression Stellan gave

Edwynne, its meaning clear: *Stay away from the engaged noble.*

Magic breathed within the room. Oradel's hands rested atop the covers, folded and still.

Then her fingers spread as if searching for something. A humming sound emanated from the gems; with a whoosh of wind, they dissolved into her body. She inhaled. For a moment she seemed like an ordinary woman. It was at that moment she lifted her head and became the queen again, her calm stare fixing everyone in turn. Her gaze stopped. "Delvar. Why did you do this?"

"You were supposed to be dead. Don't you know what a wreck this country is?" He seemed on the verge of tears.

There was no weakness in her voice as it lifted. "We will begin as we intend to go on. I told you I would have no part of your plan—"

Rage twisted his expression. "Small-minded obsessive fool! I know you. You despise the greater good—"

"As you disregard everything but yourself. Which one of us has done more to improve the lives of citizens?" Her tone was pure steel. "To that end...Delvar, I hoped you could pull yourself from this downward path. Now, I realized I should have forced you to obtain help long ago." She stood tall and sketched a magical symbol in the air. "I shall summon your colleagues from the Isle of Wizards." The effort exhausted her, and she slumped against the bed, her new strength clearly waning.

Sariva watched the light through half-closed eyes. A door opened in the air itself, allowing a trio in shimmering robes to glide through.

"Delvar," said the first mage, a tiny dark-haired woman in a saffron robe. "You are under arrest for twisting magic to your own ends, ripping through the minds of others, and attempted murder, as well as umpteen acts of petty selfishness and cruelty."

"Will you execute him?" the queen asked, weary.

The second mage, a youth in violet, looked up from binding Delvar's arms with a system of complicated knots. "Do you order us to?"

The queen shook her head. "If you can place him somewhere he can do no harm...I'd prefer that. I'm selfish. He was an ordinary man once, right?"

"Do you believe that?" asked the woman in saffron.

"I don't know. But I'd like to think no one is born irredeemably cruel."

The third mage, a bald man with skin like stone, nodded. "If only he had been content with an ordinary life."

"I'll kill you. I'll kill you all, you pathetic know-nothing fools with your exaggerated—"

The woman in saffron placed a hand on his head. "Shhh."

Rage seemed to dim from his eyes, and he blinked in confusion. "Who are you? I knew you once."

"It matters not. Come, my colleagues and I are here to ask your opinion on matters of finance."

The woman wove a low keening melody, minor key shimmering; the other two supported her, building rhythm and a deeper tune. They stepped through the door. It closed behind them.

Sariva tried to curtsy sitting down. "Milady—I mean, Your Highness—might I help you with anything? Would you like some hibiscus tea, a persimmon, any help signing paperwork or stuffing envelopes?"

Oradel smiled. "No, thank you. But I could do with some food, and it would be a pleasure to finally tell you everything that needs to be told."

Sariva stood, a concept with which her body severely disagreed. Her vision grew fuzzy, and she collapsed to the ground.

Several days later, Sariva tumbled into awareness when a warm weight landed by her side.

"There's to be a ball! To celebrate the restoration of the queen and the safety of the queendom, and I've got a new dress with a ribbon crown and flounces, and my slippers will be dyed to match! It's the biggest celebration of Queen Oradel's rule so far."

Having grown up with younger brothers, Sariva was used to this routine. At least Mattie wasn't sticking grubby fingers up her nostrils. Bless small mercies. "Yes, a ball will be lovely," she replied, rubbing her eyes. Even though her pillow looked tempting, she knew she would be excited. Eventually. After a few good strong glasses of tea.

"You don't seem too excited," said Melisant from the corridor, a smile playing about her lips. Except for a bruise on her high forehead, she looked little the worse for wear.

"I am, honestly. I'll try to find a dress the court hasn't seen yet." She shook out her plaits and stifled a yawn.

"How crowded are the shops today? I want to buy some beads—they can do so much for a neckline—but if everything good has been bought up—"

"What a sweet, innocent child you are. You saved the queen's life, and you don't even think she'd be willing to buy you a new dress?"

Sariva covered her mouth, surprised. Even her new dresses for court had been meticulously altered castoffs. She threw open the window beside her bed and took a steadying breath of the after-rain air. "That's so kind of her. I'll be ready in a moment, just let me wash—"

"You've slept for nearly a day, of course you ought to have a moment!"

"Mattie is right. Take as long as you need."

While she was still dressing, a maid came into her room with a letter. Crisp handwriting on a plain envelope, clearly from Dorenia Maddox. "Right then," Sariva whispered. It was written with impeccable penmanship: *Dear Lady Sariva, I hope I will have the honor of your company at tonight's festivities...* She folded the letter into neat triangles as she sank into an upholstered chair. It was time for her real life to resume.

When she had her own daughters, she would be able to tell them a wonderful story. A lady fell in love with a squire, and they went on an adventure. They fit together like two parts of an embroidery hoop even though they bickered about nearly everything. And even though they couldn't stay together, the ending made it no less beautiful. She rubbed her eyes and tried not to hiccup; the hiccup came out anyway. *People do worse every day. They do worse to survive.* She would bear this. She had to.

They could write to each other, and she'd see Edwynne every time she came to the palace. Edwynne teasing the other squires and yelling commands to her trainees. Edwynne jaunty and confident in her smart Queensguard uniform.

Outside the window, every plant in the garden was blooming. Grapes swelled next to dates, which swayed below heavy blood oranges and bright sunny lemons. Everything grew at once with no regard to the season. The air itself seemed to shimmer with life. She wanted to dance on the warm stone paths and tame a wild cat. The city was free, and she wanted to be free with it.

She saw Stellan on a low settee with a blanket-wrapped Ava draped over his lap. The young Desert noble suffered from mosquito fever due to her stint in the underground chambers, and Stellan stayed at her side, encouraging her recovery.

"Come on, love. One more spoonful," Stellan said, waving a bowl of porridge. "Cardamom's still your favorite, isn't it?"

Ava sighed but took the spoon anyway. "I feel like a newborn camel."

He beamed down at her, his handsome face wrinkling as he tried not to laugh. "You won't bite me, will you?"

"Only by your request," she teased with mock innocence. She tapped his nose with the spoon, and a last bit of porridge dripped onto his nose and made him chuckle as he rubbed it off.

They seemed so happy together, and they didn't notice her as she slipped silently past.

Even on days off, she knew, Edwynne liked to practice. She found the squire moving through a staff-work sequence in a wide clearing.

Edwynne noticed her approach. "I read that play you said I should read. The one with the battles," she said, resting her staff against a date palm and putting her hands in her pockets.

"Is that how you're going to refer to Amaldia's tragedy, one of the seminal works of our era?"

"Well...yes. Anyway, everyone says it's worth notice for the melodies and the poetry. But you ought to have told me there was a brilliant patter song about winter campaigning, and it's so true to life how they're all tending their stumps and trying to find greens. Honestly? I liked it."

The response caught her off guard. "What?"

She wrinkled her freckly nose. "Come on, you don't think a brainless fighter like me can appreciate high art?" And, before Sariva could shoot back an indignant retort, "I'm kidding. It was kind of beautiful, actually. In a way, dying for someone is like getting married. No one can ever separate you afterwards."

Sariva had never seen Edwynne sad before. Angry or hurt, sure, but not this contemplative stillness. She fumbled for something to say. "Did it scare you? Reading about Rhysling drowning?"

"A little. Maybe it would be worse seeing it onstage. The reviews say they have an illusionist mage making scrim move like water." She spun her staff. "But then I did some more reading, and you know how converts join the Goddess faith? By bathing in running water. Drowning? That's like extra conversion."

Sariva couldn't hold back a smile. "I'll let you have it."

"You're not letting me have anything." She fished around her neckline for a thin chain and held up a Northern moon pendant, the metal in Queensguard green and white. "My adoptive parents sent this to me. They encouraged me to start studying for a late coming-of-age ceremony." She seemed at peace when she smiled.

"So you're on speaking terms with them again?"

A one-shouldered shrug. "I sent them a letter asking for an apology. A real one. Guess I'll see what they write back, but at least I have Stellan. And your brothers—your family—did you get a chance to talk to them?"

She couldn't help smiling. "Yes. Things are becoming a lot easier with Dorenia's support. Everything's set for when I—"

When I get married, she didn't want to finish.

Edwynne picked up her staff and started spinning it again, her mouth a firm line. "It's fine. I get it. You were willing to marry an evil wizard to protect your family. This is just another chapter in the tragedy of noble, self-sacrificing Sariva Al-Beroth, whose grand solutions never involve being happy." She rolled her eyes.

Damn. Once again, Edwynne had cut to the core of the matter. Hadn't she always told herself love mattered more than duty? But what could she do? You don't understand, she wanted to say, it's not like that—but what else could she do? "I'll see you at the ball."

Edwynne's mouth hinted at a smile. "At least we've got tonight."

★

Edwynne had never been subjected to maids or beauticians before. But today, she was under the command of a small squadron. Heroines, apparently, couldn't wash themselves with a bucket of dishwater behind the barns like normal people. She'd squirmed in her chair as they fussed around her. "This is taking ages. Can't you put a hat on me and be done with it?"

"But wait until we're done. Any special girl you want to impress will fawn over you for sure. Is that a bruise, or did you just take a roll in the dirt?"

"Maybe both."

When they finished, she hardly recognized herself. With gold dusted on her eyelids and cheekbones, she looked like a newly forged rapier in sunlight, illuminated and dangerous.

"Now with your hair arranged, your garments can be the finishing touch. Would you like a dress or a Queensguard uniform?"

Edwynne hated dresses, but would a uniform look any better? Most of the boys were much broader across the shoulders, and she'd look like a child playing dress-up in her father's clothing. Still, at least she'd be able to move. "The uniform, I suppose." But once she'd put on the green-and-white uniform, her reflection astounded her. The jacket hugged her figure, and the sleeves were the perfect length. "It's had bits taken off! I never knew a few stitches could make so much difference!" She had to show Stellan.

Tomorrow, she'd go back to her messy self, sweat stained, eating with her fingers, and perfectly comfortable. But just for today, she liked pretending she came from a different world.

Stellan glanced at her and looked away, pretending to be preoccupied. "Pardon me, have you seen my squire? She's a great lanky girl in a hand-me-down tunic—"

"Come on, dumbass. You know me." She slugged him in the shoulder, and he grinned down at her.

"Well, the ball's starting. Shall we?"

★

Sariva's dress, white as a rose, had a daringly low neckline, and a green glass pendant on braided silver glistened above her perfect breasts.

Sariva must have interpreted her staring as shock because she dipped her head, a shy smile curling her lips. "I know. I've never seen myself so dressed up before either." Then, gathering her dignity, she asked, "Would you please take the honor of escorting me into the ballroom?"

Edwynne didn't know how to respond. "I thought... You're supposed to confirm your engagement."

"Yes," Sariva said quietly. "We'll be leaving the palace soon so I can view Dorenia's home. I did save you a dance though."

Everyone cheered for Sariva and Edwynne as they crossed the marble floor. Candles flickered between the pillars, reflecting off shawls spun with silver thread and necklaces of seashell and amethyst. A gathering of harpists strummed an intricate quartet. The queen herself rose to offer the pair a nod and raise her glass. In return, Edwynne bowed, and Sariva curtsied deeply.

Despite Sariva's perfectly made-up face and shimmering white gown, her eyes held a sadness she couldn't hide. As the music grew livelier, Edwynne wanted to pick at it like a hangnail. "Sariva, I know you. And I know you're a stubborn little bitch. You didn't listen to Vered when she told you to drop it. You didn't listen to Delvar when he told you Queen Oradel was beyond helping or to literally everyone telling you to stay away from the old palace. So what has changed now? Why the sudden willingness to listen to others?"

She shrugged, a helpless half gesture. "I just... My family is depending on me. We need this marriage for my little brother, so he can get seen by better doctors and live in a less musty house. And Dorenia needs someone to handle hosting dinner parties. If I fail to do my duty, I'd let everyone down."

"Brave, noble, stupid Sariva. Since when does your duty include making yourself miserable? There has to be a way we can still be together, even with the wedding."

"Maybe."

"Well, have you tried asking? Have you tried anything except suffering nobly in silence?"

"Ed, can we just dance?"

"Fine."

Edwynne had never bothered learning formal dance. She always ducked out of lessons, especially when asked to follow while the older boys took turns leading.

But Sariva led flawlessly, and Edwynne twirled with her, feet and heart light. *Stay with me*, she willed. She prayed it too, even though she didn't know exactly how to pray. She tried to memorize Sariva's face, the little pieces of jet-black curls escaping her plaits, the glitter on her cheeks and the shine in her eyes.

The dance ended too soon.

Sariva bit her lip, twisting her fingers together. "I need to go see Dorenia and finalize the marriage contract."

"Promise me you'll at least try to be happy. Promise me you'll keep being a stubborn bitch."

She only replied, "I'll try."

★

Edwynne was right.

Sariva had spent days, weeks probably, thinking of herself as superior to the other girls, contemplating the poetry of duty before love.

But it couldn't hurt to ask. And broaching the issue of emotional entanglements with her bride-to-be posed much less risk than facing death at the hands of a malevolent wizard or ravenous ghost.

"Have you seen Miss Maddox?" she asked.

Some minor minister pointed her outside, where Dorenia sat on a stone bench in the night-cool palace gardens, her shoes next to her feet and glasses perched on the end of her nose.

She ought to return inside. Return to the story she'd written for herself, a treadmill where she had to keep working even when all hope was lost.

But Edwynne had dared her into defiance. "Good evening. Do you have a moment?"

Dorenia put down her book after marking her place with a leaf. "Oh, thank the stars. I thought I'd need to go inside and search for you, and it's so hot and crowded in there. Did you have a chance to review the marriage contract?"

It would be so much easier to let protests wither in her throat, to go along with what she'd agreed to. Yet, unlike the poor people Delvar had puppeteered, she had a choice. "Actually, I was wondering if we could discuss it."

Dorenia made a well-go-on gesture.

"I'm happy to help you by fulfilling my responsibilities. Talking to the people who work for you, making sure everything on your land is used productively. Everything we agreed on." She'd gone too far to back out now. "Except I can't love you."

Dorenia adjusted her glasses. "So don't. You're a teenager I've basically hired to manage social interactions for me. I've never said anything about love."

She hadn't. Maybe happy endings, even if Sariva ignored them in stories, could exist in reality. After gathering up her skirts, she ran through the gardens, through a side door, and into the party.

"I'm trying to eat here," blurted an indignant Lisette as Sariva ran past.

Sariva didn't feel a sudden wince in her chest or a tightness on the back of her neck as if a thousand nasty eyes were watching her closely for any sign of surreptitious Northernery. Who was Lisette? Just a young noblewoman from an uninteresting province who spent too much on clothes and bragged about her accomplishments. This wasn't an enemy powerful enough to deserve acknowledgement. She just kept walking.

It seemed like hours before she could finally slip away from the feast and be alone with Edwynne, who'd spent most of the ball finally achieving her dream of filling her pockets and bag with food that could be easily stored.

"There you are! I was looking for you all night... Everyone wanted to dance with me, and they were asking where you were. I wish I'd danced with no one but you." Sariva caught up to her, laughing as freely as a bird might soar above the evening breeze. She traced her hand down Edwynne's jacket buttons. "You're going to be a splendid knight, you know that?"

"When we met, you thought I was disgusting. What was it? Badly dressed and uncouth? Less competent than Mattie?" she joked.

Sariva shrugged. "Manners and clothes...one can wield them like armor. But they don't make the warrior."

"I think I had the wrong idea about you too. At first." Edwynne fidgeted. "What I mean is, I still don't care for everything you do. Dresses and evenings on the town and aged sweet wine. But what we share is so important to me. You're kind to people, no matter their rank. You'll risk your life for what you believe in. What I mean is, I think I would rather argue with you than be flattered by anyone else."

"I'd rather have you than anyone else," Sariva murmured, cupping her face, "so that works out quite well..."

Whatever came next, for either of them, they had each other.

About Ennis Rook Bashe

Ennis Bashe is a queer disabled graduate of Sarah Lawrence College, proud cat parent, and prolific writer of romance novels and novellas. Their poetry has appeared in *Strange Horizons, Liminality Magazine, Writers Resist*, and *Cicada*, and their short fiction has appeared in *The Future Fire, Mirror Dance*, and *Resistor* Vol. 2, among others. Find them on Twitter at @RookTheBird, and sign up for their newsletter at www.tinyletter.com/rookthebird.

Facebook
www.facebook.com/Ennis-Rook-Bashe-101331775552479/

Twitter
@rookthebird

Also from NineStar Press

Give Me Grace by Bethany A. Perry

It's been six weeks since Halloween. Six weeks since Grace stumbled into the ER, almost dead and begging for help. Six weeks since she lost every single memory, including her own name.

Taken in by the mysterious Sisters of the Order of Saint Raphael the Healer, Grace's wounds are dressed and she is assured her memories will return—in time. But does Grace want her memories back? Maybe she's chosen to forget them, maybe there's a reason. The sisters hide things from her. They whisper things about her.

When a demon forces its way into the convent, it declares that Grace is a demon too. Grace demands answers. Answers that may reveal not only who she is, but that the sisters might not be who they say they are, either.

Fair Youth by M. Dalto and Laynie Bynum

Billie tried to make a small town life as a doctor's fiancée work for her, but the dream of trading in Kentucky for the glitz and glamor of LA and selling her screenplays was too strong to fight. Unfortunately, the devil hides behind every corner in the City of Angels and she finds nothing but cockroach infested hotel rooms and broken dreams.

Everything changes when she meets an enigmatic and illustrious fellow writer named Kit. Struck with attraction and intrigue, Billie begins to question not only her dedication to her past life, but also her own sexuality. Kit comes with amazing connections and Billie's work is getting more recognition than ever, until a powerful studio executive sets his sights on more than just her screen-plays. His infatuation could cost Billie her career and, maybe, one of them their lives.

Foxfire in the Snow by J.S. Fields

Born the heir of a master woodcutter in a queendom defined by guilds and matrilineal inheritance, nonbinary Sorin can't quite seem to find their place. At seventeen, an opportunity to attend an alchemical guild fair and secure an apprenticeship with the queen's alchemist is just within reach. But on the day of the fair, Sorin's mother goes missing, along with the Queen and hundreds of guild masters, forcing Sorin into a woodcutting inheritance they never wanted.

With guild legacy at stake, Sorin puts apprentice dreams on hold to embark on a journey with the royal daughter to find their mothers and stop the hemorrhaging of guild masters. Princess Magda, an estranged childhood friend, tests Sorin's patience—and boundaries. But it's not just a princess that stands between Sorin and their goals. To save the country of Sorpsi, Sorin must define their place between magic and alchemy or risk losing Sorpsi to rising industrialization and a dark magic that will destroy Sorin's chance to choose their own future.

Connect with NineStar Press

www.ninestarpress.com

www.facebook.com/ninestarpress

www.facebook.com/groups/NineStarNiche

www.twitter.com/ninestarpress

www.instagram.com/ninestarpress